D0092958

The BULRUSH MURDERS

The BULRUSH MURDERS

A BOTANICAL MYSTERY

By REBECCA ROTHENBERG

Carroll & Graf Publishers, Inc.
New York

First Carroll & Graf edition 1991

Carroll & Graf Publishers, Inc.
260 Fifth Avenue
New York, NY 10001

Library of Congress Cataloging-in-Publication Data
Rothenberg, Rebecca.
The bulrush murders / by Rebecca Rothenberg. — 1st Carroll & Graf ed.
p. cm.
ISBN 0-88184-749-6 : $18.95
I. Title.
PS3568.0862B85 1991
813′.54–dc20 91-30689
CIP

Manufactured in the United States of America

PART I
WET SEASON

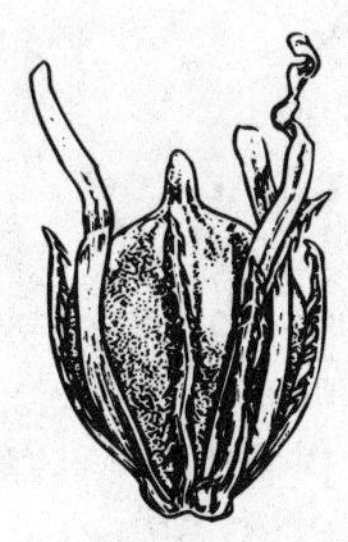

CHAPTER 1

All airports were alike, Claire thought, shifting her hips wearily on the scratchy nubby-weave upholstery (Pacific blue; Logan's had been mid-Atlantic gray). Like happy families. Actually, she had always thought Tolstoy got that wrong. It was miserable families that were all alike, misery that was forever the same: the infinite loop, the doorless room, the pit yawning under the feet. *Phil, you bastard . . .*

Damn. That was the problem with traveling—too much time to think. She took a resolute breath, reached for her briefcase, set it on her lap, and popped the latches. Inside was a manila folder containing copies of her CV, her last article, and a scrap of paper, soft and furred from many foldings. This she removed, smoothed, and studied. STAFF RESEARCH POSITION, it said:

> The University of California's College of Agriculture is seeking qualified applicants for a one-year position, beginning February 1, at its Citrus Cove Experimental Field Station. Applicants must have PhD in microbiology, biochemistry, or related field, with strong background in mycology. Previous experience in agricultural research desirable. The Citrus Cove Experimental Field Station is located in the eastern San Joaquin Valley, in the heart of California's citrus and stone fruit industry. The University of California is an affirmative action employer; qualified minority and female candidates are encouraged to apply.

It had come to her like a note in a bottle in the back of the November issue of *The Journal of Agricultural Biology,* and she knew it by heart. Gratefully she leaned back in her fuzzy chair and slipped into the familiar daydream: *The Grapes of Wrath*. True West. The Golden State (here she glanced briefly at the anonymous decor of San Francisco International and closed her eyes again), endless vistas, postcards of sunny, impossibly vivid orange groves framed by majestic, snow-covered mountains . . . and a vision of herself, Claire Sharples, sun browned and confident, leaning back in the saddle—no, no, that was ridiculous, but . . . a jeep, okay? leaning against the hood of her jeep—on a high, windswept hill, the fertile green valley stretched out below her. Claire Sharples, led out of captivity and into the land of milk and honey and citrus and stone fruit. Only what was stone fruit?

Suddenly the carefully contrived image wavered as, unbidden and unwelcome as always, the desolate, obsessive thoughts washed over her and her stomach knotted helplessly. *Phil, you bastard, how long, how far do I have to go to get beyond you? Three thousand miles? Is that enough? Do I have to get a job in Fiji?*

"Good evening, ladies and gentlemen," came the ageless, unaccented voice from the State of Airport. "Golden West Airlines announces the departure of its 9:40 flight from San Francisco to Fresno. We apologize for the delay. All aboard, please."

She woke in darkness, fumbled for the light, and squinted without comprehension at an orange swag lamp floating before her like a blob of ectoplasm.

Oh, right. Motel. Fresno. Job interview. *Job interview!* In a panic she grabbed for her watch, but she was still on Boston time; it was only five A.M. and the guy from the field station wasn't picking her up till eight.

But sleep was out of the question. Therefore shower and blow-dry the hair. Slip on the dress. She scowled at herself in the mirror; maybe a little eyeliner to balance those jet-lagged hollows under the eyes? There was nothing she could do about the basic material, but then it didn't pay to be a truly pretty woman in science anyway. It upset people; they discounted you or hit on you or resented you or dogged your steps. Even she had contended with this over the years, and she was nothing special, just sort of fiftieth-percentile attractive: body, tall and lean—good, not disruptively female; eyes, okay—startlingly light green under dark brows; hair, unruly

—which happened to be fashionable this year; face . . . well, face. Interesting, maybe, and intelligent, but the nose was too broad and the mouth too sardonic for beauty.

All in all, however, her looks had served her well in her career, and only rarely did she wonder wistfully what it might be like to be too pretty.

Wondered if that would have made the difference with Phil.

Out into the emptiness of a very early morning in a very strange city. The coffee shop's parking lot was deserted save for two big rigs and an unloaded lumber truck, hinged back on itself like a bear trap. No surprises there; last night Fresno had winked at her like one big garish truck stop flashing through the taxi window. An hour and a half later she had forced down greasy eggs and white toast and was rereading the *Fresno Bee,* half dozing despite anxiety and multiple cups of coffee, when someone spoke.

"Dr. Sharples?"

She looked up into a face that jolted her awake.

Mulcahey? My God!

For one wild moment it seemed that that Dr. Donald Mulcahey, Nobel-aspiring microbiologist and tyrant, had sensed his post-doc's treasonous impulse toward defection and pursued her across a continent . . . but of course that was insane, this wasn't Mulcahey, this was—

"Ray Copeland, Dr. Sharples. From Citrus Cove."

Pulling herself together she nodded, somewhere registering the fact that if Copeland himself, the field station's manager, had come to meet her they must want her. But really, Mulcahey could have been this man's evil twin. Same thinning hair carefully pulled across a lumpy pink scalp; same truncated nose, long upper lip, incongruous rosebud mouth that was petulant in her boss but friendly and sort of endearing in Copeland, who smiled and stuck out his hand.

"Welcome to California."

As they walked to his car he chatted nervously.

"It's about a thirty-mile drive, but I think you'll enjoy it—we go through some pretty country. Have you eaten? They'll have doughnuts and coffee. . . ." They rounded the building into the morning sun. For a moment she lifted her face to its warmth, closed her eyes, opened them—and gasped.

"What . . . ?" said Copeland, concerned; then, following her gaze, "Oh. You flew over them yesterday, you know."

"It was dark," she answered, voice unsteady. Because there, to the east, beyond the spiky palm trees and the telephone lines and Golden Arches and stoplights and billboards and other works of man, were *mountains. Big* mountains. Blue below and snowy above, as far north and south as the eye could see.

"The Sierra Nevadas," Copeland said unnecessarily. "That's what makes the central valley. Three-hundred-sixty miles of the best farmland you ever did see."

They weren't headed for the flat center of that vast valley, he explained, opening the massive door of his Buick and tucking her in. Citrus Cove sat in the Sierras' western foothills—*in the heart of California's citrus and stone fruit industry,* Claire intoned to herself, thought she might ask about stone fruit, decided she'd wait.

South out of Fresno and almost immediately the pizza huts and discount tire stores began to alternate with orchards. And suddenly there was nothing but trees, endless rows of them. Copeland named them: the dusty silver were olive; the knobby, arthritic ones pistachio; those bare, delicate networks of rose and gray almonds—or stone fruit, like peaches and apricots (Claire suppressed an exclamation)—and the dark green were citrus. Obviously. Their bright fruit gleamed in the glossy foliage like Christmas balls.

South, then east, then south again; trees, a vineyard, more trees—and always, beyond, that great wall of blue, defining the landscape with an inevitability that made Claire wonder how she had lived her thirty-two years without it. Back home she oriented herself by the Charles River, the Atlantic Ocean, Newburyport, Waltham—a mental map, not palpable like this. Back home . . .

Back home at this very moment she would be hunched in her office at MIT, contemplating the color gray. As in battleship gray, the color of her cubicle walls, or steel gray, her desk where it showed underneath the computer output and the Xeroxed articles, or sullen gray, the Charles in January. The glowering gray of the sky, the dreary gray of the icy rain no doubt beating against the window . . .

And here the air was clear and crisp and held a faint tang of smoke, the sun shone steadily, and Claire was enchanted.

Oh God, she thought, I hope I'm what they're looking for, I hope this isn't just some pro forma Affirmative Action scam and they've already hired someone from Michigan or Cornell or one of the other big ag schools—

"Brown rot," Copeland was saying. "Been having a lot of trouble with it this year. Maybe a first-rate microbiologist like yourself can help us out."

He smiled politely while her stomach lurched. Brown rot? Was she supposed to know what that was? Meanwhile they headed east again, toward the mountains, and suddenly they were at the field station, a long low brick building that reminded her of her elementary school—except for its backdrop of orange groves, lapping up against the hills like waves of a dark lake.

Her (please God) future colleagues waited to feed her doughnuts and questions in the conference room. They seemed nice enough: middle-aged middle-class middle-American, white except for one Japanese guy, male except for one female lab tech. And what they were looking for was simple: a mycologist to do research on the fungi and molds that infected local crops.

"We're mounting a big study on *Aspergillus flavus* in almonds," Copeland said. "Investigating methods of biological control. That would be your primary project."

Claire nodded. She happened to know a lot about *Aspergillus,* which could produce nasty carcinogenic toxins in a number of nuts and grains.

"In addition, you'd be responsible for some of the testing we've had to send up to Fresno in the past," Ray continued. "You know, common fungus infestations like brown rot—"

Oh, hell. Brown rot again.

"Monolinea fructiola and *laxa* are always a major problem around here."

Ah, *Monolinea!* The bailout came from Sam somebody, a thin, dark man with thick glasses, too-short pants, and a shirt buttoned tightly around his Adam's apple. In Cambridge he might have been an art student imitating a nerd, but here he was undoubtedly the real thing. Nevertheless she smiled at him gratefully. He appeared not to notice.

"The local growers frequently come to us with stubborn or atypically diseased trees," Copeland was explaining, "and we investigate them. Usually turns out the grower hasn't been treating the problem correctly, missed a spraying or something—"

Here he was interrupted by a cough. He looked sharply at the dark man and continued in a slightly louder voice. "But periodically we'll suspect we've got a new, fungicide-resistant strain on our hands. At that point we've had to call in the big guns from Davis, but if we had someone with your background working here . . . Like to see the orchards?"

Her research, their research, lunch. Tour of the lab; if she had had any doubts, that cinched it, because there, framed through the back window, was her postcard of Technicolor orange trees gleaming below snowy mountains.

By two o'clock, as they filed into the conference room again, everyone was smiling and she was sure she had it sewed up.

"Tell me something, Miss—uh, Dr. Sharples."

The light tenor voice with a faintly Southern accent belonged to Sam the nerd, who, Claire now knew, was an extension expert, whatever that might be. Having identified him as an ally, she turned toward him with a friendly expression and thus received the sandbag right between the eyes.

"Why the hell do you want this job?"

Embarrassed silence. Some people rolled their eyes and Copeland said, "Sam!" in a tone of gentle reproof, but he continued unperturbed.

"No, listen. What makes you think you wouldn't be bored? I mean, you've been doing pretty high-powered theoretical work at MIT, and you understand we don't exactly—push back the frontiers here. Our research goals are, um, modest, and pragmatic. . . ."

" 'Modest and pragmatic' sound just fine, Mr.—ah—"

"Cooper," he supplied helpfully.

"Mr. Cooper," she repeated, "and it's a fair question"—shooting him a venomous glance. She launched into a semiprepared speech that omitted irrelevancies like broken hearts and megalomaniac employers and wasted youth, and emphasized such fine intellectual points as 1) the artificiality of the dichotomy between basic and applied science, 2) the scientific value of a first-hand understanding of the consequences of one's research, 3) her frustration at being alienated from the implications of her work. "The real-world implications, I mean," she added, "social and economic, not whether it's going to get me tenure." Everyone laughed knowingly.

"You people are really in the trenches," she finished with a rhetorical flourish, "and I'd like to be there too!"

Too corny? No. Ray Copeland was positively beaming. Good-bye Boston, good-bye Mulcahey, good-bye Phil . . . Then she caught the scornful gaze of Mr. Extension Expert, and for some reason felt slightly ashamed. Maybe she had laid it on a little thick.

"And also," she added hastily, "I like the weather."

Several of the staff exchanged glances.

"You might not like it so much in six months," Copeland said. "But I think I'm safe in saying—" pause, look round the table, nod "—that you'll have the chance to decide that for yourself. If you want to."

She had it, she had it! The blood thrummed in her ears as she stood, shook hands, stammered a pleased acceptance. She looked forward to working with them. They looked forward to working with her.

Finally, mutual congratulations completed, Copeland said, "Well, we can't keep you. You've got a plane to catch."

CHAPTER 2

How long does it take to serve notice to the world that you are about to tear your life into pieces and throw them like confetti into the air? Claire gave it two weeks—the world, in her case, comprising her landlady, her mother, her best friend Carrie (who was aghast), a few other friends, the people at the lab (she was leaving a big hole but she couldn't feel guilty, and anyway, some ambitious young patsy of a grad student or post-doc would soon materialize to take her place)—and Mulcahey. This last she kept avoiding, hoping that the grapevine would accomplish the onerous task for her, then realized that he wasn't *on* the grapevine; everyone was as afraid of him as she was.

So daunting was the prospect, in fact, that by Thursday she was beginning to reconsider her decision. That evening she walked pensively to her car, automatically glancing across the parking lot to Phil's space. The gray Mercedes was there—obscenely expensive, but then it wasn't just an automobile, it was an "investment." Nothing was just what it was to Phil; everything was an investment and was expected to produce returns: in hours worn or driven or looked at—or, in the case of ephemeral experiences like meals or vacations, in status accrued and names to be dropped. He applied this same chilly pragmatism to people, though the calculus was murkier; but presumably she, Claire, had simply not fit into his life portfolio as well as what's her name, Laura. It was nothing personal. . . .

These vindictive musings were interrupted by the light, rapid tapping of a woman's high heels, and suddenly Phil and She came into view. Claire winced and averted her eyes, then forced her head up again. Phil looked sleek, happy, and healthy, and She—Laura—oh, damn, she was so pretty.

Small, neat-figured, soft brown curls, big eyes, button nose . . . Claire couldn't even console herself with the epithet "air-head," since the woman had a PhD in electrical engineering and probably pulled down eighty K a year. And *that* probably rounded out Phil's portfolio very nicely.

The next day she walked into Mulcahey's office and spilled the beans.

California again, and this time the ashes in the wind smelled like burning bridges. But the hills were, if anything, greener, the mountains bluer, the air sweeter, the sun warmer, and she was ready to begin.

And then Ray Copeland appeared, led her to the lab, handed her a stack of articles on *Monolinea* and *Aspergillus,* smiled sweetly, and shut the door.

There she sat, among the petri dishes, autoclave, microscope, and other assorted gadgets; she might have been back at MIT, except for the view. She shrugged, hunkered down, and read: not technical material only, but history, natural history, economics, politics, newspapers. She read until she was woozy, then fixed her eyes on the neat rows of orange trees outside the window, then read some more.

After two weeks she was steeped to the gills in Kaweah County lore and mighty claustrophobic. She approached Ray.

"Listen, do you have any idea when I'm going to start getting out in the field?"

"What do you mean, out in the field?"

"Well, you know, out to talk to the growers, to make some contact, get some feedback. . . ."

"There's no need for you to do that," he answered cordially. "That's what the extension people like Sam Cooper and Jim LaSalle are here for. They'll keep you busy, don't worry."

"That's not the point!" Claire could hear her voice rise with panic. "I *want* to get out into the community! That's what I talked about during my interview, you know, understanding the implications of my research."

Ray looked extremely dubious. Finally he said, "Oh, well, of course, if it's important to you . . . Why don't you talk to Sam right now and make arrangements to ride with him on some sort of regular basis?"

Because he hates me, she wanted to reply. He's hated me

since the interview; we haven't spoken two words since I arrived. Surely that can't have escaped your notice.

Still, if it was between Sam Cooper and Jim "Lock-and-Load" LaSalle, who kept cornering her in the hall to talk about his guns, she actually preferred Cooper. He was perched in a glass-walled corridor that looked out on the station's orange grove, balancing egretlike on one leg with the other bent and resting on the low window ledge and his head jutting forward. Furtively she examined his Adam's apple. My God, it was the sharpest thing she had ever seen. It looked like the nose-cone of a '56 Studebaker. It looked like it was about to poke through his skin. Didn't it hurt?

She managed to pull her eyes away and blurt out, "Sam. Could I come with you on your next field call?"

No answer. He seemed entranced by some activity out there behind the building, and when she followed his gaze she saw that they were harvesting the station's orange crop. This process began with the laborious placement of a long flexible aluminum ladder against the tree's glossy side. Then an acrobatic young man scaled it and hung like a sailor in its riggings, snapping off fruit with a quick twist of his wrist until he had cleared the area around him, at which point it all began again.

"Hard work," she remarked.

"Yeah. Haven't figured out how to mechanize it yet; the damn oranges are stuck on too tight to shake loose. Some of the growth hormones look promising—like that research you were doing with abscisic acids at MIT." This was almost gracious, but Claire didn't notice; she was thinking of a leftist analysis of the problems of mechanization of labor in agribusiness she had read recently. "Of course, that would displace a lot of workers."

"Sure," he drawled, finally straightening and looking at her. "They'd all rather be doing *that*"—jerking his head toward the picker, who was now connected to the ladder only by his left foot, curled around a top rung; his body was at a forty-five degree angle, his left hand grasped a swaying branch and his right hand stretched longingly for a shining globe about five feet beyond it. " 'Specially in the summer."

"They'd rather have jobs than not, if that's the choice," she retorted. Hell, this was hopeless. He had no intention of doing anything for her, and why should she let this—this skinny nerd, with his glasses and his Adam's apple, goad her into an argument?

"Forget it," she said, turning away. She'd ask Jim LaSalle instead, even if Jim did give her the creeps—and then, to her surprise, she heard Cooper's thin voice behind her.

"Meet me at four-thirty. I got to look at some peaches."

Through the orchards rattled the field station's Ford pickup, bearing its two silent passengers. The man would respond to a direct question with a monosyllable, and that was it. Claire wondered if it was people he didn't like or women or just her, or if, god forbid, she was stepping into some sort of messy office politics. Finally they turned right, toward the mountains (already she thought of them as a cardinal direction: north-south-west-mountains), and after a mile or two pulled onto a dirt road that cut north through rows of bare trees, all pruned back drastically into identical *Y*s. AGUA DULCE ORCHARDS, said a hand-lettered sign. PEACHES. NECTARINES. S. & C. RODRIGUEZ.

Agua dulce, sweet water . . . As Sam wrestled the pickup along the rutted dirt road, whole sections of recently encountered text floated up before her eyes (she had a good visual memory) regarding the first visitors to the San Joaquin Valley—the Spanish, and later the Mexicans—who had taken one look at that bare expanse and had kept on riding. Good for grazing a few cattle at most, was the verdict. *But it was here all the time,* she thought, meaning, water, sweet water: a vast underground reservoir gathered from the Sierras and trapped between layers of clay just below the surface. And when the first gringo had sunk the first well, it had been there, waiting; and lo, the desert had bloomed.

Eventually, of course, demand had exceeded this natural supply, especially as agriculture spread toward the drier western foothills. Now a network of man-made aquifers crisscrossed the valley, carrying the magic ingredient to fields of instant tomatoes, instant cotton, instant rice, oats, peas, beans, and barley. . . . Just add water, thought Claire. And fertilizer. And pesticides and herbicides . . .

"This shouldn't take long," Cooper said.

"Oh, I'd much rather be here than in the lab!" she replied fervently, and maybe that loosened him up, because after a moment he spoke again. "This is the family that's been having so much trouble with the brown rot. *Monolinea.* We mentioned it during your interview."

"Right," she said energetically, to show she'd been paying attention. "You thought they might be developing a fungicide-resistant strain."

He nodded. "Ray thinks they just haven't been applying Benyl—that's the fungicide—properly. I doubt it, but I'm going to go over the spraying schedule with them, just to make sure. They need to get on it right away."

"Already? But it's only February."

Ah, a misstep; he gave a disgusted snort and kept driving.

Good intentions scattered. She reacted to that kind of contemptuous dismissal like one of Mr. Pavlov's beagles with rabies.

"We seem to have got off on the wrong foot here. Sorry if I've offended you somehow," she said icily, sounding anything but sorry.

The truck stopped dead, right in the middle of the road.

Cooper took a deep breath for a count of ten, and then turned to look at her directly for the first time that day; looked in fact as if he'd like to make her into compost for the peaches. But when he spoke his voice was controlled.

"I got nothing against you personally," he said. "I'm sure you're perfectly competent at what you do. And I'm not some hick chauvinist or misogynist, if that's what you think."

Whoa, cowboy, them's mighty fancy words! A hick chauvinist was exactly what she figured him for, and she wished he'd take off his glasses so she could read his face.

"I just think Ray's made a mistake," he continued. "He's got this bee up his . . . in his bonnet about beefing up the basic science at Citrus Cove. So he goes and hires somebody who's got nothing but highfalutin academic credentials, who's never been west of the Rockies, and doesn't know the first thing about—"

"I can *learn,* dammit! How do you think I got those academic credentials?"

That scored, or else he suddenly regretted his candor. In either case, he looked away from her and started the engine. After a moment he muttered, "Forget about your East Coast summer-fall-winter-spring. This is a Mediterranean climate; we got two seasons, dry and not so dry. By the time your cherry blossoms are out, our hills are starting to die. So yeah, this is the time to start spraying." The pickup rumbled on. "And maybe you'd better do some reading," he couldn't resist adding.

This time she kept her mouth shut.

Eventually they skidded to a stop before a shoebox of a house. A young woman appeared on the porch, trim figured, with crow black wings of cropped hair. Cooper swung down from the high cab, and Claire, who on her second week of work was still Dressing for Success, slid down awkwardly after him, tugging at her skirt. Jeans tomorrow, she vowed silently.

As the woman carefully descended the stairs the illusion of youth melted. She dipped and bobbed on a hip frozen by injury or arthritis, and as she neared Claire saw the same maze of fine lines that mapped the faces of the older men at the station. What kind of heat, she wondered apprehensively, or bone-dry air or general harshness incised those lines? *You might not like it so much in six months. . . . Our hills are starting to die. . . .*

Meanwhile Sam was stooping to receive an embrace. "Hey, Silvia, *¿como 'stas?"*

The woman—Silvia, presumably—released him and patted his shirtfront fondly. It was a distinctly motherly gesture, and Claire could see now that she was probably in her early sixties. "Where you been, *m'hijo?* Ain't seen you since November. Since we lost the trees." Her voice was hoarse and forceful, and her accent rolled like her gait. The strong inflection and pure vowels fell exotically on Claire's ears.

"I know, I know. . . . When'd you put up the shed?" A newly painted equipment shed stood about fifty feet behind the stucco house.

"Carlos and Arturo built 'er, last month. My Christmas present." She grinned, a flash of white against brown. Then she turned to Claire, who was trying to lean casually against the truck.

"This man never did have no manners." She held out her hand. "I'm Silvia Rodriguez. I own this place—me and my husband."

"Claire Sharples," said Claire, stepping forward before Cooper could redeem himself. "I'm—I just started working at the field station. It's, um, it's a very nice orchard."

"Where's Carlos?" Cooper asked, unabashed. "And Tony?"

Silvia waved vaguely toward the trees. "Carlos is out somewhere fixing a broken pipe. Tony . . ." She trailed off and shrugged. "Tony *said* he was going out to help him a couple hours ago. Which means he could be anywhere between here and Los Angeles" (los An-hay-lace, she pronounced it) "and if this is an official call, have a seat."

Settled on the cold concrete steps, Claire listened to the other two talk about fungus diseases of fruit until she felt faint from boredom. Finally they stopped, and Silvia pulled out a pack of cigarettes.

"Those things'll kill you," Cooper remarked with mock severity; really, he was behaving a lot like a human being. Claire, however, he continued to ignore.

"Hey, I'm down to three a day," Silvia protested, enumerating them on her fingers: one at noon after she served the men lunch and they returned to the orchard, and two in the evening, out here on the stoop where a breeze might pick up. Claire looked at her. At that moment it was plenty breezy, bordering on downright chilly.

"In the summer, you know," Silvia turned to her. "I don't know if you ever been here in summer, but the sky gets hard and . . . and shiny, like a fryin' pan. At least when it's dark it don't seem so hot." Claire began to wonder if this were some local hazing ritual designed to scare Eastern greenhorns. Could the summers be that bad?

They all sat in silence, Silvia smoking until the strip on the western horizon was glowing like her Camel. Somewhere over there, Claire thought, conjuring the map of California in her mind, somewhere beyond the orchards and the fields of cotton and tomatoes and alfalfa, beyond Salinas and . . . and Monterey, maybe? Anyway, somewhere over there the sun was sinking in the sea. She'd like to see that.

As if reading her mind, Silvia spoke. "When I was a little kid people told me the sun set in the ocean. But I never seen the ocean, not till later. So I always imagined her slipping into a slot about two feet off of Monterey, just like a little ol' pillow in a pillowcase."

Claire laughed. It was incongruous and touching, somehow, to hear childhood fancies recounted in that gravel voice.

"Of course later," she continued, "when I went down to LA—"

"During the war," Cooper interjected.

"Right, in 'forty-three, then I seen how foolish I was. 'Cause we use to watch the sun set from Santa Monica Pier and it was *far,* like it was setting off of Hawaii. But if you was in Hawaii it would seem like it was settin' near, oh, maybe Japan. And if you was in Japan. . . ." She stopped, her geography exhausted.

"Well, sometimes," Claire heard herself say, "sometimes it seems that life's like that, that when you chase after something it moves away as fast as you close in."

Good God, had she really said that? Worthy of *Readers Digest,* and barely grammatical! But after two weeks of total social isolation, her internal censor was rusty.

Anyway, it was okay; Silvia was nodding agreement. That's what she'd decided, way back then, she said. And that's why she had come back here to the eastern San Joaquin, to live her life three miles from the little town where she was born.

Here, in the shadow of the Sierras on this cool evening, seemed to Claire not a bad place to have lived one's life. It was growing dark, and aromas rose on the damp air—also the faintly sour, scorched smell she noticed every morning. Very, very humbly she asked about this.

"Crop burnoff," answered Cooper tersely.

"Dirt farmers!" Silvia added with disdain. She began to chant in a singsong voice. "Plant your crops, grow 'em, cut 'em down, burn 'em off; plant 'em, grow 'em, cut 'em, burn 'em; plant grow cut burn—" Sam laughed and she broke off, looking across the drive to the dark mass where her orchard began. "Trees, now, trees is different. Trees are with you for a long time, like family."

"Better than family," Sam bantered. "If Tony was a peach tree he'd stay put, instead of buzzing around on his bike making trouble."

Silvia shook her head and sighed. "You don't know my boy, Tony," she said to Claire, determined to include her despite Cooper. "See, my first, Frank, he was killed in Vietnam, and then my three girls all married and left Kaweah County. So Tony's all that's left. My baby, you might say." She grinned wryly, but her voice had softened. "And I guess he's a little spoiled. Carlos thinks so anyway; he's hard on the boy. But Tony ain't a bad kid, he's just . . . he's . . ." She faltered and stopped. "One thing about Tony," she said finally. "He's beautiful. Ain't he, Sam? I don't know how that ugly old man and me made Tony."

The smell of smoke was sharper, nearer. Much nearer. Claire looked questioningly at Silvia who mumbled, "Wind's shifted," but nevertheless stubbed out her cigarette and wearily rose. The three of them walked around the house, Claire and Cooper slowing long-legged strides to Silvia's.

As they approached the new shed the smell was stronger and Claire's eyes began to smart. Some careless farmer had started a grass fire, she thought, noticing how the sun's last rays still glowed in the shed's windows.

Only the sky had darkened five minutes ago. And anyway, the shed faced south. A minor sun burned behind those windows. They were lit from within.

It was Claire who first began to run, racing ahead, so intent on that light growing brighter by the second that she almost stumbled over a couple of sacks in the drive, fertilizer or something—

No. Not fertilizer. A man, facedown, his left arm crumpled under him.

"Tony!" screamed Silvia, then stuffed her fist in her mouth because it clearly wasn't Tony; the red light showed a long, angular body, a middle-aged face—and a dark, sticky wound an inch above the eye.

Sam dropped to his knees beside the inert figure. Silvia lowered herself awkwardly and lifted his head.

"Arturo," she whispered, looking at Sam; then, scrupulously remembering Claire, "my brother-in-law. He was helping Carlos today." He stirred a little and moaned softly, and Claire's heart started beating again.

Now they could see flames quickening inside the building. A window exploded with the sound of a thousand wind chimes. They had to call Carlos, call the fire department, run for the hose, but for the moment they all were mesmerized, watching the flames snake out the window and lick the roof. Above their carnivorous crackle a motorcycle rumbled and then grew fainter, as if taking off across the fields toward the mountains. The sound registered subconsciously and was somehow unsettling, but Claire didn't have time to think about it. Cooper was calling to her.

"Hey, give me a hand here!"

The two of them hoisted Arturo's limp form between them,

staggered toward the house, and more or less dropped him on the grass by the front door. He raised himself on his elbows, head bobbing slowly like a toy turtle's.

"*¿Como te sientes, hijo?*" asked Silvia.

"I'm okay. Some son of a bitch jumped me as I was comin' in from the orchard," he said weakly, and Claire looked around nervously.

"Who?" Silvia demanded, but Arturo simply shrugged, then groaned again at the movement. Silvia struggled to her feet.

Meanwhile, Sam had turned on the hose and was playing it on the shed roof. "You got any flammables in there?" he called to Silvia.

"No. But—*ay, Dios,* the truck's parked in back. Goddamn it!"

"I'll move it! Call the fire department!" He caught Claire, who had wandered up uncertainly behind him, by the elbow and shoved the hose in her hand. "Don't get too close," he said, sprinting off, and in a moment she heard another engine.

The stream from the hose hissed and disappeared in the blaze, as impotent as Claire herself felt at the moment. What was she doing here? Why was she not home in my nice safe cubicle? When Cooper appeared again he was carrying a small fire extinguisher scavenged from the truck. She saw him silhouetted against the flames for an instant; then he darted inside.

Not smart. The fire had been tugging at the roof, pulling off morsels, and suddenly the whole west side caved in with a shower of sparks that sent Claire scrambling backward. Then, equally instinctively, she moved toward the structure, pulling the hose and silently cursing. *Stupid son of a bitch,* she cursed silently, *what does he think he's going to do with that pea-sized extinguisher? It was just a fucking storage shed, no lives at stake . . . until now . . .*

The hose literally pulled her up short, jerking violently as it was extended to its full length about ten feet in front of the shed. She looked at it for a second, bewildered. Then with a decisive movement she turned it on herself, gulping as the cold water saturated hair and clothes, and then plunged toward the open door—

And almost collided with Cooper, who had stumbled through the doorway and was doubled over, coughing his lungs out, his shirt smoking. Grabbing his ropy upper arm, she dragged him toward the hose and soaked him down, perhaps more thoroughly than was absolutely necessary.

"Stop!" he gasped, feebly holding his arms in front of him before dissolving in another spasm. Merciless, she kept spraying.

"¡La chingada!"

The hose was yanked roughly from her hands and she turned to receive a faceful of alcoholic fumes. Carlos Rodriguez had returned, just in time to save Mr. Cooper from double pneumonia.

And just in time to see the shed's north and south walls collapse. "What the hell happen' here?" he asked frantically.

Claire had to catch her breath before she could reply. "It started about fifteen minutes ago—" she began, when Silvia's voice cut in.

"*¡Borracho!* You been drinking while your house was burning!" she spat, arms folded across her chest.

"A couple lousy beers, after work. *You* were *here*—how could you let this happen?" He aimed the hose directly on what was left of the shed.

Claire tried again. "It started about fifteen minutes ago—"

"Forget the damn shed, Carlos." Silvia's voice had an edge that might have had nothing to do with the present emergency, as if she were picking up the thread of a standing argument. "Just make sure that grass don't catch. Where's Tony?"

Tony . . . why was that thought disturbing? Suddenly Claire remembered. The wayward Tony rode a motorcycle. Tony fought with his father. She had heard a motorcycle right after the fire started.

"He left a little while ago."

On his motorcycle? Claire wondered, and looked at Silvia and then at Sam, who was breathing hard but otherwise seemed all right. Had they heard it too?

Silvia opened her mouth to reply—and help came clanging up the driveway.

The firemen knocked down the last wall and sprayed foam on its smoking remains. The paramedics trundled Arturo into a yellow ambulance and, upon being informed that he had no health insurance, trundled him out again. They attempted to examine Sam, who looked like he might be suffering from smoke inhalation and have insurance, but he shook them off. A sheriff's deputy wrote down everyone's name, conferred with the firemen, and reached the preposterous conclusion that a stray spark from a burning field had ignited the shed.

Silvia, Carlos, and Sam burst into protest, all speaking at once.

"But the nearest fire was miles away!" "What about Arturo?" "That fire was set, Jimmie, and you know it!"

The deputy shrugged. He was a blond in his mid twenties, about Claire's height. "I don't have no way of knowing where the closest field fire was," he said in an accent that was California with a hint of Arkansas. "And as for your brother-in-law, the paramedics say he'd been drinking. Who's to say he didn't fall over his own feet?"

"Listen, *huerito—*" Carlos began, clenching his fists, but Sam broke in.

"Jimmie, you know somebody plowed under a bunch of their saplings a few months ago?"

"Sure, Mr. Cooper—Sam—everybody knows that. I just don't see how it relates to this incident." He shrugged again. Claire felt herself grow hot despite her dripping clothes.

"Look, isn't there some way you can check the shed for an incendiary device? Or, um, flammable liquid of some kind?"

He looked at her and consulted his clipboard.

"Miss Sharp, is it?"

"Sharples. Ms." *(BS, MS, PhD, if you want to get technical, buddy.)*

"Mmm. Well, sure, we could do that. If we had any reason to suspect arson. Which we don't."

She started to argue, caught sight of Sam's frown, decided she was learning an important lesson in the politics of Kaweah County—or maybe just the politics of a man with a gun—and shut up.

The law departed, as did medicine, finally persuaded to take Arturo to a farmworkers' clinic that had an emergency service. The professional firefighters started packing up and the four amateurs moved in toward the smoldering ruin—Silvia and Carlos, to see what could be salvaged; Claire and Sam purely for warmth. They were both shivering.

"Was it really necessary," Sam asked through chattering teeth, "to soak me to the skin?" He peered at her in the slow strobe of red light from the fire truck. "And how the hell did *you* get so wet?"

"I hosed you down because your clothes were smoking," she replied with dignity, calling in her debt of gratitude. When it was not forthcoming she added with resentment, "And I hosed myself down because I thought I was going to have to go in after you!"

"That's ridiculous. It was perfectly safe—"

"So incredibly fucking *stupid*—"

Their voices rose to modified screeches. Silvia and Carlos turned to stare at them, and they stopped. Claire surveyed herself. Her nifty blue dress was wringing wet and didn't seem to be wicking very well, her stockings were shredded, she had two angry red weals on her shin and inner arm where cinders had landed, and her face, if Sam was any guide, was streaked with black. Her hair clung damply to her skull but soon would dry in god knew what configuration.

Cooper had removed his glasses and was wiping a sleeve across soot- and smoke-reddened eyes. He looked up at her.

"Well," he said with the ghost of a smile, "how did you like your first day in the field?"

PART II
DRY SEASON

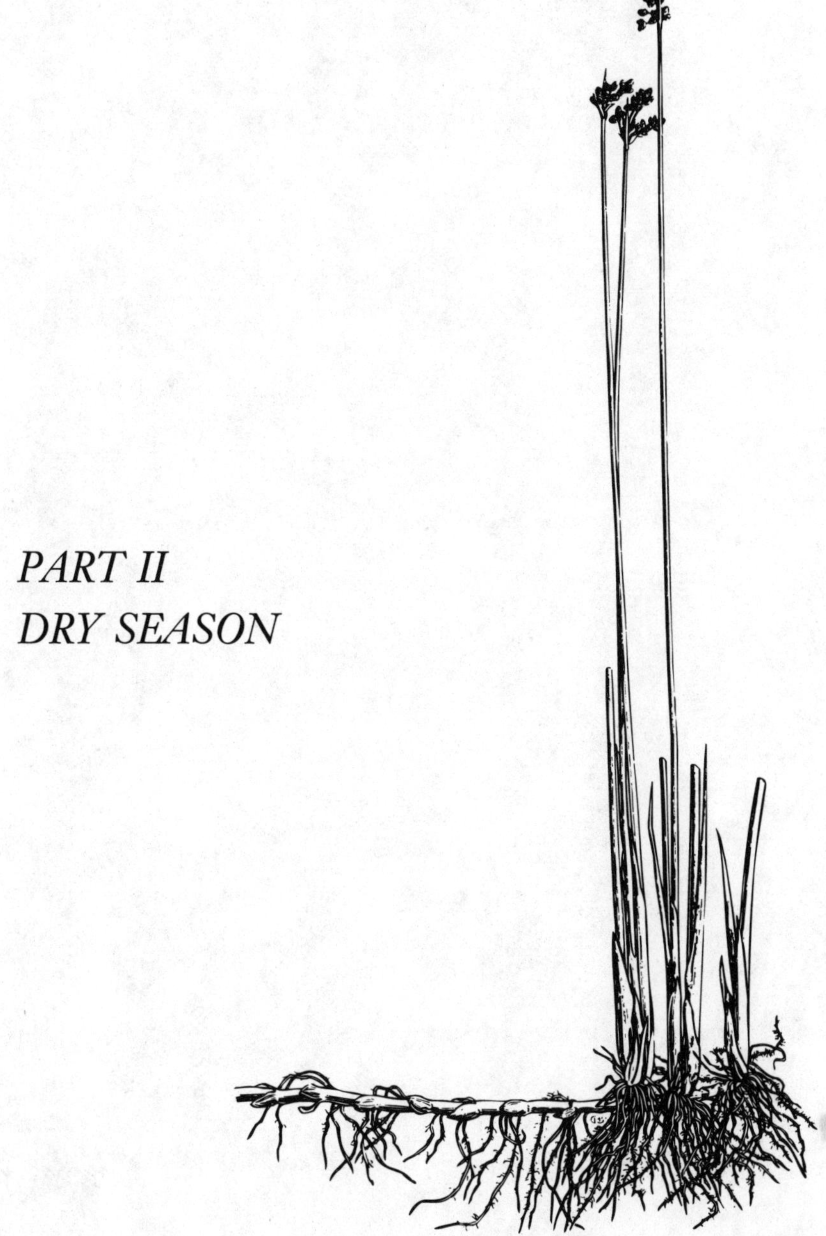

CHAPTER 3

JUNE 15, said the Parkerville B of A sign, and then, in rapid succession, 2:52, 38° C—Claire did a quick mental calculation —100° F. She sighed. It felt like 200 as she drove north along J-25 in the station pickup, whose windshield was smeared with smashed insects like huge globs of rubber cement. Sweat rolled in rivers down her sides and soaked the small of her back, and her hair lay in damp ribbons on her forehead.

The majestic Sierras on her right had started to fade around May. A line of clouds like snowcaps marked peaks now obscured by the acrid haze of the valley: part dust, part smoke from crop burnoff, part chemicals it was better not to think too much about, and part plain old smog with its peculiar aluminum smell. The lush green hills of February were bone dry and yellow. Wrinkled, folded, covered with bleached stubble, they resembled the carcases of enormous animals. (Actually, they fascinated her, those hills; she had taken dozens of photographs of them already.)

She slammed on the brakes as a huge farm vehicle lumbered onto the road in front of her and began to crawl northward at approximately seven miles an hour. Irritably she flicked on the radio, conducted a short, futile search for something worth hearing, and flicked it off again. Well, at least Sam wasn't with her, so she didn't have to listen to the goddamn Bakersfield station.

She had liked country music back in Cambridge, where it was tastefully sandwiched between Bach and Charlie Parker, but lately it had come to represent everything she loathed about this place. Aside from its obvious musical shortcomings, it was so . . . so bogus: all those jaded professional musicians pretending to be simple country folks singing to all those cable TV installers and bank tellers pretending to be cowboys. As far as she could tell, the only real cowboys and simple country folks in the neighborhood were the Mexican farm workers. And they had their own radio stations.

Of course, she would never voice these sentiments to Sam. Oh no. At present they were operating under a precarious truce, and although she was having her own problems with this, she certainly was not going to jeopardize it by criticizing his taste in music.

A little camaraderie-in-disaster had lingered between them after the Agua Dulce fire. And then, on a single April afternoon, she had managed to sabotage both this and her prospects of ever again working outside the lab.

"Meet me at one-thirty. I'm heading out to Hanford West to talk to Bill Hanford," he had said, and Claire had been at the truck at 1:07. Finally, the Hanfords! For months she had read about the county's first family—its landed gentry—and the news was not good. Only last week the *Bee* had reported Bill Hanford's citation by Cal OSHA for not providing minimal sanitary facilities, i.e., a couple of portable toilets and a little clean water to wash in, for his farm workers. She pictured Hanford clearly, his squat frame, his bulbous nose surrounded by little piggy eyes—Rod Steiger as a mean, ignorant Southern sheriff.

Imagine her surprise when she and Sam were greeted at the gate by a tall, athletically built, undoubtedly handsome man. Maybe this wasn't Bill Hanford.

"Howdy, Bill," said Sam.

Oh.

"Howdy, Sam. Who's this?" turning a disconcertingly blue gaze on her.

"Oh, uh, Bill, this is Sharples—Claire Sharples. She's our new microbiologist at the station and she's kind of getting a feel for things. . . ."

"How do you do," Bill Hanford said warmly, taking her hand. His eyes were vivid against his tanned face and they crinkled when he smiled. "Glad to have you in Kaweah County. We need all the beautiful intelligent women we can get."

Give me a break, she thought, except that something besides her brain was lapping it up. It was impossible not to react to Hanford's physical presence, and Claire felt the pressure of his hand long after he had removed it.

"So what you got?" Sam had asked, and he and Bill examined some maturing leaves. After a moment he remarked, "Looks like zinc deficiency," and Bill nodded.

"That's what I concluded. Too late to do anything this year."

"Mmm. A little zinc sulfate applied next fall will do the trick." Bill nodded again.

Claire squared her shoulders. Just because Hanford looked like a movie star, talked like a Harvard grad, and had flattered her shamelessly was no reason not to do what she had decided to do.

"So, Bill," she said casually, though she could hear her voice trembling, "going to plow some of this season's profits into Port-O-Sans?" Then she had held her breath, amazed at her own temerity.

The effect had been gratifyingly dramatic. Sam stared at her with horror; Bill shot him a brief, questioning glance, cleared his throat, and eventually responded.

"Oh, you read about that. That was really all a misunderstanding. It's very frustrating: I told my foreman to take care of it and he just didn't get around to it. When you run an operation on this scale, Miss Sharples," he added with a smile at once disarming and dismissing, "you have to delegate authority. And that puts you at the mercy of your employees. Sam, good to see you. Talk to you soon."

She had to steel herself not to cringe when Sam slammed the pickup door.

"If you *ever,*" he had said through clenched teeth, "*ever* pull a stunt like that again you'll be on a plane back to Boston so fast your head'll spin! Who the hell do you think you are? You've been here three lousy months—"

"Somebody had to do it," she had retorted, "and it obviously wasn't going to be you. Yassuh, Marse Hanford, nossuh, Marse Hanford—"

"It's not my job to do it!"

"No, and you just do your job. Like a good German."

She regretted this as soon as it was out. He had formulated a scorching reply, she could see that, but for some reason never delivered it. Instead he said in an almost normal voice,

"Look. I have to work with these people. Some I like, some I don't. Hanford's better than most."

"Maybe. But that business about delegating authority for the toilets—"

"Was bullshit," he conceded, starting the engine. "Yeah. Okay."

Yeah, okay, he had said, but he had reported the incident to Ray as soon as they had returned to the station, and she had been yanked from the field. Until today.

Recovering her credibility had been a tough battle, she thought, speeding up to fifty as the tractor finally pulled off and disappeared into an orange grove. After the, um, exchange at Hanford's, which she was willing to admit might have been a lapse of judgment inspired by healthy reformer's zeal, Ray decided she was a loose cannon, which was a moderate position, considering that her other colleagues now referred to her in private as Hanoi Claire. A few liberals, however, were willing to allow that she was not actually seditious —merely ignorant and naive.

Well, she was ignorant. As blithely as she had told Sam she "could learn," the actual day-to-day operations of commercial agriculture were proving more complex than she had anticipated. The technology itself—the diseases, pesticides, fertilizers, herbicides, irrigation systems, and so on—was overwhelming enough, not to mention the legal and political intricacies of water rights, pesticide registration, labor contracting, et cetera, et cetera. She was learning, but compared to people like Sam and Jim and Ray, farmers' sons and local boys all, she was still a complete novice.

Frankly, she had begun to wonder whether this struggle to leave the lab was worth it. She *liked* laboratory work; it was what she was trained for, and no one questioned her competence or performance.

And the lab was air-conditioned, she thought wistfully, once more pushing her hair off her forehead.

But she had kept pressing Ray, recognizing something here that had to be confronted, something that transcended mere reason or politics, something that linked the good ol' boys of Citrus Cove to the old boys of MIT and Cornell: the protection of the male prerogative.

So yesterday Ray had decided she could be trusted again to

accomplish certain extremely simple tasks on her own. Like picking a half dozen fruit and placing them in plastic bags, her current mission.

She turned east on 170. A few miles ahead was the new State Water Project dam, which had created a long, still raw-looking lake, Lake Prosperity. From there the road wound along the river through hills of pale grass and dark oak to the little town of Riverdale, where Claire now rented a tiny wooden bungalow. From Riverdale it rose abruptly into the mountains themselves. But her destination was here, on the fertile alluvial plain of the river, where citrus and fruit orchards stretched for acres in all directions. And just ahead of her, behind the billboard that said TRELTAN—BECAUSE CLEAN HAY PAYS, was the sign for Agua Dulce.

A hundred yards up the dirt road she stopped for a moment to take a look at the fruit trees running in long diagonal avenues along either side of the so-called road. From the truck the peaches—Elbertas, she thought—looked normal; on closer inspection, however, she could see that most of the still-immature fruit had small, circular brown areas, some of which had already begun to develop the grayish fuzz of mycelia. As predicted, the Rodriguezes once again were fighting persistent *Monolinea.* She picked several obviously infected specimens, sealed them in plastic bags, placed them in a Styrofoam cooler, and continued up the road.

When she pulled up before the house Silvia was hanging out washing on a line that once had been strung between the house and the shed, and now was strung between the house and a two-by-four driven into the blackened ground where the shed had been. She looked up and waved a greeting.

"Wanna buy an orchard?" she called, laughing raucously at her own joke.

While Claire had hoped that the drama of their first encounter might mean she and Silvia could become friends—she was beginning to want a friend with something like despair—so far it hadn't happened. Maybe it was the age difference, or maybe Silvia fit into too many of her romantic categories (Latina. Ex-farm worker. Struggling small farmer), or maybe she, Claire, was just too far outside of Silvia's experience; in any case, each time they had met there was mutual shyness and constraint.

But today she sensed the looseness that she remembered from that first visit and smiled warmly, thinking, Maybe this time.

"You're not really thinking of selling, are you?"

"Well, we don't want to sell. Only sometimes we think we're getting too old for this, you know, *no vale la pena,* it's too much trouble. And since none of our kids wants to work the farm—"

This last comment was aimed pointedly to Claire's right, and she turned to see Tony Rodriguez leaning lazily against the side of the house, hands in pockets.

Ah. Here was the reason for Silvia's relaxed mood.

Claire knew Tony. Soon after the fire she'd been at Parkerville's pitiful excuse for a record store flipping through the jazz bin—she had not yet realized that the selection never changed—when out of the corner of her eye she had spotted a young man with familiar deep-set eyes. As he paid for his Def Leppard album the clerk had called him "Tony," and she'd identified him as Silvia's "baby." After that she saw him fairly frequently—around Parkerville, at the record store, or at Casey's, where he usually drank too much. Eventually her sidelong stares had become so obvious that she'd had to introduce herself.

He *was* a wild kid; Silvia hadn't exaggerated. But although Claire remembered the sound of that motorcycle roaring off into the hills during the fire, she couldn't bring herself to mention it to a soul. It seemed perfectly harmless and natural that he might prefer such teenage pursuits as tearing around on his ancient but perfect Harley-Davidson—and listening to heavy metal, and hanging out at bars and pool halls—to sweating away in his parents' orchard.

And as the days ticked over and she developed a distinct empathy with the misfits in conservative rural communities, she liked to think that she and Tony shared a sort of outsider's sensibility. She liked to think that Tony was an essentially decent kid who cared about Silvia and Carlos, despite his rhetoric and his poses. She liked to think . . .

She liked to think about Tony. Because Silvia hadn't exaggerated there, either: her "baby" was spectacular.

Silvia was attractive, but where her features were blunt and strong, her son had a finely modeled, almost feline, face—high cheekbones, short upper lip, sulky inviting mouth, delicate chin—and, of course, his mother's wonderful eyes. He was slim and muscular, and his adolescent-macho swagger would have been laughable on someone less astonishingly good-looking. But lounging against the wall in cutoff T-shirt and tight jeans, he had the raw appeal of a dark James Dean.

And he was also ten years younger than Claire. Twelve. Well, thirteen. But the attraction was purely aesthetic, she told herself: she just wanted to . . . to photograph him.

"Howdy, Claire," he said with a grin that nevertheless caused her a pang.

"Hi, Tony. How's the Hawg?"

"She's just fine. Maybe I'll take her down 99 tomorrow, straight down to Los Angel-eez. Hey, Ma," he called to Silvia, "don't you want to come down to LA with me? I'll put you right on the back of the Harley."

"¡Ay, que barbaridad!" exclaimed Silvia, laughing. "You're crazy!"

"C'mon, Ma, you can be my *chola,"* Tony teased. "It'll be just like the old days." He turned to Claire. "She used to live in LA, you know."

"Yes, I know."

"Yeah. And it was great. Exciting. Not like this place. Tell her, Ma," he urged, "tell her what it was like. Tell her about the car."

"¡Ay, m'hijo, she don't want to hear about the car!"

"I do!" Claire said, intrigued by the prospect of another of Silvia's reminiscences. "Tell me."

A little more pro forma coaxing and Silvia had settled herself on the front stoop.

"Well, a long time ago," she began, classically, "during the War, I went down to LA, like I told you. I worked in a defense plant that made shell casings. I lived with an aunt down there—I was just a kid, sixteen years old, younger than you, *m'hijo.* Anyway, after the war ended and the men started coming back, there was this guy, Freddy—"

"Alfredo," murmured Tony, correcting a deviation from the text.

"Right, Alfredo Ruiz," Silvia repeated, "and all the girls were wild for him because he had a car. A 'forty Ford—he'd bought it before the war. But I could tell he liked me—"

"Because you were the prettiest," said Tony. "The prettiest girl."

Claire looked at him sharply. Even her dazzled eyes had perceived him as a surly and cynical young man, but right now he was dreamy and childlike. Another pose?

"Pues, I don't know about that," Silvia replied briskly. "I think it was because he couldn't figure me out. See, I went out with him a few times, but then I wouldn't go out with him no more. And the reason was, he had this fancy car, sure, but it was always filthy! He never washed it. And I said to myself, what kind of guy has a car like that and don't bother to keep it clean? So finally I told him, look, I'm not going out with you again till you wash that car! Well, he looked at me like I was crazy, but the next Friday night he pulls up in front of my aunt's apartment and his car is shiny and clean, like new. So I said, okay, we'll go out.

"And so we went out dancing," she said. "And afterwards when we walked back to the car, you know what I saw?"

Claire shook her head like a child, and Tony was listening raptly as if he had not heard this story a dozen times before.

"The whole left side of that Ford was still covered with dust! That crazy *vato* had only washed half the car!" Silvia exclaimed, and Claire and Tony burst into laughter. "There was a neat line right down the middle. It must of took him twice as long as washing the whole car." She paused and added, "That's when I knew he was in love with me."

"But you didn't marry him," Tony half chanted.

"No." A shadow flitted across her face. "No, I came back up here and married your father."

As if on cue there was the rumble of an engine and an old Ford truck rolled into the driveway. Carlos Rodriguez emerged from a cloud of red brown dust.

Short and barrel chested, he wore the traditional working uniform of jeans, boots, and checked shirt. A straw cowboy hat was perched over his mahogany-colored face. His dark, almost black, eyes were set close above a triangular nose, giving him a comical look, and Claire always expected him to be funny. But Carlos was a very serious man.

He scowled when he saw Tony.

"Where were you today? We could of used you, clearing out those ditches. Frank would of been there!"

Tony mumbled something that sounded suspiciously like Fuck off, and Carlos exploded.

"*What* did you say to me?"

"I said I'm not Frank! Frank's dead, in case you hadn't noticed!"

A short silence followed this statement.

"I got some business in Parkerville," Tony muttered. "I'll be back when I'm back."

"You mean you're going up to Riverdale to get drunk and kill yourself on that machine—"

But these paternal protestations were lost in the roar of the Harley, and they watched its blue smoke and dust disappear down the long dirt road.

"I tell you, Silvia, if that kid don't change his ways he's going to wind up in jail! Running with that crowd, doing drugs—you think I don't know what he's up to?" It sounded like a well-worn argument.

"There's nothing wrong with Tony," Silvia retorted. "He's just bored."

"Bored? Why don't he get up off his ass and do an honest day's work; maybe then he wouldn't be bored—"

"There's other kinds of life than this! Tony's not a farmer!"

"Yeah, well *I'm* a farmer, *we're* farmers, and this is a farm, and we could use a little help—"

"Speaking of help," Claire interjected hastily, "I see you're still having trouble with brown rot. How have you been treating it?"

Successfully distracted, Silvia turned away from Carlos. "Well, John Martinez—he's our PCA—he sprayed with Benyl in February and April," she replied, "and he's coming out tomorrow for a preharvest spray."

Claire nodded. Many growers, she had learned, relied on these certified Pest Control Advisors to lead them through the maze of pesticide regulations, tell them when and what to spray, and supply the equipment and the crew to do the job. And it was, in fact, John Martinez, who worked out of Kavoian's Feed and Supply in Parkerville, who had contacted the station. He had been nonplussed by the persistence of the fungus infection at Agua Dulce, and was worried that a strain of *Monolinea* was developing there that was resistant to Benyl, the current state-of-the-art fungicide.

Claire held up her plastic bags. "Well, I've got some samples here I'm going to take back to the lab, do some tests," she told them. "We'll lick this thing, don't worry," trying to convey a confidence she didn't really feel.

"Yeah, sure," said Silvia, smiling, but her eyes were worried. No one would have mistaken her for a teenager right now, at any distance. "I sure hope so, anyway. Carlos and me, we're kind of desperate. We've had a little bit of bad luck the last few years, and if we don't have a decent harvest this year . . ." Her voice trailed off.

"Hey, you've got the best mind in the county working on it," Claire joked, climbing into the truck. "How can we fail?" But her face was as worried and distracted as Silvia's as she drove out. Tony's dust still hung in the air and she inhaled his gritty wake all the way to the highway.

CHAPTER 4

When she pulled into the field station parking lot a car alarm was warbling, *wheedle-wheedle-wheedle,* and two hubcaps were gone from Jim LaSalle's powder blue Silverado pickup. He's going to be pissed, she thought unsympathetically, automatically checking the other cars in the lot: her own Toyota, Ray's burgundy Buick, and Sam's old blue Valiant. Too bad Sam was still here. For reasons of her own she was trying to avoid him, but it wasn't going to be possible today. She trudged up the stairs and into his office.

He was talking to Jim and Ray, settled in a characteristic pose: long legs propped on desk, glasses sliding down nose, polyester shirt of a strange lime-green color buttoned tight around his thin neck. (Did he have an infinite supply of identical ugly shirts or did he rinse that one out every night?)

"Hey, Jim, you're missing some hubcaps."

"Shit!" He leaped up from his chair and tore out the door. "Those goddamned greaser kids!"

Sam was having as much trouble suppressing a grin as she was—some things are funny when they happen to somebody else—but Ray said severely, "This is becoming really annoying. We never used to have trouble like this."

Jim stomped back into the office. "Thank God they didn't scratch the paint. But you're going to have to hire some security guards, Ray."

"We're probably better off spending the money to reopen the municipal pool," Sam said equably. "Kids get mighty bored here in the summer, Jim. As you must remember."

"Why can't they swim in the irrigation ditches like we did?" Jim retorted, and Claire decided to call the meeting to order. Without ceremony she dropped her plastic bags on Sam's desk.

"What does that look like to you gentlemen?"

"Brown rot, classic case of," said Jim. "That from Agua Dulce?"

"Yep."

Sam stared at the bag in dismay and Jim gave a a smug, told-you-so grin. "Well, I'm damned if I know what their problem is," he said. "Nobody else is having trouble like this; it was a pretty wet spring, but if they'd treated it right from the beginning . . . God knows if they're treating it at all. Carlos don't know his ass from a hole in the ground, near as I can tell. Pardon my French," he added, for Claire's benefit. She winced.

Claire had to work with Jim on the *Aspergillus* project, and she tried hard to like him, she really did. But there were certain obstacles.

Jim looked like an eight year old. Not a midget or a dwarf, just a forty-year-old man whose face had stopped changing in 1956. His reddish hair stood straight up in a kid's brush cut; his thick freckled skin was smooth and, as far as she could tell, hairless; his mouth was small and mischievous.

And out of some kind of compensatory effort to raise his macho quotient, he was a gun freak. He had a gun rack in the back of his Dodge pickup. He had a large collection of modern and antique guns, the centerpiece of which was an old Colt .45; and he talked about this gun frequently. Sometimes he even brought it to work.

And finally, he was a patronizing sexist bigot who toadied to the big growers and contemptuously dismissed the small growers. But maybe that was just her own cultural bias.

"They've been spraying regularly," she said defensively.

"Yeah? With what? Bordeaux mixture? Baking soda?" Jim retorted sarcastically, loosening the Western string tie he affected. He had an irritating way of gritting his teeth while he talked, so that his mouth barely opened. The effect was of a bad ventriloquist.

"Now, wait a minute, Jim," Ray interjected. "I happen to know that they've contracted with Martinez from Kavoian's, and they've been using Benyl, same as everybody else. They're putting a lot of money into that orchard. I don't know where they're getting it, to tell you the truth, or how long they can keep it up—"

"I'll tell you where they're getting it," Sam interrupted.

"Silvia's working at the cannery again, and the Grange persuaded First National to extend Carlos a little more credit. They're in hock up to their eyebrows."

The cannery! Claire's heart sank; no wonder Silvia looked tired. You came upon those dark satanic mills if you followed a railroad track deep into the heart of the groves and orchards, and maybe Sam was right; maybe there was some work humans shouldn't have to do.

"Yeah," Jim was saying, "everybody's got problems. But some people know something about growing peaches. I mean, *we* all know"—here he glanced at Claire—"that it's a lot of work to take care of an orchard. And they don't have any crew except themselves and that punk kid of theirs. Did they even clean up their trees after harvest last year? Remove the mummies, to get rid of the conidia? That's probably their problem, right there—"

Sam frowned and Ray, peacemaker as always, interjected hastily, "Now, Jim, they're doing a pretty good job with that place, considering they don't have any money. Carlos gets his brothers over from Alma—"

"Okay, okay, Ray," Jim said, resting his hands on his Monsanto belt buckle. "They're swell folks; they're great farmers. So answer me this: how come they have uncontrollable brown rot and nobody else does? Huh?"

Claire couldn't remain silent. "Because they might have developed a Benyl-resistant strain!" she burst out. "That's what we're trying to find out! I mean, that's just bad luck, it could happen to anyone—"

"Only somehow it always happens to the Rodriguezes," finished Jim. "Let me tell you something, their problem isn't luck, it's incompetence—"

"But they *have* had some bad luck, Jim," Ray said. "Right from the git-go. And now that equipment shed burning—"

"Bad luck!" Jim snorted. "Carlos was drunk and fell asleep with a cigarette in his hand!"

Claire gasped and began to protest, but Sam had beaten her to it.

"And what about the two dozen saplings that got 'dozed into the ground last November? I suppose that was Carlos's fault, too!"

Jim waved a dismissive hand. "Kids' prank. Like you said, things get boring around here." He smiled as he scored the point. "Face it, Sam, the Rodriguezes aren't smart enough to make up for the fact that they didn't start with enough money. They barely had enough to buy that land in the first place, they can't get credit, they try to do all the work on a shoestring using Carlos's family instead of a competent work crew, so of course everything is half assed. In my opinion, if they can't afford to take care of their trees they should sell out right now. That's good land they're sitting on, and they can't make it produce. They should just sell out!

"No," he continued, anticipating Claire's rebuttal, "no, spare us your sentimental notions, Dr. Sharples. Farming is not some picturesque hobby. It's a business, probably the most important business in this country, and it's already got enough problems. There were a dozen bankruptcies filed in the east valley this year, and I hate to tell you how many acres of prime land we lost to developers. To build tract homes and . . . and country clubs, for Christ's sake! What do these people who move up here to get away from it all think they're going to eat when all the farmland is gone?"

Claire paid less attention to the speech, which she had heard before—one of Jim's few redeeming traits was a passionate opposition to development of agricultural land—than to the fact that in his agitation he had moved his mouth in almost normal fashion. She had begun to wonder if his jaw were wired shut.

He took a breath and continued, "If people like Silvia and Carlos don't have the resources to run their own farm, frankly, we can't afford to subsidize them."

And with that he left. Ray rose, mumbled something apologetic, and followed.

Claire erupted, so angry she forgot that she was avoiding Sam.

" 'Can't afford to subsidize them!' How the hell does he have the nerve to say that? How does he think his precious Hanfords and all the other big growers around here survive? Subsidized water, subsidized prices, subsidized low-interest loans, payments in kind. Man, this is Welfare City! If you ask me," she said a little more calmly, "Jim just can't stand the fact that the Rodriguezes are Mexicans who own land. He probably thinks that's a violation of Holy Writ or something!"

"Well, that might be part of it." Sam straightened in his chair, smiling slightly at her hyperbole. "Jim really has it in for Carlos and Silvia. I've never been able to figure out why. But then so do a lot of other people—not because they own land, but because of the way they got it."

Claire raised her eyebrows.

"Sure," he said. "Haven't you ever wondered how the Rodriguezes came to be *patrones* instead of *campesinos?* Agua Dulce is Reclamation Act land. A few years ago somebody lit a fire under the Feds, and they decided to get tough and enforce the 1902 Act. They do this sporadically, you know. So they made the Hanford brothers break up a thousand acres the water lease had run out on."

" 'Course," he added, "the Hanfords managed to retain most of it through the usual means—dummy transactions, holding companies—but when the smoke cleared, Carlos and Silvia were holding the deed to sixty acres of prime delta orchard land, right smack in the heart of Hanford Farms, Incorporated."

"But what's wrong with that?" asked Claire. "Wasn't that the whole point of the Act—to encourage small farming? The Rodriguezes were entitled to that land!"

"Oh, yeah, they were entitled to it. Technically. Only nobody ever takes that part of the Reclamation Act seriously, the part about breaking up land into smaller parcels. As far as the Hanfords and everybody else are concerned, it's just cheap water, no strings attached.

"Except Carlos and Silvia, they took it seriously," he continued. "Especially Silvia. You know, Carlos had worked on the Hanford Delta Farm for twenty years—finally ended up as foreman—and when the water lease expired she decided they should own a piece of it. So she talked to these yuppy lawyers in Fresno, and it turned out they were just looking for a nice test case to come along. And they talked to some friends in Sacramento, who talked to some people in Washington, and the next thing anybody knew Carlos and Silvia had their little farm. Boy, was Bill Hanford pissed!"

He glanced at her as he mentioned the name and she flushed, but said acidly, "Well, my heart goes out to the Hanfords, left with a measly ten thousand acres scattered all over the county."

"No, I guess they won't miss sixty acres, though it's valuable land, especially with the new dam," Sam replied. "They just thought it was a bad precedent. The thin edge of the wedge, so to speak. All the same," he continued thoughtfully, "Jim's right about Carlos and Silvia. They ought to sell—no, no, not because of incompetence, but because of money. Times are tough right now, even for the big growers like Hanford. Well, let's face it, times are always tough. . . ."

Oh, no, not the times-are-tough speech. She prepared herself for the rationalizations that would inevitably follow.

"Look at what happened a couple of years ago," Sam was saying. "A lot of peach growers around here were wiped out because the biggest canning company decided to start buying their canning peaches from South Africa instead of locally. They gave their growers a little warning, told 'em they better start putting in another crop, but of course most people couldn't afford to do that. It's not like annuals, where you can just decide to plant beans instead of cotton this year; trees are a big investment of time and money. . . ."

(Like family, Silvia had said.)

"Well, Silvia was lucky that time; they grow for shipping, not for canning."

Claire shifted her weight restlessly; she knew the moral of this story. "But periodically everyone's luck runs out," Sam droned on. "LA stops eating peaches, or the harvest is too good and you can't get a decent price, or the crop is destroyed by some natural disaster. . . . If you don't have enough capital to survive a cataclysm or two, to diversify and be flexible, well, you're just not going to succeed. The sooner Silvia and Carlos get out, the less heartbreak they'll suffer. Small farming's—"

"Dead in this country," she finally interrupted in exasperation. She had heard the party line on small farming ad nauseam over the past few months, and she still didn't buy it. "Look, you've told me yourself that most of that economies-of-scale argument is crap, that it's an artifact of the whole, well, apparatus—the legal and financial and technological arrangements that favor big, capital-intensive operations—"

"That doesn't make it less true."

"And it doesn't make it fair, either!" Claire said heatedly. "I mean, if Carlos and Silvia got a little support from the people who are supposed to help them, maybe they could make it! But everybody around here is too busy kissing Bill Hanford's ass to care about scum like the Rodriguezes!" she concluded furiously, and grabbing her samples from Sam's desk, stalked downstairs to the lab.

Surrounded by the cool and sterile tools of science, her righteous indignation drained away. Why had she yelled at Sam? He had been in a rare good mood, he had been almost expansive, and in spite of her present ambivalence toward him—which she was not going to think about—he was the closest thing she had to a friend in the whole desolate expanse of Kaweah County. But her anger seemed so close to the surface lately, seeping up like oil through a shale field when she least expected it.

As she sat miserably staring at the floor, there was a light tap behind her. She turned to see Sam leaning against the doorway, his face unreadable behind his heavy glasses.

"Feeling better?" he inquired mildly.

"No, actually, I feel terrible." She took a deep breath. "I'm sorry, Sam. I was angry at Jim and I guess I took it out on you. And I'm worried about Silvia. She's always so . . . so indomitable, but today she seemed old and scared."

"Yeah," Sam said shortly, sitting on the lab bench. He jiggled his right foot, the first sign of nervous energy she had ever observed in him. Usually he was very still, very contained, very . . . repressed.

"You know," he remarked after a minute, "In spite of what you may think, I like Silvia and Carlos. As a matter of fact, I probably like them better than you do. I think they're just an abstraction to you, some kind of symbol of—of Third World oppression or something."

He held up his hand as Claire started to protest. "Okay, maybe that's unfair. All I meant was, I've known them a long time; their son Frank and I, we sort of hung out together when we were kids. . . ." He paused a moment. "And I've bailed Tony out a couple of times," he concluded with a faint smile.

"But Jim's right," he continued. "You still have a lot to learn about farming. It's not some kind of—of moral sweepstakes, where the nicest people win. Take my folks." He stood up and walked to the microscope, where he fiddled with the knobs. "A couple of real sweet, hard-working people. They came out here from Oklahoma in the 'thirties, and saved for twenty years to buy a pitiful little piece of land—their own farm, a dream come true," he said with only a hint of mockery.

"Well, after fifteen years they were bankrupt. Five more and they were dead. That's the romance of small farming in a nutshell, and I can see it happening all over again, with Carlos and Silvia, and . . . damn it, Jim's right about that, too! They'd be better off selling out, and I wish to god they'd just do it!" he ended angrily.

"See you tomorrow," he muttered after a short silence, and walked out.

CHAPTER 5

Claire sat pensively for a few moments, then roused herself and began to prepare a nutrient medium for the Agua Dulce *Monolinea (Monolinea rodrigueza,* she had dubbed it). While her hands mechanically mixed and autoclaved, her mind reviewed the conversation with Sam. Funny how agitated he had become on the subject of the Rodriguezes. He must really be worried about them. It was kind of touching, actually; usually he was reserved to the point of autism. And like so many people out here he was a second-generation Okie; she hadn't realized that. It explained the slight southwestern accent.

Three petri dishes now contained a mixture of potato agar, a little streptomycin to suppress imperialistic bacteria, and a solution of Benyl, the latest superfungicide from the Pennco Co. arsenal. Another three held agar and antibiotic, but no fungicide. She would allow the dishes to set for twenty-four hours, streak them with *Monolinea* from the Rodriguezes' peaches—and wait. If the *Monolinea were* Benyl resistant, she would expect to see some growth on the treated medium after three or four days; the untreated control dishes, of course, should exhibit luxuriant crops of *Monolinea* and whatever else had come along for the ride.

It was about seven o'clock when she finished, and the heat still rose from the asphalt parking lot as she walked to her car. But up in Riverdale it might be starting to cool off, she thought hopefully, heading north. Lately her work days had been getting longer and longer, because of the heat. . . .

No, not because of the heat. Because there wasn't much to do but work. Even before the Hanford incident had made her anathema, her so-called social life had peaked and fizzled.

Well, she had been warned. "Kaweah County!" her friend Carrie, a native San Franciscan, had exclaimed. "It's the kind of place you pass through on your way to somewhere else. It's boring, hot as hell, bleak, the people are conservative, racist, sexist. . . . Well, look, I can understand why you want to get out of here for a while, but—doesn't Marin County need agricultural biologists?"

But it wasn't that people weren't "nice," Claire thought resignedly, turning east on 170 once more; on the contrary, they had been painfully nice, treating her as if she were a foreign exchange student or had some terminal disease. They just didn't know what to make of her, these pleasant, God-fearing, Rotarians—nor, to be fair, did she know what to make of them. A staunch Democrat, sometime socialist, and New England Unitarian, she had never been intimate with a devout Republican in her life. There were a few agonizing social encounters—like the dinner with Ray Copeland and his wife, Nora, during which they had all struggled heroically to find some common ground but finally had lapsed into shop talk—and then her relations with the community sank by mutual agreement to the level of distant but cordial.

Of course, she had her photography and her records and her work, and she went for long walks on the weekends. And there were occasional sublime moments—like this drive home, when the late afternoon sun shot through the tall grass so that, looking up, she could see whole hillsides radiant, like fields of white light. . . .

But she was lonely.

This was such a novel sensation that she scarcely recognized the symptoms. Always it had seemed to her that she had too many social ties and obligations, had to struggle fiercely, even ruthlessly, for the solitude necessary to her work. But now—well, obviously she must be lonely now, she reasoned, accelerating as the road began to climb.

Otherwise, why would she be dreaming about Sam Cooper?

Those damned dreams . . . Her tires squealed as she took a poorly banked curve too fast. It was nearly impossible to maintain a—a professional working relationship with someone about whom your subconscious was regularly churning out steamy fantasies. Take last night's erotic classic. . . .

Absorbed as she was in the edifying exercise of recalling these details, she failed to notice the line of impatient cars accumulating behind her. The irate squawk of a horn startled her and she pulled over to let the parade pass.

Anyway, she thought, resuming her journey, what was really exasperating about these dreams was that they were so —ridiculous. In the past Bill Hanford and Phil had both, not surprisingly, made the odd guest appearance in dreamland, and she was awaiting the debut of Tony Rodriguez.

But Sam Cooper!

It wasn't the first time something like this had happened, or she would have been more concerned: from time to time her treacherous unconscious had fastened on some complete wimp, of the type that abounded in science and that she had spent her life avoiding. Then she would suffer these daily waves of embarrassment until she became attached, in fact or fantasy, to a more appropriate person.

So she just had to ride this out. Because lonely she might be, frustrated she surely was, but nevertheless she had certain standards in these matters, and she deserved more than Sam Cooper. Sullen, funny-looking—

Well, no, he wasn't always sullen. Today, for example, he had been almost friendly, and when he condescended to talk to her, he was quite articulate. And at least he would actually converse instead of insisting on that moronic flirtatious banter that Jim LaSalle seemed to feel was *de rigueur* with females. And he was intelligent, she conceded, passing the motels and beer and bait stores that marked the outskirts (and the in skirts, for that matter) of Riverdale. And she had gradually realized that his political opinions actually were somewhat less Neanderthal than the prevailing norm. And fundamentally he wasn't bad looking: a bit gawky, but that was kind of appealing.

No, the basic, insurmountable problem with Sam, she decided, pulling into her driveway, was that he had no *style.* It was a shame that something so superficial could be so important, but after all, she was a photographer—an artist, in a modest way—and Sam assaulted her aesthetic sense on every front. Look at the clothes he wore! He couldn't be much older than she was—late thirties at most, but he dressed like a high school science teacher from the fifties: polyester pants, polyester sport shirts, heavy-rimmed Roy Orbison glasses. She half expected to see a slide rule hanging from his belt. And look at the kind of music he listened to—that country-western crap—and—and the kind of women he liked.

Ah, yes. The kind of women he liked. Not that she cared,

but the stupid clod clearly lacked the, um, sophistication to appreciate her somewhat angular charms, preferring instead the blatant appeal of that vapid Dolly Parton clone he was with at the Memorial Day picnic. She slammed the front door viciously behind her.

The house was hot enough to bake bread in, but its ambience was, as always, comforting. Her records. Her books. Her photographs on the wall, her food in the refrigerator: it was a little island of Claire in the midst of an alien sea. She listened to Coleman Hawkins, made herself an omelette, read *The New York Review of Books,* and went to bed at ten. If she had dreams, she didn't remember them.

On Friday Sam was absent from the station—up in Fresno or Davis, probably—and she was able to work undistracted. Her work, after all, was the redeeming feature of her stay in Kaweah County, the reason she didn't go scuttling back to Cambridge in defeat. "Modest and pragmatic," as Sam had described it all those months ago, but nevertheless absorbing and satisfying.

Almost embarrassingly satisfying, considering how committed she had been a short time ago to the cutting edge of theoretical microbiology.

But then she had never had the single-minded drive that marked most of the successful scientists she knew. She liked biology, she worked hard at it, but it was by no means an obsession. In fact she sometimes wondered if she hadn't been riding the academic trolley to the end of the line simply to satisfy her father, who was dead and therefore insatiable, or her mother, who was merely insatiable.

Water under the bridge; undoubtedly anyone who is moved to do anything has had too much or too little mother or father. Whatever her particular surfeit or deficit, Claire had long ago become a microbiologist, and right now, every time she went outside to work—into the station orchards or, better yet, out in the field—she felt a little thrill of illicit pleasure, as if she were getting away with something. After all, everyone knew that "work" wasn't performed in broad daylight out in the world; it took place under perpetual artificial twilight, in a completely synthetic environment. So what she was doing must not be work.

Even hanging baited traps from trees to monitor insect

populations, as she was doing at this moment, was still new enough to be fun, though it was hot work. Ray Copeland gave her a friendly wave from a window. Whatever his shortcomings as a small talker, as a boss he surely beat Dr. Donald Mulcahey hands down.

(Carrie had been right about that, too. "I can think of only one thing worse than moving to Kaweah County," she had said. "Telling Mulcahey you're going to do it!" Claire winced unconsciously as she remembered that parting scene. "You know we're doing Nobel caliber work here, Claire," Mulcahey had said, his ruddy complexion deepening to a blistering scarlet. "What are you going to do, lead 4-H groups?" he had asked wittily. "Don't assume this job is going to be waiting for you when you come crawling back in six months," he had offered generously. "You won't publish a single paper while you're gone," he had predicted, firing his parting salvo. "I know!" she had replied fervently, shutting the door.)

After an hour of manual labor she sought refuge in her cool den, and at about seven-thirty inoculated her six petri dishes with fungus from the Agua Dulce peaches, using a cotton-tipped swab to streak each plate. Then she headed for her Friday night ritual of dinner at Casey's, her friendly neighborhood bar.

Riverdale being sort of a tourist town, Casey's was sort of cosmopolitan, meaning fist fights on week nights were rare and an unescorted woman could drink a couple of beers and leave the premises unscathed in body, if not in reputation. And Claire had long since ceased to care about her reputation. The usual motley vehicles were already pulled up in front of the bar when she arrived: Tony's Harley, gleaming like a piece of Bauhaus sculpture, several panel trucks, a green Forest Service pickup (some park ranger down for a night on the town), a couple of big, sleek sedans.

Casey's was cool, smoky, and still relatively orderly. She quickly spotted some of the humans belonging to the machines outside: Tony, leaning against the bar and talking to a chubby mustachioed fellow whom she recognized as one of the regulars, next to him the brick-red crew cut of Jim LaSalle, and at the far end a blond giant in a park service shirt standing with a couple of men in shiny three piece suits that looked like the sedans outside. She ordered a burger and a beer—no quiche and white wine at Casey's—and settled at a corner table, nodding to Tony in passing.

The jukebox was producing its inevitable nasal whine *(The Whites,* she thought; *god, I'm beginning to know them by name!)* and she ate in her usual splendid isolation. The regulars had learned not to approach her, and she had so perfected her polite-but-firm refusal that she could dismiss untrained newcomers in thirty seconds. She wouldn't have minded some high-quality interaction, but since that was unavailable—

Completely without warning a sneak attack of nostalgia blindsided her, knocked her to her knees, and plunged her into excruciating memories of herself and Phil. Walking arm in arm down Brattle Street, bundled against the cold. Sipping espresso at the Blue Parrot after an orgy of Fassbinder films. Lying entwined in his Back Bay apartment, watching the lights flicker on the river. And the talk: heady, stimulating, urgent—

The music's monotonous bass line had changed from a rapid to a slow thump, momentarily distracting her. "Pardon me, you left your tears on the jukebox," a male voice was intoning, "and I'm afraid they got mixed up with mine. . . ."

She giggled, and the spell was broken. Quickly she wrenched her mind to some other topic: Sam, she thought wildly, what would Sam be up to on a Friday night? Probably out with Babette or Trixie or whatever her name was—

"Mind if I join you?" A voice mercifully interrupted this equally dangerous train of thought, and she looked up to see Tony standing in front of her.

"Please do," she replied gratefully. "I was beginning to bore myself."

He swept a chair around and straddled it, cowboy-style. "I got something I want to ask you," he announced, seeming strangely excited by comparison with his usual affectation of languor. His eyes were very bright and his face flushed. Maybe Carlos was right after all; he seemed pretty wired on something. Or maybe he was just a little drunk.

"Fire away," she said with some apprehension.

As it turned out, however, Tony was perfectly lucid, and his burning question strictly professional. He wanted to know about brown rot and, more specifically, about Benyl. "What is that stuff, anyway?" he said. "How come it's such hot shit? It's costing my old man an arm and a leg."

"Yeah, it's very expensive," she replied, touched by his concern—this boy could not have torched his father's shed; how had she even considered it?—"but it's also supposed to be very effective. It's a systemic fungicide, so you can use it as a dormant spray early in the spring as well as later. . . ." She stopped suddenly, feeling foolish. Tony undoubtedly knew these details a hell of a lot better than she did.

"So how come it's not working out at my old man's place?"

"Well, we're not sure, but we think maybe the fungus—the brown rot—at Agua Dulce might be resistant to Benyl. That happens all the time, you know—fungi develop immunity to fungicides, insects develop immunity to insecticides—it's a constant losing battle against evolution," she concluded somewhat pedantically. And now let's talk about Iron Maiden, she thought. Or Us.

But Tony was dissatisfied. He stared moodily at his beer, his long lashes shadowed against his cheek, and Claire was once more stirred by his . . . his beauty, there really was no other word for it. It was hard to believe that in twenty years he would look like his father, that smooth skin furrowed and seamed like a dry riverbed, like the corrugated hills that obsessed her.

He looked up. "See, I was wondering—"

"Hey, Tony," a voice called from the bar, "Buddy here says he wants to buy you a drink."

Tony hesitated for a moment, then rose abruptly.

"I got to go. I'll be back in a minute," he said and sauntered up to the bar.

Oh shit, thought Claire, don't get your nice face smashed in again, Tony. For some time now she had been noticing the bulky figure of Bill Hanford's brother Wallace, known to all as Buddy (*he* was the one who looked like Rod Steiger) propped against the bar. Buddy's belligerence rose with his blood-alcohol content, which must have just reached some kind of threshold. Evidently he and Tony had been having sporadic Friday night brawls ever since the Rodriguezes had moved into Agua Dulce, and since Buddy had about fifty pounds on Tony and was a mean son of a bitch, Tony always came out the loser.

Sure enough, in about five minutes she heard Buddy's low

growl rumbling something that sounded like "Tijuana Trash," a favorite local epithet, and then Tony's voice, high and angry above the din of the bar. She turned just as Tony launched himself at the older man.

He was stopped in mid trajectory. With the dexterity of long practice Mickey the bartender and another peacekeeper moved in to pin his shoulders back, while the park ranger clamped a sequoia-sized arm across Buddy's chest to prevent him from throwing a punch at his helpless opponent. Claire glimpsed Tony's face through the thicket of restraining limbs: eyes glittering, lips drawn back in a snarl, he looked both magnificent and slightly ridiculous. Buddy, red and heaving, was merely ridiculous.

Tony shrugged off his captors and stalked out of Casey's with a certain amount of dignity. In a minute Claire heard the Harley roar off toward the valley.

It was probably a prudent time for her to depart, too, and she walked out into the cool night. To her right a silver half moon was rising over the dark mass of the Sierras, and she could smell the musty, rich scent of the river.

Loud voices shattered this peace, and the two men in suits who had sat at the end of the bar pushed past her into the parking lot, the shorter one giving her a cold, cursory glance as if she were a bug, and an uninteresting bug at that. Same to you, buddy, she thought, swallowing her anger; funny how some men seemed to think it was their god-designated assignment to let you know you just didn't meet their standards of female pulchritude. Of course, they were just as insulting if you did . . . Wait a minute, she knew this creep!

In the neon light the pale jowly face glistened under the thinning dark hair. He looked like a stubby young Richard Nixon . . . and she had had that thought before. Where . . . ?

Oh, yes. The zoning hearing.

Once, out of sheer lonely desperation, she had accompanied Jim LaSalle, of all people, to a county zoning commission hearing, of all things. She hadn't followed the details of the proposed project, something called Golden Hills Golf Course & Estates, too closely. Bill Hanford had been there with Buddy, and Claire, like many of the women in the room, had spent the evening surreptitiously watching Bill. (Her conscience kept reminding her that he was a slimy weasel.) Only after the meeting ended without LaSalle launching into his usual antidevelopment oratory did she realize that this probably had been out of deference to her, and suspect that she had just been on a date. Apparently the experience was as uninspiring for him as for her, and was not repeated.

But the point was, this greasy fellow had made the presentation! Van Houten, Van Horn, some similarly snooty name . . . and he had had a pretty blond surfer boy as an assistant.

She examined the guy's current companion, a powerfully built man with blunt, Latino features who was climbing into the Buick. No, certainly not him. The car spun away, nearly backing over her first so that she had plenty of time to read the yellow bumper sticker: I ♡ GOLDEN HILLS.

CHAPTER 6

It was early yet—not even eleven—and Claire was restless. Seeing Tony had reminded her of how much she really did want to photograph him, with Carlos and Silvia if possible. Maybe tomorrow she would work up enough nerve to drive down to Agua Dulce and ask him. It might tickle his adolescent vanity.

Sam's remark about her attitude toward the Rodriguezes came suddenly to mind. "Some sort of symbol of Third-World oppression," he had said. The memory made her squirm; it had been uncomfortably acute. Yes, of course she romanticized them, but was that why she wanted to photograph them—because she saw them as *things?* Silvia, the Noble Third-World Woman? Carlos, the Victimized Farm Worker? Tony, the Hot Young Stud? After all, at the best of times photography could be patronizing, even exploitative; that's why she preferred inanimate subjects like landscapes.

But the Rodriguezes were *so* photogenic. . . .

With a small philosophical shrug signifying the triumph of art over moral scruple she mentally posed them in front of their house, imagining their dark skin tones—Tony's velvet and light absorbent, his parents' drier, more reflective—against the white plaster. After a moment she let Oscar Peterson loose on her turntable and pulled out the stack of prints she had accumulated since March.

Hills. More hills. Undulant hills, serrate hills, leonine hills, tectonic hills . . . ah, here was something different: an overexposed and underinspired shot of a sunflower against a barbed wire fence, saved purely for sentimental—make that historical—reasons.

The fire at Aguea Dulce had inspired a mild thaw in Claire's relations with Sam, and he had begun to actually invite her along on his field calls. But his attitude hadn't evolved so far as to make the experience pleasant. So for weeks they had driven from station to orchard to ranch to station in stony silence, her desperate attempts at conversation met by silence. Finally, one day in April as they were traveling to a nearby citrus grove Claire had noticed some tall yellow flowers growing by the roadside. *"Helianthus annuus,"* she'd muttered to herself, a habit she had acquired during the preceding weeks.

"Helianthella californica," Sam had corrected absently, "the leaves are completely diff—" He had broken off and turned to stare at her, the pure hard light of fanaticism beginning to shine in his eyes.

"You interested in native vegetation?" he had inquired casually.

"Yes. That is, I know the New England flora pretty well. I don't know anything about California but," she'd added cunningly, "I'd like to learn."

"Like to see a typical riparian woodland habitat?" he had asked. Now Claire's street dead-ended at the river, and on many afternoons she walked along its cool banks. Most of those big-leaved river trees—alders, cottonwoods, sycamores, maples—had close East Coast relatives and were familiar to Claire. But did she say, "Oh, no thanks, I already know all that stuff"? No, she did not. Sam had by then turned off onto a side road without waiting for her reply, and they had spent a pleasant day walking along the river above the dam.

Soon she began to accompany him on his regular weekend walks, hiking into the Sierras to watch spring move up the slopes: magenta redbud, then creamy plumes of California buckeye, luscious yellow Fremontia, and finally starry dogwood. To her surprise she actually enjoyed Sam's company on these excursions. He was relaxed and entertaining, knowledgeable about local natural history and rarely boring. Only occasionally did he pull out his thick *California Flora,* a taxonomic guide to the state's native plants, and spend several intent minutes "keying" some bit of greenery to establish its exact species (he always knew the genus). Claire, being a picture-book botanist—flip through the pictures until you find something that looks like it—bore these episodes with amused patience.

Privately and only half facetiously she attributed Sam's improved personality on these outings entirely to his wardrobe. Rather than his usual body-and-soul-constricting polyester he wore cotton T-shirt and jeans. He must feel better; he certainly looked better.

And then, after a month of mountain walks, Sam had said, "Let's try something different," and turned south. Soon the orchards and citrus groves gave way to bare camel-humped hills, dotted first with black-and-white cattle and then, increasingly, with oil wells like locusts, dipping and sucking in slow rhythm. Turning west, they had threaded through this surreal swarm, holding their noses as they passed the feed lot ("Cowschwitz," Claire murmured before she could censor herself), gradually descended, and finally came into the heart of the valley itself.

The basin, Sam had called it, but The Great Depression might have been more apt. Here, he'd told her, an ancient inland sea had slowly receded, leaving a mosaic of shifting, shallow lakes and expanses of impenetrable marshes, called tulares, that had sustained native tribes and frustrated travelers for centuries. Now, of course, the tulares were no more: diked, drained, and reirrigated, the area was entirely agricultural—currently it was California's "cotton bowl."

But it looked like Mars. This was the essential paradox of the central valley, Claire had realized that day: immensely productive land that somehow managed to look absolutely barren. It was monstrous, in a way. The rolling hills around Citrus Cove clearly were good, fertile land, as humans had traditionally understood that concept, but the valley . . . flat as a stamp, its soil white with alkali salts, to Claire it was the featureless landscape of a nightmare. But to the entrepreneur farmers of the twentieth century it had seemed as inviting as a vast blank sheet of paper, and with great energy and ingenuity they had imposed on its bleak character their own equally bleak but more regular, more profitable, arrangement.

As they had rattled along the narrow gravel roads, she was repeatedly amazed by the juxtaposition of stark white flats on their right—the land in its unirrigated state—and acre after neat, lucrative acre of uniform, synthetic-looking cotton plants on their left. She had tried to capture this bizarre image on film—her most successful attempt hung on the wall across from the couch—but finally was defeated. Its enormous scale demanded some other medium. Like aerial photography, preferably through a bombsight, she thought grimly.

Predictably, however, the basin was Sam Cooper's favorite ecological habitat—not, of course, the cultivated areas, but the small islands of native vegetation that somehow managed to survive in the chinks of agribusiness. He rhapsodized over the flora of the alkali sinks: stunted, tough little plants only a botanist could love, plants whose common names—pickleweed, saltbush, iodineweed—reflected their hostile environment and their lack of charm. From time to time he'd remembered to say things like, "Agriculture could learn a lot from these halophytes," or, "It's amazing how this *Atriplex* has adapted to these saline conditions," which hadn't fooled Claire for a minute. There was no practical reason for his interest; it was infatuation, pure and simple.

But his real passion, botanically speaking, was marshland vegetation. The fact that the marshes had all but vanished from the central valley some years ago didn't deter him in the least. What remained, he loved, and they spent hours wandering through a nature preserve where the tulare habitat had been painstakingly recreated and maintained. The dense, endless stands of rushes stirring softly in the hot air and the sudden harsh cries and wing beats of marsh birds moved Claire, almost against her will, by their eerie beauty.

"This used to cover the whole basin," Sam had said in the hushed voice their surroundings seemed to require, and Claire'd looked at him with wonder. How could a man obsessed by a vanished landscape work for the industry that had destroyed it? It seemed awesomely perverse; she would have to ask him about it sometime.

"The marsh flora must look pretty familiar to you," he'd continued, and she had examined the wall of vegetation.

"Well, I recognize the cattails, but what's that?"—pointing to the tall, slender, spiky rushes that towered over them.

"That? That's *Scirpus, Scirpus acutus!*" Sam had answered, surprised; then, seeing her blank look he'd rattled off some common names. "Tule," he'd said, pronouncing it "too-lee." "Hardstem, bulrush—"

"Bulrush!" Claire had exclaimed, "So that's a bulrush. Ever since Sunday school I've wondered . . . but I've never seen it before in my life."

"Really? Niehaus says it's endemic to the Northeast, too." Then he had launched into a lengthy and esoteric discussion of the various species and subspecies and hybrid species of *Scirpus,* of which he had made an extensive and, Claire thought privately, totally unnecessary investigation. She had continued to snap pictures in self-defense.

Funny, she thought now, flipping through the prints, despite the desolation of the landscape she had gotten some good shots that day. The one on the wall—those wide, windswept vistas; this, of a huge white bird—a heron, she guessed.

She stopped abruptly at the next photograph.

It was of Sam. He was looking up, probably following the heron, unaware that he was being photographed. She studied the face dispassionately, noting the wide mouth, usually tight, here relaxed; the sharp nose, high cheekbones, deep-set eyes (he hadn't worn his glasses that day—"I only need 'em to read," he had said), and the way his stiff hair grew low on his forehead. It was almost an Indian face, and she wondered if there had been a little Seminole, a little Trail-of-Tears, somewhere in his Oklahoma background.

On that day they had conversed more than ever before; even exchanged, very tentatively, a few personal facts. She had talked about Mulcahey, she remembered, and about her family, and . . . oh yes, about Phil, a little. In turn she had learned that Sam was separated from his wife, had a couple of kids who lived in LA, had gone back to school on the GI Bill after Vietnam . . . no details, just the bare outlines of their lives. Still, it had been a beginning of a—a friendship, at least. She had looked forward to more outings.

Only it hadn't been a beginning, evidently. Oh, relations were cordial again—they had recovered from the Hanford incident—but the hikes had stopped. And the dreams had started.

Well, the whole thing was ludicrous and humiliating, she thought, impatiently putting away her photographs. If Carrie knew the high point of her social life in Kaweah County to date was native plant walks with someone like Sam Cooper—worse, that she was *dreaming* about him—she'd probably hire one of those what do you call it—deprogrammers to come and haul her back to Cambridge. Claire poured herself a generous glass of white wine and went to bed.

Saturday she rose at six as always, savoring the morning coolness. She made herself a cup of real Cambridge coffee from her treasured and rapidly diminishing supply, grabbed her camera, and headed west on 170. She had decided to shoot a roll down on the river before driving to Agua Dulce and importuning the Rodriguezes.

On her right Lake Prosperity sparkled serenely in the early sun. A few fishermen were out, but the weekend hordes of water-skiers and speed boaters had not yet arrived. As she was passing the west end, just before the dam, a familiar blue car caught her eye. Sam's Valiant was parked off the road, and beyond it was the battered black-and-white Chevy that represented one-third of Riverdale's police fleet. Sam must be fishing with Tom Martelli, the chief of police and (like everyone else in the county, evidently) an old friend.

Though it was an odd place to fish . . . Then she saw a county sheriff's pickup, and then a state police car and an ambulance. Her stomach tightened uneasily as she pulled off the highway. A knot of people was gathered on the end of the narrow concrete dam, watching the tow truck from Ernie's Chevron operate some kind of winch from shore. She stopped the car and ran toward the lake. A terrible idea was forming in her mind.

It was with tremendous relief that she recognized Sam's spare figure in the crowd.

"Sam, what's happening?" she called out. "Has there been an accident?"

He turned, walked very slowly toward her, and halted at the end of the dam. She looked up at him. Even behind his dark glasses his face looked drawn and fatigued, and suddenly she was frightened again.

"Sam—?"

"It's Tony Rodriguez," he said shortly, stepping onto the shore. "He finally managed to kill himself on that goddamn bike."

CHAPTER 7

Afterward when Claire thought about that morning it was like trying to reconstruct a hallucination. Sounds and actions had taken on sinister meanings she couldn't quite grasp: the incessant whine and clank of the winch; the squeal of brakes as passing motorists noticed the action and pulled off for a closer look; their avid faces, distorted like Diane Arbus photographs, peering past the highway patrolmen who were holding them at bay. She seemed to keep asking Sam questions without comprehending his answers.

"But what happened? What is the tow truck doing? Are they looking for—for him?"

"No, they've got the body." Sam jerked his head in the direction of the ambulance. "Two kids found . . . it . . . floating above the dam about an hour ago, came up to the east end of the lake, and got Tom and me. We were fishing. Right now they're trying to pull out his bike."

"His bike?" Claire repeated stupidly.

"The crazy son of a bitch tried to ride across the dam last night. Went right over the edge. Broke his fucking neck," he said savagely, but Claire was too dazed to notice his tone.

"Last night? But I saw him last night at Casey's. I talked to him," she insisted, as if making some important point.

"Yeah, well, Casey's is probably where he got a snootful."

"No, he wasn't drunk," said Claire, remembering, "at least not very drunk. Not too drunk to make it over the dam; he told me he did that all the time."

"Well, he didn't do it this time," Sam said harshly. "So somewhere he had some more to drink, or to smoke, and then when he was really loaded he got this bright idea. Ride across the dam! Better than Disneyland! Jesus, what a stupid kid!

Almost as stupid as his brother, who was the dumbest bastard who ever lived—"

His voice caught, and he sat down abruptly on an outcropping of granite, shading his eyes with his hand as if the light penetrated even his dark lenses.

Claire looked at him helplessly. As always, she felt paralyzed in the presence of strong emotion, including her own. Impulsively she reached out to touch his shoulder and then stopped herself. Instead she stood numb, tears stinging her eyes, unable to cry.

They remained motionless for several minutes, Sam rigid, staring at the ground, unaware of her presence. Presently excited conversation roused them, and they turned to see that the tow truck had done its job. Tony's Harley lay dripping on the shore. Sam stood up and walked over to it, with Claire following rapidly.

The bike, better designed for life's rigors than its rider, had escaped injury. *Each thing kills the man who loves it,* Claire thought confusedly, looking down at it, shining like some treasure salvaged from the deep, the seaweed intertwined among its chrome spokes. . . . Wait a minute, seaweed? In a lake?

"Sam, what—" she began, but Sam was already on his knees, examining the long, green, whiplike plants.

"Scirpus," he said briefly, rising. "And *Allenrolfia,"* prodding a waterlogged succulent with his toe.

"Allenrolfia?" echoed Claire, but the county sheriff interrupted these botanical irrelevancies.

"Look, let's get this bike up on the truck and get it out of here. We can examine it later, down in Parkerville," he barked.

"But, sheriff, that's *Allenrolfia.* Iodineweed," Claire said urgently.

"So?"

"So it doesn't grow around here. It grows down in the alkali sinks. How did it get on Tony's bike?"

The sheriff stared at her with hostility. He had a round pink face and a round, presumably pink, belly, and in spite of his regulation General MacArthur sunglasses and Wehrmacht boots was somehow unimpressive. "Who the hell are you?" he asked succinctly.

"I'm . . . my name is Claire Sharples, I work at the Citrus Cove Sta—"

"Yeah, well let me tell you something, Miss Sharp. When he wasn't making some kind of trouble, this Rodriguez kid was riding that bike. At one time or another he probably traveled every road in this county. So yesterday he was down in south county tearing up some weeds. So what?"

So what? Claire thought about the Harley as she had seen it last night, outside Casey's. . . .

"Listen, sheriff—"

"Look, lady, I've got a major traffic jam about to happen here and I'm going to get this area cleared and get the hell out. If you've got something to say that has some bearing on this accident, stop by the office in Parkerville later. I'll be happy to talk to you then." He dismissed her with a curt nod.

During this interchange Sam had disappeared. Claire saw him sitting behind the wheel of the Valiant, head resting against the back of the seat, sunglasses off, eyes closed. He opened his eyes as she approached.

"Sam, about that tule," she began hesitantly.

"Jesus, Claire," he said wearily, "forget about the tule. It's not important."

Claire persisted stubbornly. "But listen, Sam, last night I saw Tony's bike in the parking lot at Casey's."

"And?"

"And it was sparkling, immaculate, just like always, no ugly green weeds wrapped around its spokes. So that means that Tony must have picked up the tule and the iodineweed after he left Casey's. And why would he have gone down to the basin at eleven on a Friday night, just to ride around?"

"Because he was nuts," Sam answered dully, replacing his glasses. "It seems totally in character to me. I don't know what's bothering you." He started the engine.

"I'll tell you something else about that tule, if you really want to know," he said, revving the motor.

"What?"

"It's not even ordinary *Scirpus acutus*. I think it's the *Scirpus validus* I told you about that day . . . that day we went to the marshes. Remember, I said I thought I'd documented its presence in one place here in the central valley?"

Claire looked blank. "Oh, yes . . . Tell me about it again."

"Well," said Sam, sitting upright and switching off the engine, "there seems to be some confusion about this particular species." A note of animation entered his voice. "Munz used to say it was rare, located only up in the northern counties; now he says it's endemic to the Santa Ana riverbed down in LA. But this stuff I've found seems to conform to his description all right: culms compressible, scales rusty-colored and—"

"Yes," said Claire patiently, "but where? Where did you find this, um, *valentus,* whatever . . . ?"

"Validus," corrected Sam, "and I'm not saying it is. It might only be a hybrid; these things hybridize all the time—"

"Where did you find it?"

"I told you that day; I even pointed out the road. At the old abandoned migrant camp, remember? At Amargosa Springs."

She vaguely remembered the name. "Was that a place Tony knew about?"

"Sure. We go—used to go—duck hunting there. . . ." Sam's voice trailed off. He started the engine abruptly, and drove away.

After Sam left, Claire sat in her Toyota for nearly ten minutes, staring at the lake, incapable of movement. Finally, acting on the vague belief that the familiar journey would be somehow reassuring, she continued down the hill to Parkerville. But she had forgotten she would have to pass the entrance to Agua Dulce. Oh God—Silvia. By now she would know.

Try not to think of the terrible grief unfolding at the end of that long dirt road. Think about—think about tule. *Scirpus acutus,* or *validus,* as the case might be. Should she stop at the sheriff's office? What would she say? Sam's explanation was undoubtedly correct. Tony had spent the last hours of his short life riding through the basin for the same reason he had done everything: because there was nothing else to do in this god-awful backwater.

The lush orchards on her right gave way abruptly to an area which had mystified her the first time she had seen it: a huge bare field, marked at regular intervals by charred circles about six feet in diameter. Row after row of them ran off into the horizon, like the Sea of Holes in *The Yellow Submarine.*

"What is that?" she had asked Jim LaSalle one day. "Are they preparing to put trees in or something?"

"Nope," he had replied, amused by her ignorance, "that's

where the trees used to be! This was an almond orchard. The Hanfords cleared it off last year."

"Were the trees diseased?"

"Oh, no, perfectly healthy ten-year-old trees. Bill Hanford just didn't like the way the almond market was looking. We had bumper crops a couple of years in a row, and the price really broke. So he decided to do something else with the land."

At the time she had been mildly appalled by the thought of all those trees put to the torch—but now, suddenly, she was consumed by white-hot rage. She hated this place, where everything was a commodity; this place, which wasted its water, its trees, its fruit, its children. . . .

Shaking with emotion, she skidded to an abrupt stop in front of an abandoned roadside stand. GRAPEFUIT. ORANGES, the faded sign said, 5 LBS/$1. SWEET PEACHES IN SEASON.

She rested her forehead against the steering wheel. Tony was dead. How could she comprehend that? She couldn't; she couldn't even weep for him. That release seemed to be unavailable to her. She hadn't cried for years, not since her father had died, and now her eyes smarted and her throat tightened but no tears flowed.

Eventually she pulled back onto the highway and continued west, then turned south on 99, driving with apparent aimlessness. When she hit the tiny hamlet of Roosevelt—two bars, a general store, and a dusty quarter mile of farm workers' shacks—and turned westward again, she thought, *I guess I'm going to Amargosa.*

There was only one problem with this plan: she didn't know where Amargosa was. All she knew was that on their trip to the marshes Sam had pointed to a dirt road, identical to dozens they had passed, and had muttered something about tule. She seemed to recall that he had also talked about its being one of the seasonal villages of the local Indians, and had made some joke about that—yes, that's right, he had said it was a "seasonal village" during the Depression, too; that there had been a federal camp for the Dust Bowl migrants. . . .

Fine. So where was it?

After roaming around the back roads of the desolate flatlands for close to an hour, she came upon a configuration of cottonwoods and an ancient barbed wire fence that looked familiar. She turned onto the deeply rutted dirt road and followed it for several torturous miles of potholes and gulleys. Just as she was beginning to wonder how much longer her muffler could cling to the bottom of her car, she rounded a curve and saw a clearing containing the scattered debris of old buildings. She had arrived at Amargosa.

She got out of her car and stood for a moment, listening. The air was very hot and still, with the curiously dead quality she had felt that day in the marshes, as if the rushes that lined the road and pressed in on the camp captured all motion and translated it into their own sibilant rustling. As she walked slowly toward the clearing, she noticed a confused overlay of tire tracks in the soft dirt of the road. She had no idea how recent they were or what kind of vehicles had made them, except that one imprint, single and narrower than the rest, must be a motorcycle track. Brilliant, she thought disgustedly, and picked her way through the scraps of plywood, corrugated tin, ancient tar paper, and two-by-fours.

She surveyed this ruin and began to reconstruct it in her imagination, resurrecting the tents and rickety shelters, populating them with ragged children and hollow-eyed adults. It would have been remarkably like the present-day camps she came upon from time to time, half hidden in the midst of an orange grove or an orchard. In the fifty years since the Depression the lives of farm workers hadn't altered much. Their numbers had dwindled, and their ethnicity had changed, but then the Dust Bowl migrants themselves had been only one brief passage in the procession of peoples who had come to harvest the crops. The Chinese. The Japanese. The Filipinos. American blacks from the South, Sikhs, Yemenites—and, of course, Mexicans. A WPA camera crew wandering the San Joaquin Valley today would photograph brown-skinned faces rather than Dorothea Lange's gaunt Okies and Arkies.

The memory of those haunting images made her shiver in the hot sun. In this sad place it was easy to believe that watchful, hungry eyes stared at her from just beyond her field of vision, and try as she would to shake off this strangely superstitious notion, the feeling of dread persisted.

Unsure of what she was seeking, she nevertheless forced herself to explore further. Beyond the clearing, partially hidden by a flourishing salt cedar, she found a long, low shed, still relatively intact: it even had a functioning door. This she pushed open slowly, and then stood blinking in the darkness. As her eyes gradually adjusted, what she saw bewildered her. Stacked against the far wall, in neat rows reaching nearly to the low ceiling, were about ten forty-pound sacks bearing a familiar red logo: BENYL.

Why would somebody be storing fungicides way out here? she wondered, walking toward the pile of sacks. She stopped abruptly. From somewhere behind her had come a faint creak, like the opening of a door, that shattered the silence like the crack of a rifle. She whirled, heart thudding, rushed to the door, and peered out. Nothing. Just that her vague sense of being watched was suddenly unbearable.

Claire had never thought of herself as a particularly timid person. But now she was filled with blind, unreasoning, primordial terror. She sprinted across the clearing toward the haven of her Toyota, flung herself into the car, and tore down the dirt road as fast as she could without concussing herself against the roof, constantly watching the rearview mirror for signs of pursuit. But the dust behind her was impenetrable.

It was early afternoon when she returned to Riverdale. For several hours she wandered aimlessly around the house, too exhausted to think constructively, too overwrought to rest, but at about six-thirty she fell into a brief, feverish sleep. And after all these months she dreamed, finally, of Tony.

Strands of seaweed hung about him like holy medallions. He smiled, walked toward her, loomed over her, his eyes swimming in his face like dark fish, his cold mouth closing over her own. She awoke with a galvanic jump, heart pounding, sweat soaked. Incredibly, it was only seven-thirty and still unbearably hot. Her house, usually so soothing, seemed like a stifling prison. Panic and claustrophobia swept over her. She had to get out, go somewhere!

But where? None of her usual emotional remedies was available. No old friends to drop in on, no all-night bookstores or Bergman movies, no little clubs with hot jazz—

Eventually she picked up the phone and dialed a long string of digits, and three time zones and three thousand miles away, another phone jangled in an empty Cambridge apartment. On a Saturday night Carrie would be out to dinner or at a movie; she might even be down on the Cape for the weekend. Claire hung up the phone.

The thought of rocky beaches and cold, clean seawater made her even more desolate. After a moment she dialed again. She let the phone ring ten times; just as she was about to hang up, sick with disappointment, a voice answered gruffly.

"Yeah?"

"Sam—this is Claire."

"Yeah?"

Relief gave way to mortification. *This is a big mistake,* she thought, but plunged on. "I was just wondering—" *Wondering what? Wondering if you could pretend to be my friend for a while?* "Uh, wondering if you were going to be around tonight . . . if it wouldn't be an imposition or anything—well, I was thinking maybe I could stop by. . . . I wanted to talk to you about . . . something," she ended lamely.

Dead silence. Then, "I'm not going anywhere," he said.

Well, that sounded like an invitation to her! "I'll be right up."

Sam lived in the foothills above Riverdale, about fifteen minutes away. Claire pulled into what she thought was his driveway, but the small house—cabin, really—looked dark and deserted. *Maybe he snuck out the back,* she thought. Then she saw the red glow of a cigarette, and, as her eyes became accustomed to the fading light, the silhouette of someone sitting on the porch steps. She walked up the path, drinking in the blessedly cool air and the friendly sound of crickets.

She stopped in front of the steps, feeling extremely awkward. Finally she said inanely, "I didn't know you smoked."

"I don't," Sam's voice came quietly out of the darkness, its faint twang more noticeable than usual. "Just a little backsliding is all. Have a seat."

She sat down beside him.

"Now what did you want to talk to me about?" he said, these welcoming pleasantries completed.

Claire took a deep breath. "Well, that was somewhat misleading. Actually, I just wanted some company. I was feeling kind of upset."

Absolutely nothing followed this remark. It was as if she had spoken in Urdu.

"About Tony," she added.

Still no response. *Oh, this was pointless; I should never*

have come, she thought. *What the hell did I expect? Sam's cold and uncommunicative at the best of times; tonight he's undoubtedly absorbed in his own grief. I should make some excuse and leave—*

Suddenly he rose. "Afraid I finished the Scotch," he said. "Want a beer?" and he walked into the house without waiting for a reply. In a moment he returned, switched on the outside light, and handed her a Coors. *I'll just drink it and leave,* she thought, and then, seeing Sam for the first time, drew in her breath sharply. He looked ghastly; his thin face was like a death's head. It must be the yellow porch light, which drained him of color.

He turned to see her staring at him.

"You look pretty tired," she said, embarrassed.

"A little tired, a little drunk." A pause. Then, "I talked to Silvia and Carlos."

"Oh." Of course. Somebody had to tell them about Tony, and Sam was the logical person. "How . . . how are they?"

"How do you think they are, knowing they raised two sons too stupid to live past the age of twenty?" he said brutally.

Claire was shocked. This was not the response she had expected. "Two sons . . . I thought Frank was killed in Vietnam!"

"Oh, yeah, he was killed in Vietnam. Sure was." He stood and leaned against the wooden pillar. There was a long pause. Finally he said, "Frank wasn't dumb, in spite of what I just said. But he had no imagination, and he was absolutely fearless. Maybe those qualities are related, I don't know. Anyway, they made him a great football player and a great soldier. Oh yeah, the army just loved him. Ate him right up. Promotions, bang bang bang; medals, bang bang bang—only the last medal was posthumous. One bang too many." He grinned at his own joke.

Claire winced. "Were you with him?" she asked timidly. She had always been afraid to ask him about the war—well, she had always been afraid to ask him anything remotely personal. But somehow the enormity of the day's events had eroded her tact.

"No," he said, "no. Jim LaSalle was in his unit, and some other guys from around here, but I was a couple hundred miles away. In Thailand. We all enlisted together, but I got smart," he said with a sneer. "I learned Thai and took myself out of combat. But like I said, Frank had to be where the action was." He sat down again.

"Sorry if I raked up bad memories."

He shook his head. "Oh, it was a long time ago. It's just that—" He halted. The silence stretched out until Claire wondered if he would complete his thought.

"Guess I've got a guilty conscience or something," he said presently in a low voice. "Like maybe if I'd been there I could've restrained Frank's kamikaze impulses. I could usually do that. Anyway, when I first came back from Thailand I started having this dream." He paused again, then proceeded with difficulty. "See, I'm fishing, up along the river—the way it used to be before the dam—and I snag something, something big. So I reel it in, and it's a—a person, a man, and I turn it over . . . and it's Frank. Dead. Gray and swollen, like he'd drowned in the river.

"Well, I just stand there, staring down at his dead face, not really understanding what's happened . . . and then, real slow, he opens his eyes and looks at me. And smiles."

He laughed shakily and drained his beer. "Scares the shit out of me, every time."

Claire shuddered, remembering her dream of that afternoon, and Sam continued. "When I saw Tony today . . . he looked so much like his brother. . . ." He stopped.

They sat quietly for several minutes. Presently she said, "I went to Amargosa today."

"Amargosa! Why the hell . . . oh, the tule." He shook his head in disbelief. "Nancy Drew, girl microbiologist."

Trust Sam to find the remark most likely to keep me at a distance, she thought with resignation, but she was too tired to react. Even Sam seemed to regret his witticism, for in a moment he asked, "See any *Scirpus?"*

She roused herself to answer. "Plenty of *Scirpus acutus,* at least that's what it looked like to me. I didn't get a chance to look for your *validus,* because I got distracted."

"By what?"

"Well, first of all I saw lots of tire tracks, some of which might have been the Harley's, only I couldn't tell when they were made. And then—there's an old shed down there beside a salt cedar—you know the one I mean?"

"Sure."

"There were about ten sacks of Benyl stacked up in there.

Does somebody own that land? I couldn't figure out why anyone would be storing fungicide in the middle of nowhere."

"Well, yeah, somebody owns the land—no such thing as free land around here—but I'm not sure who it belongs to right now. Used to be Hanford property, but I believe they sold it a few years back. I'm going to get another beer," he said, rising.

She followed him into the house and collapsed on the couch. She was very, very tired, she realized, but nevertheless she surveyed the pleasantly rustic room with a certain amount of curiosity. Not many clues to the character of its inhabitant, but plenty to his activities: lots of books, scholarly journals, newspapers strewn about; fishing gear in one corner, a shotgun and some cartridges in another, a couple of Geological Survey maps on the wall. But no works of art or other frivolous objects of adornment. Then she saw a framed color photograph at the end of the couch. She leaned closer to examine it; her eyes were having trouble focusing. Two small blond boys smiled out at her. "To Dad, from Shannon and Terry," one had written in a round, childish scrawl. Sam's kids. Did he ever see them? she wondered. She would ask him sometime. . . .

"Anything else interesting out at Amargosa?" Sam called from the kitchen, interrupting her reverie.

"No," she answered sleepily. "It's kind of a creepy place, though. I kept thinking that someone was watching me." She omitted a description of her terrified and unheroic dash for the car.

"Probably the ghost of Clarence Cooper," she heard Sam say, as if from a great distance, "my father. He lived at that camp for a couple of months in 'thirty-nine. . . ."

But she never heard the end of this interesting bit of personal history. When Sam came out to hand her a beer, she was asleep on the couch.

Tantalizing odors and a strange, repetitive noise gradually permeated her consciousness. She woke stiff and momentarily disoriented, realizing after several seconds where she was and what had happened—and that Sam had covered her with a blanket, which both embarrassed and pleased her. She staggered toward the kitchen, source of the wonderful smells (coffee and bacon) and the strange sounds (Sam, singing, by god, a country song, whose refrain rose and fell monotonously. *"'If you're tryin' to break my heart, you don't have very far to go. . . .'")*

"Hi," she said awkwardly. The singing stopped abruptly.

"Good morning," he replied politely, pouring a bowlful of eggs into a pan.

"I guess I sort of crashed and burned, as we used to say in my youth."

"Fell into a drunken stupor after one beer, is what I'd say. Hate to think it was my conversation. Have some coffee."

The coffee tasted strongly of ancient aluminum percolator, but it hit the spot. "Eggs and bacon coming up," he continued, then peered at her suspiciously. "You're not a vegetarian?"

"I make an exception for bacon."

"Good, because this is all soy filler anyway. Grab a plate."

They sat on the back stoop and ate in silence, Claire too preoccupied to make her usual attempts at conversation. Her analytical powers worried at the puzzle of Tony's last hours, the iodineweed, and anomalous sacks of Benyl. Meanwhile, a less disciplined part of her brain was absorbed in contemplation of the fine, sun-bleached hairs on Sam's forearm, his long legs in soft blue jeans, the pleasant, lightly sweaty smell of his T-shirt. . . .

With a shock she became aware of this subversive mental activity. *I've got to get out of here,* she thought urgently and stood up.

"Thanks for the hospitality and the breakfast. It was delicious, I need to be getting back, I've got some work to do, see you at the office," she said breathlessly.

Sam looked even blanker than usual. "Sure," he said, rising slowly, "anytime. See you Monday."

She hurried to her car, slightly ashamed of her ungraciousness. But it had been a matter of self-preservation. Nocturnal fantasies, however spectacular, were one thing, but to lust after Sam Cooper in broad daylight, in full possession of her faculties . . . what was the matter with her? Had heat and loneliness burned out important circuits in her brain?

She headed west on 170. Well, she reasoned cautiously, she was upset about Tony. That had made her vulnerable, and Sam, in his peculiar way, had been unexpectedly kind. He had told her his dream; he had covered her with a blanket. . . .

She pulled herself up sternly. Sure. That was what was dangerous about Sam: his unpredictability. Very occasionally that aloof manner was punctuated by flashes of warmth, all the more touching for their rarity. It's just random reinforcement, a highly effective technique for training dogs and other dumb creatures, she thought resentfully, remembering her behavioral psychology. And furthermore, when someone was as reticent as Sam it was natural to feel, well, flattered, even grateful, when he did share a confidence.

Somehow this ingenious and scrupulous analysis didn't seem to fully explain the fact that her adrenaline was pumping like an eighth grader's.

She turned into her driveway and sat, perplexed, considering. Phil, now . . . she approached the subject of Phil very carefully, as if navigating a mined harbor. Phil was what you might call an overtly sexy man. Not crude; but somehow his bearing implied—in a discreet, civilized, professorial manner, of course—that he was interested in women, that he could show them a good time, so to speak. But Sam seemed so remorselessly asexual. . . .

Well, obviously he wasn't. He had fathered two children, and there was what's her name—Darlene, Loretta—who hardly seemed like a platonic companion, but it was so difficult to imagine, it was the dark side of the moon. What was he like, under the reserve and the Dacron? Passionate? Selfish? Inept? Romantic? It was intriguing, it was tantalizing, it was driving her nuts—

Great, she thought disgustedly, getting out of the car. Two excellent reasons for being attracted to someone: masochism and curiosity. To hell with the surly bastard anyway, she thought, working up a little therapeutic righteous indignation, and proceeded to mop the kitchen floor.

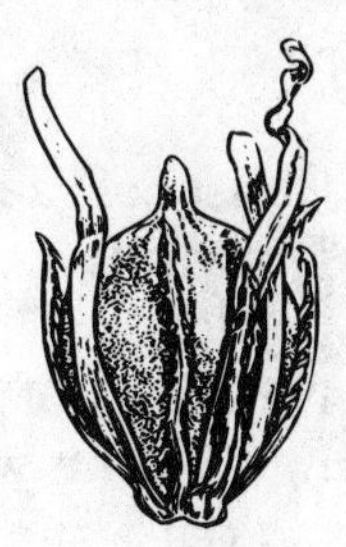

CHAPTER 8

Claire slept very badly that night. Doggedly she lay in bed long after the sun rose, clinging to the faint hope that she might capture a couple of solid hours, but at nine, feeling slightly deranged, she made her way to the station and headed straight for the lab. All she wanted to do was shut the door, turn up the air-conditioning, and read something very technical and unambiguous. She didn't want to see anyone, or talk to anyone.

Inevitably she ran into Sam immediately.

She collected herself and regarded him warily. He certainly appeared to be his usual unalarming, unappealing self; nevertheless she anxiously monitored her reactions. Elevated pulse rate? Hot flashes? No, she concluded with relief; yesterday had just been some weird hormonal blip after all.

"Hi," she said, and attempted to walk past him to the stairs.

"I was just coming to see you." She halted reluctantly. "The county sheriff, Cummings, wants to talk to you," he said.

"To *me?"* She stared at him in amazement.

"It's kind of a long story. Come into my office and I'll explain.

He perched on the edge of his desk while Claire eyed him apprehensively.

"Tom Martelli just called," he said. "The county coroner's office finished the autopsy on Tony."

"Autopsy?" she repeated weakly, the finality of the word making her feel sick.

Sam was regarding her unsympathetically. "Look, you want to hear this or not?"

"Of course," she said unconvincingly.

"Okay," he said, ticking the points off on his fingers. "One.

Cause of death: asphyxiation due to water in the lungs. Drowning, in other words. No surprise there. Two. Blood alcohol level of point-oh-five, well below legal intoxication level. No traces of anything else, either." He looked at Claire. "You told me he wasn't drunk. You were right."

"Yes," she said, "but I thought he might have been high. Guess he was just excited. Go on."

"Three, there were extensive head injuries, not inconsistent with hitting the edge of the dam as he fell off his bike. Not inconsistent with some other possibilities either. I'll get to that in a minute."

She waited, her own head throbbing ominously.

"Well, as far as Cummings was concerned, Tony alive was just a pain in the ass, and Tony dead was a problem solved. So he didn't want to waste too much of his feeble brain power on the, uh, incident. But I told Tom Martelli about the sacks you saw out at Amargosa, and Tom told Cummings, and Cummings suddenly got very agitated."

"I don't understand. . . ." said Claire confusedly.

"Drugs," said Sam briefly.

"See, Cummings now feels that Tony may have been bashed somewhere else and dumped in the lake," he explained in a level voice, "which in fact is a much more plausible explanation of the head injuries and the iodineweed on the bike and the fact that there were a lot of prints on the bike that weren't Tony's. And so on."

Bashed on the head and dumped in the lake . . . She sat down abruptly. Well, of course; wasn't that what had been in the back of her mind since she had seen the *Scirpus* on Tony's bike that morning? Wasn't that really why she had made her apparently aimless pilgrimage to Amargosa? Then why was she so shocked? Why did she feel she had been hit with a blunt instrument? She winced at the unfortunate phrase and tried to concentrate.

"So he got this inspiration about your sacks," Sam was saying. "He figures they were filled with, um, drugs, and that Tony's death was somehow connected with them."

Claire was silent for a moment. Then, "What does he mean by drugs?" she said.

Sam looked at her.

"I mean," she continued, "is he talking about marijuana? Because that stuff in the shed sure didn't smell like marijuana." Sam gave a brief, half-conspiratorial smile of acknowledgment. "And if he means cocaine or—or heroin, well ten forty-pound sacks would be—hell, I don't know, billions of dollars worth."

"He doesn't know what he means," Sam said flatly. "He just thinks this could be a major coup for James T. Cummings—Million-Dollar Drug Ring Uncovered by Rural Sheriff. It's probably bullshit. I mean, an international cocaine-smuggling operation headquartered in—in Roosevelt, God help us. . . ." Laughing in spite of himself, he picked up the phone, dialed and handed it to Claire.

She answered the sheriff's questions mechanically.

"That's right—about ten sacks. Marked Benyl. No, I didn't check to see what was inside them, I—something startled me. . . . Yes, all right. You're welcome."

She hung up the phone and looked at Sam. "You know," she said slowly, "it's really not such a bad idea. In some ways that area is ideal for smuggling: it's remote; small planes fly in and out of there all the time—"

"Oh, it's plausible," Sam interrupted. "I just don't believe it. I mean I don't believe Tony was involved; I don't think he would have gotten mixed up in drug-dealing in any major way. . . ."

On the contrary, Claire was thinking, it seemed exactly what Tony would have done. What future did a poor Chicano kid have in Kaweah County? Any kid, for that matter? Stealing hubcaps from the field station parking lot was a pretty pathetic source of amusement; no wonder half of them left for LA or San Francisco as soon as they were old enough to reach the Trailways ticket counter. Tony was bright and rebellious, and faced with the prospect of working in the fields until his back gave out—or at McDonald's or the packing house until his mind gave out—he had probably decided that a little drug dealing looked pretty attractive. Claire couldn't really blame him. And it would certainly explain his violent death. Sam was just letting sentiment cloud his judgment.

Some of her skepticism must have communicated itself to Sam, who stared mutely at the floor and looked stubborn.

"Then why was he murdered?" she asked bluntly. "*If* he was murdered."

"There are lots of reasons for killing someone," he replied. "But I'll tell you one thing: if this international drug ring theory of Cummings's keeps him investigating the case, then I think it's a fine hypothesis."

Reasons for wanting to kill someone. Something came burbling up from her subconscious, and before she was able to censor it she blurted out, "Buddy Hanford!"

Sam looked at her. "That was the first thing I thought of," he admitted. "In fact, I asked Tom Martelli to check it out, and *he'd* thought of it too and had already called up to Casey's—Buddy's usually up there on Friday nights. But it won't wash. Buddy and Tony had a fight, all right, as per usual, but after Tony left Buddy stayed there drinking until two, at which time he was too drunk to stand. Somebody had to drive him home, so he didn't get home 'til three, and when we found Tony at six this morning the body . . . well, they could tell he'd been dead more than three hours."

Claire listened dumbly to Sam's account and nodded intelligently, but in fact her tenuous grip on the reality of this conversation was slipping away. "I'm going down to the lab," she managed to say when he had finished, and escaped into the hall where she pressed her forehead against the cool, tiled wall. Then she walked slowly downstairs.

At around two o'clock she returned to Sam's office. His phone began ringing as soon as she closed the door, and he pounced on the receiver.

"Yeah, Tom," he said. "Uh-huh—oh, is that so? I bet he's pissed off. . . . No, I don't know what to think, but I'd say she's pretty reliable. . . . Yeah. Oh, listen, Tom—what did he drive out there? That Chevy? Okay. So long."

He looked at Claire. "That was Tom Martelli," he said. "Cummings just got back from Amargosa. They didn't find any sacks of anything out there. He claims the shed was totally empty."

She stared at him in dismay. "Sam, they were there! Somebody must have moved them—I told you I had the feeling I was being watched!"

"Oh, I believe you. Cummings doesn't, of course—but he's faced with a real dilemma: he likes this drug-smuggling idea a lot, but he thinks you're a hysterical female." He was too absorbed to note her scandalized expression. "I just wish I knew what the hell was going on."

He sat thoughtfully for a moment. Claire was momentarily distracted by a noise behind her; she turned just in time to see Jim LaSalle's unmistakable face disappear from the doorway. When she turned back to Sam he said, "Got anything real pressing this afternoon?"

"No . . . why?"

"Because I think we should take a drive down to Amargosa."

CHAPTER 9

An hour later they had turned down the narrow dirt road that led to Amargosa. After several rough miles, Sam suddenly said, "Pull over here and park. I want to take a look at some of the tracks you saw Saturday."

Claire complied, and stood looking attentively at the dirt and gravel road surface. After several moments of this futile exercise she exclaimed, "This is impossible. I don't know what I'm looking for, and in this soft dirt it's complete chaos—"

"Calm down," Sam said. "Let's start with something easy."

They squatted side by side in the dust, Claire uncomfortably aware of Sam's arm almost touching her own. "Here are the tracks we just made," he said. "So here you are, coming in on Saturday"—pointing to similar, fainter marks—"and here" —walking across the road—"here you are, leaving."

Claire followed dutifully behind him. "You learn this in the army or what?"

"Are you kidding? All I learned in the army was patience . . . and enough Thai to keep me out of Vietnam. Look, somebody drove out after you; the tracks are on top of yours. Not those, those are Cummings's Chevy, but these—big tires, wide wheelbase, could be a pickup or a van—"

"So maybe there *was* somebody here on Saturday watching me!" she interrupted excitedly. Then, as Sam eyed her reprovingly, she said, "Oh. We don't know when it went in. But," she added, brightening, "we could look for its inbound tracks. If they're under the Toyota's, then it must have been here while I was here!"

This neat theory proved difficult to test, however, since they found some marks which appeared to be under, and others which appeared to be over, her own.

"Well, either this guy came in twice or we don't know what

we're doing," Sam said, standing up. "Where was this motorcycle track?"

They trudged up the road and rounded the bend. There was the camp: a pitiful assemblage of firewood, nothing more; no ghostly aura, no sensation of watchfulness. She walked to the side of the road and pointed.

"Looks like a bike, all right," he agreed. "We'll assume for the sake of argument that it's the Harley. So where did he go?"

The track ran clearly past the ruins and then vanished abruptly in a patch of gravel beside the storage shed. About ten yards ahead was a green strip of marshland, marked by cattails and tule, and beyond that, gleaming whitely, the flat, barren alkali sink. Claire advanced uncertainly.

"Wait a minute," Sam said. "Let's check out the shed." He pushed open the door.

Even in the dim light one thing was immediately obvious: the building was empty.

"The sacks were here!" Claire said positively. "Piled up against the far wall."

Sam didn't respond. He had stooped to pick up some minute object from the earth floor.

"What is it?"

He held out his hand. In the palm lay several bent, heavy-duty staples.

"Oh," she said, disappointed. "That's not too informative."

"Mmm," he replied enigmatically. "Come on. I'll show you some *Scirpus validus*. Unconfirmed. That is, if *it's* still there."

They walked to the stand of tule and stood looking up at the tall rushes. Suddenly Sam pointed to a particularly undistinguished specimen. "There," he said, stepping gingerly into the muck, "see how it's a little shorter than the other *Scirpus?* And feel the culm—the stem—it's much less rigid than the hardstem."

Gently he bent it toward her, delicately cupping the dry, feathery spike in his hand so that she could examine it.

For some reason Claire found this gesture extremely unsettling. "Oh—oh yes," she stammered, leaning forward and carefully clasping her hands behind her. "I see . . . and the end is sort of . . . rounder."

"Exactly," Sam replied enthusiastically, pulling out his

hand lens. "The spikelets—" He stopped abruptly, eyes fixed on the ground.

She followed his gaze. There, in the damp earth beside his right foot, was the clear imprint of a motorcycle tire.

"Guess this is where he picked up the tule," Sam said.

They followed the track onto the alkali flat, where it soon disappeared on the hard-packed earth. "And there's the iodineweed." He indicated a patch of the knobbly succulents.

Claire surveyed the desolate terrain. Out here the glare intensified the heat so that it was staggering, and she was feeling a little shaky anyway. The sky was hard and shiny. Like a frying pan. She finally knew exactly what Silvia had meant.

"I'd like to sit down in some shade for a minute," she said weakly.

Sam wasn't listening. "I think I see something," he said, striding away from her and stopping at a spot seemingly identical to every other spot in this featureless landscape. As she approached wearily, however, she saw what he had noticed: a roughly circular mound of some powdery substance, almost imperceptibly whiter than the white alkali soil. He knelt, rubbed the stuff experimentally between his fingers, and tasted it.

"Cocaine?" she asked, unable to keep the excitement out of her voice.

He looked up at her. "I'm not sure," he said. "But I think it's Benyl."

On Tuesday, Claire saw Sam only briefly. He had dutifully reported their discovery to Cummings, he told her, and Cummings had been utterly indifferent.

"Oh," said Claire. "He say anything of interest?"

"Yeah," Sam replied shortly, "he told me the investigation was proceeding normally, and if I wanted to know anything I should read the newspaper."

"I see. Mind your own business. Nice guy."

"He's a jerk," replied Sam. "He's always been a jerk. But he's very popular in certain circles. Anyway, Tom Martelli told me a couple of things. Not much happening, really—a few very dubious reports about Saturday night: somebody claims they heard a motorcycle near the dam, somebody saw a suspicious-looking vehicle parked there at two in the morning, somebody heard shouts—nothing very reliable. And Cummings is checking out Tony's drug connections. Real and imagined.

"I've got to go," he said after a moment, walking away. Then he stopped and turned toward her.

"Tony's funeral is Thursday. Nine A.M., St. Xavier's in Alma." And with that he was gone, leaving Claire unaccountably depressed and confused.

At Amargosa yesterday she had once again felt that they were forming some kind of alliance. But on the way home Sam had been preoccupied and secretive, as if their relationship had regressed instantaneously to its initial state of sulky grunts. *(I might have known,* she thought, *that he would freeze faster than he thawed.)* And now he was excluding her completely from his ideas about Tony's death, which, she supposed, was his right, but somehow she had thought . . .

Well, never mind what she had thought. At least the strange fascination he had exercised over her id seemed to have vanished at last. She hadn't dreamed about him since . . . since Saturday, since Tony had died, and this was a great relief. Really a tremendous relief, she repeated, wondering uneasily what her subconscious was up to now.

CHAPTER 10

At three Wednesday morning she sat up in bed and remembered her *"Monolinea rodrigueza."* In the upheaval following Tony's death she had sort of forgotten about the problem; but now, suddenly, she was seized by a feverish and completely irrational obsession with the experiment. It was all she could do to prevent herself from driving down to Citrus Cove at four in the morning to look at her petri dishes; it was as if . . . as if, in some obscure fashion, they were connected in her mind with Tony.

Or maybe it's just a respite from Tony, she thought, walking into the lab at seven-thirty A.M. A neat, solvable problem, a nice clean experimental design. She pulled out the tray of petri dishes.

They were fairly dramatic. The untreated dishes were beginning to grow healthy colonies of mold—blue *Rhizopus,* white and brown *Monolinea*—while her Benyl-treated samples were absolutely clean. In short, what she beheld was a textbook example of an effective fungicide.

Of course, it had only been—what—four and a half days since she had streaked the plates; she should give them a few more days before she drew definite conclusions. After all, she might walk in Friday and find luxuriant fungus all over the Benyl-treated samples. Still, it was interesting.

Sam looked up from his morning cup of coffee and newspaper when she entered. "Just informing myself about local events," he remarked, throwing down the paper in disgust.

"Nothing about Tony, I presume."

He didn't bother to answer; clearly he didn't want to talk about Tony. Suppressing her disappointment she said, "Well, I've got a more conventional problem for you. Come down to the lab for a minute."

She showed him her six petri dishes.

"Of course it's much too soon for definitive conclusions," she said apologetically, "but it's a suggestive pattern and I thought you might . . ."

Her voice trailed off as it became obvious that Sam was not listening. He was staring at the petri dishes as if mesmerized, and for the first time that morning she thought about the implications of the test. If the Agua Dulce *Monolinea* wasn't Benyl resistant after all, what did that mean?

"Could Martinez's people have sprayed improperly? Not covered the trees thoroughly or something?" she asked.

She had to repeat the question.

"What?" Sam said, rousing himself. "Seems unlikely. He's a competent guy. A bit heavy-handed with the chemicals, like most of these PCAs, but . . ." He lapsed into silence again. After a few moments he said, surprisingly, "Tell me exactly what happened Friday night at Casey's."

Startled by the non sequitur, Claire nevertheless told him. Tony had come over to her table. They had talked about brown rot. He had quarreled with Buddy Hanford and had left the bar a little before eleven.

Then she told him again, searching her memory for details. And again. Finally, wearily, she said, "That's it, that's the bottom of the barrel. Without hypnosis or sodium pentathol."

Sam frowned discontentedly. "And Silvia had told you Thursday that Martinez was going to be out there for a preharvest spraying on Friday."

"That's right," she said, mystified.

He stood up abruptly. "I'll see you later," he said, and walked out.

She stared at the door for several seconds. Then, with a cry of frustration and rage, she sprinted after Sam.

She caught up with him in the hall and grabbed his arm.

"Wait a minute!" she said, breathless with anger. "You can't just leave me hanging like that!"

Jim LaSalle eyed them curiously as he passed by, but Claire ignored him.

"I realize I'm only an outsider," she continued bitterly. "I didn't grow up here, I haven't known everyone in Kaweah County all my life, I didn't go duck hunting with Tony when he was three, but goddamn it, I cared about him! I liked him, and—and he liked me!" she exclaimed, with unconscious pathos. Sam looked at her with a strange expression, but she was too excited to notice. "I want to know what happened to him," she concluded heatedly. "I want to know what's going on!"

"I don't know what's going on—" he said quickly.

"Well, you sure as hell have some ideas!" she said, her voice rising again.

There was a short silence. Claire realized she was still hanging on to his arm, and released it hurriedly.

"Okay," he said finally, "okay. We'll talk about it. Only not here. Not now."

"When and where?" she insisted, pressing her advantage.

He hesitated. "After work . . ." he said doubtfully.

"All right," she said. "You come to my house for dinner. At six-thirty."

"Yes, ma'am," Sam said with a trace of amusement. "I'll be there," and suddenly she was aghast at her own belligerence.

"I guess that correspondence course in assertiveness training finally paid off," she said weakly.

Sam grinned at her in a friendly fashion and walked into his office.

Claire arrived home feeling somewhat ambivalent at the prospect of another human invading her little island. Nevertheless she performed certain perfunctory gestures of hospitality: she stacked newspapers, straightened photographs and paintings, and carried dirty dishes to the kitchen, where she washed a head of lettuce and set it in the colander to drain. Then she sat down on the living room sofa and began to think.

Why had Sam asked her about Friday at Casey's? Did he think Tony had transacted a drug deal there? Unlikely; Sam was not particularly enthusiastic about the international drug ring theory. It must be something else. And what was that about the spraying at Agua Dulce, what did that have to do with anything? Why did he have to be so goddamn enigmatic?

She was feeling more frustrated by the minute, and her mind was whirring uselessly like a disengaged gear. Wisely she decided to leave the subject entirely, and allowed her thoughts to wander.

* * *

They wandered to the topic of Tony's funeral the following morning. Much as she hated ceremonies, she felt the need to pay some sort of tribute, and anyway it was only a church service. She would skip the graveside event, unable to face the irony of Tony's remains being laid to everlasting rest just where Tony had least wanted to be: in the synthetic soil of Kaweah County.

Speaking of synthetic soil . . . she contemplated with mild distaste the photograph of the basin which hung opposite her, noting how the narrow white Road to Nowhere bisected it perfectly, separating the dense rows of cotton on the left from the arid desert on the right. Looks like a fertilizer advertisement, she thought. Before and after. The miracle of modern agriculture. Better farming through chemistry—

Suddenly her eyes glazed over. For a full two minutes she stared unseeing at the wall; then, still in a trancelike state, she picked up a pad and began to write.

She was surrounded by balls of crumpled yellow paper when Sam showed up twenty minutes later carrying a grocery sack.

"I was afraid you might only have Perry-er," he said, proferring a six-pack of Bud somewhat shyly, "and I've been thinking about cold beer for the last two hours." He detached a can and sat across from her.

"Mmm," she replied absently. "Listen . . . have you ever developed a theory that felt really solid, really persuasive—only you just didn't have any data to support it?"

"Sure," he replied quickly, "all the time. You might say that's my preferred modus operandi: 'pole-vaulting to conclusions,' as a professor once said about one of my papers."

She laughed at the remark, but something uncharacteristic in its tone startled her and she glanced at Sam sharply. There had been an undercurrent of—what? Self-consciousness? Boastfulness? No, she suddenly realized: defensiveness. He had sounded defensive. It was as if he were saying, look, I write papers too, I'm a bona fide scientist too, even if I didn't go to some fancy Eastern school.

Sam—so competent, so smart, so completely on top of things—defensive? With her?

It was her second revolutionary notion in under an hour, and it took a lot out of her. Several seconds passed before she was aware that Sam was talking.

"I said," he repeated patiently, "let's hear it!"

"Hear what?"

"Don't be coy. This spurious theory, obviously."

Focused again on the matter at hand, she swallowed nervously. Sam might be a—a pole-vaulter, but she had long ago ruthlessly suppressed any such tendencies in herself; the mild antagonism of many of her older male colleagues had taught her to be meticulously careful in her work and her thinking. And what she was about to say was pure conjecture.

Opening a beer, she said, "Let me show you my, uh, observations first," and handed him a page of neatly written notes. "Then you can judge for yourself."

On the sheet of yellow lined notebook paper Sam read:

1) The Rodriguezes have had bad brown rot this year. They've sprayed Benyl, and preliminary tests suggest that their *Monolinea fructiola* is not resistant to Benyl.

2) There were sacks of something labeled Benyl in the shed at Amargosa on Saturday. By Monday they were gone.

3) There was a pile of Benyl (we think it was Benyl) behind the shed.

4) Tony hung out at Amargosa.

5) On Friday, John Martinez sprayed the Agua Dulce trees.

6) At Casey's Friday night Tony asked questions about the treatment of brown rot. Later that night he rode out to Amargosa (we think).

7) The Rodriguezes are extremely unpopular in certain circles in Kaweah County. Also, their financial difficulties are well-known.

Sam handed back the list without comment. Claire took a deep breath and said, "Okay. The theory.

"I was sitting here staring at that photograph"—Sam swiveled to look at the picture—"and thinking about how dependent this whole business is on various chemicals—fertilizers, herbicides, soil additives, fungicides, insectides, and so on. Hardly an original thought, but suddenly I started to wonder what would happen if certain crucial substances were just . . . removed from the whole process. Sort of a very simple form of industrial sabotage, you might say: it would be so easy to substitute something inert, useless, for a . . . a fungicide, for example. Even if the switch were eventually detected, no one would suspect anything other than incompetence or some innocent mix-up. And in the meantime, in spite of frequent applications of this stuff, the disease would just get worse and worse."

She cleared her throat, then continued. "I think it would be hard to pull this off on a large scale. You couldn't ruin, say, the whole Hanford peach crop; the logistics would be too complicated, and growers like the Hanfords have such massive resources that a few seasons of brown rot wouldn't really hurt them. But small farmers, people who just barely hang on from year to year—that's another story. Especially if your victims were unpopular anyway. Everyone would just suspect that they were screwing up, not treating the problem appropriately. Or that they had developed some new superstrain of fungus, in which case everyone would be scared and angry.

"Anyway," she said, gulping her beer, "not to be labor the point, I think that's what has been happening at Agua Dulce. Somebody has substituted something for the Benyl they're supposed to have used out there. I think the actual substitution was made out at Amargosa; the Benyl sacks were emptied behind the shed and filled with . . . something, I don't know what . . . and stored out there until needed. Not a bad idea; it was deserted, and sheltered.

"Except that Tony used to go out to Amargosa from time to time. And he saw the sacks and, like me, wondered what they were doing out there. Only, unlike me, he figured out that something funny was going on at his parents' orchard.

"I think Friday, after the last spraying, after talking to me, he somehow put two and two together and rode out to Amargosa to check out those sacks. And somebody either followed him out there or was waiting for him. . . ." Her voice trailed off. Her audience was silent, and she felt as if she had just presented a very dubious seminar.

"What do you think?" she asked, when it became apparent that spontaneous applause was not forthcoming. "Solid but plodding? Brilliant but erratic? Completely harebrained?"

Sam's voice interrupted this self-review. "And just who do you see as the mastermind behind this nefarious scheme?"

She winced at the sarcasm but plowed on. "Well, it would

have to be someone who knew something about agriculture—about peach cultivation in particular—and had access to the machinery, the supplies used in spraying, or could hire someone with access and who had some motive for wanting the Rodriguezes off their land. . . ." She paused uncertainly, then continued in a rush, "Well, I hate to be redundant, but the name Buddy Hanford comes to mind!"

Sam drained his beer with maddening slowness. Then, "It does, doesn't it?" he said.

She looked at him in amazement. "You mean, you agree? With the theory?"

"Sure I agree. In fact, you've forgotten, uh—" he glanced at her notes—"Point eight. The staples."

"The staples?" said Claire, bewildered.

"Yeah. Benyl stacks are chain stitched. Like dog food bags. But if you wanted to empty those sacks and fill them with something else—"

"You'd have to staple them!" finished Claire. "Sam! That's brilliant!"

"Hardly," he said derisively. "I'd say it's a lot more impressive that someone who knew nothing about agriculture or Kaweah County six months ago, arrived at the same conclusions as—as—"

"As yourself," she said, grinning. "Thanks. High praise indeed."

They both sat thoughtfully for a moment. Then Claire said, "You know, attached as I am to this theory, professional integrity compels me to point out a few holes."

"It seemed pretty convincing to me," said Sam. "What's the problem?"

"Well, first of all, Buddy himself seems to have an alibi for the time of Tony's death."

"Oh, well, obviously he's hired someone to do the actual physical labor: getting hold of the Benyl, hitting people over the head, that kind of thing," Sam said bitterly.

"Right, that's what I figure. But more importantly, we don't yet know for sure that the Agua Dulce *Monolinea* is not Benyl resistant—"

"Come on, Claire," Sam interrupted impatiently. "We both saw those petri dishes—"

"We don't know for sure," she repeated stubbornly. "We'll know Friday. And anyway, even if the Benyl does turn out to be effective, we need to show that it wasn't used at Agua Dulce, that something else was, in fact, sprayed. Someone should do a chemical assay of that fruit, and our liquid chromatography spectrophotometer has been broken for two weeks. I keep telling Ray about it—"

"No problem!" Sam interrupted eagerly. "I'll take some samples from Agua Dulce up to Fresno on my way to Berkeley Friday. I know a chemist at USDA who'll do an assay for us."

"You're going to Berkeley?" Claire said irrelevantly.

"Yeah, for a couple of days. Hey, I gathered up some of that stuff we found behind the shed at Amargosa. Anna can check that out, too, just to confirm that it really is Benyl."

"Anna?"

"The chemist. Anna Cheng. Any other problems?"

"Oh . . . well, yes. Several. First, is it possible that Martinez and his crew could have sprayed Carlos and Silvia's trees three times and not have noticed they weren't working with Benyl? Or do we have to assume that they were involved in the substitution? If so, we're talking about a major conspiracy here. And I just don't understand the mechanics of spraying well enough to know. . . ."

"Well, I do," Sam replied promptly, "and yes, it's perfectly possible that they wouldn't notice: they all wear protective clothing and respirators, so they don't have much contact with the stuff. If it came in Benyl sacks, they'd never question that it was Benyl. However, I think somebody from Kavoian's —Martinez himself, maybe, though I can't believe it—has to have been involved in making the substitution. And by the way," he interjected hastily, as Claire was about to present problem four, "I seem to recall that the word dinner was mentioned this afternoon. Or was that just a ploy to get me to talk about Tony?"

"Oh," said Claire contritely, rising. "Sorry. It'll just be a minute—want another beer?"

She attended to culinary details and in a few moments returned to the living room with two trays bearing steaming bowls of chili and green salads. Not exactly a gourmet menu, she thought, and it certainly wouldn't have met Phil's standards, but it would have to do. Simple country fare for simple country folks. Sam was staring thoughtfully at her photograph of the basin.

"You take this?" he asked.

"Yes, when we went down to the marshes. I got some good pictures that day—" She stopped suddenly, flustered. Sam didn't notice.

"You ever take any color pictures?"

"Sometimes. But I like to do my own developing, and I like black-and-white."

"Kind of artistic," commented Sam. She couldn't tell if he was being sarcastic.

"I'm afraid we have to eat in here, I don't have a dining room table. In fact, I don't have a dining room." Apologetically she handed him his tray.

They ate in silence for a while. Then, feeling she could no longer suppress her next question without suffering physical damage, she said abruptly, "Sam. Speaking as an expert and a local boy, do you think Buddy Hanford is capable of something like this?"

"Absolutely," he replied indistinctly, his mouth full. "Morally, temperamentally, financially—"

"How about intellectually?"

"Huh?"

"It's just that . . ." She hesitated, then continued, "this whole theory is pretty, well, Byzantine. And I don't know Buddy very well, but I wouldn't have described him as a subtle thinker. Assault and battery, maybe, or barn burning—" She stopped suddenly.

"Or shed burning?" suggested Sam. "Or tree 'dozing? You know, I've always kinda suspected the Hanfords. Buddy in particular. It was all a little crude for Bill. Did you see or hear anything the day of the fire that might point to anybody?"

"Well," she said reluctantly, "I heard a motorcycle—"

"A motorcycle!"

"Yes. Leaving, right after the fire started. And I thought Tony—"

But Sam had stopped listening. "Buddy rides a dirt bike!" he exclaimed triumphantly.

"He does?" She felt enormous relief.

"Yeah, all the time! Loves to go out and disrupt fragile ecologies. That son of a bitch, I *knew* he was behind those incidents, and Cummings did too! That's why Cummings never really investigated them. And that's why it's real convenient that Cummings is obsessed with this drug-smuggling idea.

Because if he thought a Hanford was connected with Tony's death, well . . ." He looked at her and quoted wryly, " 'Everybody around here is too busy kissing Bill Hanford's ass to care about scum like the Rodriguezes.' "

Claire flushed and Sam grinned at her discomfiture.

"Don't worry; it was a fair statement," he said. "I've been thinking about it seriously. I've even been reconsidering what you did at Bill Hanford's that time—no, really," when she started to defend herself. "Not that it didn't show a complete lack of sense on your part, but maybe I needed it. I mean, I try hard to be evenhanded in my work and to remember all points of view. But it's easy to get lazy and drift into attitudes that are convenient and sort of inoffensive. You shook me up a little."

Now she was really flustered. She toyed with the gluey remains of chili in her bowl.

"I still say that burning a shed is one thing, and contriving this elaborate sabotage another," she said after a while.

"You shouldn't underestimate Buddy," Sam replied. "He's not a fool. He's got the knowledge, or access to it; he's got the money to buy off whoever he needs, and we know he has the motive. He hates Carlos and Silvia because of that Reclamation suit, he hates—hated—Tony out of sheer orneriness, and he probably believes that white Americans are the master race. I mean, who else is as likely a candidate?"

Claire nodded reluctantly, and presently Sam shifted in his seat and stretched his legs. "Like I said, though, someone from Kavoian's has to be involved in this too. Someone who made the actual switch out at Amargosa."

"And, presumably, carted away the incriminating sacks after I'd seen them on Saturday," Claire responded.

"Yeah, and maybe even killed Tony the night before. See, he must have hit him with something heavy—the old blunt instrument—and then, I don't know, loaded him and the bike into a pickup or a panel truck or something, and hauled him off to the lake."

They should talk to the work crew at Kavoian's tomorrow, Sam said, after the funeral. He would drop the leaf samples with Anna Cheng on Friday morning, and Claire was to call her Friday afternoon to find out the results of her tests.

"Then I'll give you a call Saturday morning, around ten," he said. "You can tell me what she says. And also what your damn petri dishes look like—as if I didn't already know!"

She nodded, then frowned as a new and disturbing thought occurred to her. "Sam, what happens if we do plug the holes in this theory, make an airtight case against Buddy Hanford? I mean, if the sheriff is in Hanford's pocket . . ."

"We'll worry about that when it happens," Sam said grimly.

She nodded again, unhappily. Their mutual construction bothered her. It seemed plausible, all right; the failure was not of logic but of character. Buddy's, to be exact. She just couldn't imagine him pulling this off.

"Well, thanks for dinner," Sam said, rising.

They stepped onto the front porch. The sky had darkened and a single red star shone above the pointed roofs of the houses. They could hear the delighted shrieks of children playing and the faint, plaintive sound of a radio somewhere up the street. It was very peaceful.

Sam must have felt it, too, for he seemed reluctant to leave. He turned to her. "Claire," he said hesitantly, "there's . . . there's something I'd like to ask you."

"Yes?" she answered in a choked voice. To her annoyance her heart had begun to beat very rapidly.

He looked down at his hands. "Would you—that is, later, of course, after this is all over . . ." He stopped and gazed at her anxiously; then the words came tumbling out.

"If we went down to Amargosa some time, could you take photographs of the *Scirpus validus?* Color photographs? See, then I could send them to the Herbarium in Berkeley, and if they confirm my identification, I'll get a citation in the new Jepson *Flora!*"

Claire leaned weakly against the door frame. "I'd be delighted," she replied.

"Great, thanks a lot! See you tomorrow."

The Valiant had rattled up the street and its taillights disappeared around the corner before she started to laugh.

CHAPTER 11

At eleven A.M. on Thursday Claire closed the door of the lab behind her and collapsed limply in the splendid cool of the air-conditioning. St. Xavier's, a tiny cinder block structure in the middle of an orange grove, had been crammed with people and unbelievably hot. As soon as she had entered the church she had stripped off her jacket, and now, looking down at her bare arms and legs, she realized that her skimpy black dress was more suitable for seductions than for mourning. But when she had left Cambridge she hadn't packed for funerals.

Anyway, no one had noticed her. She had slipped quietly into the back pew and watched the proceedings like an observer, an anthropologist. An anthropologist who hadn't done her homework: somehow she had expected a gathering out of *The Magnificent Seven*—women in shapeless dresses and head scarves, men in homespun garb, sombreros in humble hand. But of course Silvia and Carlos weren't simple peasants, if such a thing existed; they were assimilated Mexican-Americans and important figures in their community, and the mourners were dressed accordingly: sober but exceedingly fashionable. And she had forgotten about the kids, Tony's friends, some of whom were downright glamorous. Two rows in front of her a stunning young woman with luxurious layers of L'Oréal-blonde hair had sobbed without inhibition, like a child. Claire had almost envied her.

She had seen Sam, dour as an undertaker himself in a somber suit, sitting next to Carlos and Silvia in the front pew. The service, conducted in Spanish and Latin, was incomprehensible to her, and her sense of discomfort and alienation had increased by the moment, until finally she had fled, overwhelmed not by grief but by the vacuum where grief should be.

But then that was the story of her life, she thought now, gazing out the laboratory window at the bleak hills. "Inappropriate affect," they called it: she felt what she shouldn't feel—with Sam, for example—and didn't feel what she should feel. At her own father's funeral she had stood numb, detached, her only emotion irritation at the drone of the minister's words, so irrelevant to the dead, so meaningless to the living.

Silvia, sitting rigidly at the front of the church, had she been consoled by that soft, relentless flow of ritual language? Had it helped her to feel that her loss was part of God's plan or something, that she was a member of a—a Community of Souls, or whatever she believed?

Claire hoped so, but she doubted it. Halfway through the service Silvia had broken down and had to be helped from the church. *"Mi hijo,"* Claire had heard her moan as she passed, *"Maté a mi hijo. . . ."* What did that mean, *maté?* She would have to look it up when she got home—

She caught herself and almost burst into hysterical laughter. "Look it up." Right, that was the answer to everything. Name something and you controlled it, you imposed order on chaos. No mistaking which "community" she belonged to—not of souls but of namers, the Community of Scientists: a bunch of . . . of self-absorbed misanthropic misfits who retreated from the demands and ambiguities of the world into their self-created, logical, orderly systems, devising technical solutions to spiritual problems. They were all alike: Mulcahey, Ray, her co-workers at MIT. . . .

And me, she thought. I'm like that. Sometimes I think I'm not because—why? Because I'm female? Because I have the vocabulary to talk about feelings? But I'm just like them: give me a tough intellectual puzzle and I perform like an integrated circuit; put me in a situation requiring an emotional response and I fall apart. Or else I convert it to a . . . an algorithm, a model, a problem I can solve. Something I can "look up."

Slowly she paced the length of the room, her heels percussive on the concrete floor. Into this black mood walked Sam.

He halted abruptly when he saw her. "You look nice," he said awkwardly.

"Thanks," she answered dully; then, making an effort, "So

do you." And in fact he was dignified and almost handsome in the dark trousers and crisp white shirt of his good suit.

"You left early," he said, after a pause.

"Yes . . . I didn't think anyone saw me, coming or going."

"I saw you." Another brief silence.

"Listen," he said, "I'm going to Silvia and Carlos's. Do you want to come?"

"Now? Won't we be intruding?"

"Naw. It's traditional. The whole family'll be there."

"Oh," she said distractedly, then, after a pause, "Sam. I've been thinking about this—this theory of ours. Doesn't it seem to you a bit, well, glib? Like an academic exercise?" What was the word she had used last night? Byzantine?

Sam frowned in puzzlement and replied, "No . . . I think it's pretty tight, pretty logical, assuming we can verify a few—"

"Of course it's logical!" she exclaimed fiercely. "Logic is our stock-in-trade! The point is, is it true?

"Look," she continued more calmly, "we'd both like to think that Tony's murder and the problems out at Agua Dulce—the saplings, the fire, the *Monolinea*—are linked somehow. Because it's more—elegant, more parsimonious, if you like, to construct a single unifying theory that explains both. And because you . . . well, *we* don't want to believe that Tony died for something as sordid and commonplace as a drug deal. But isn't that really as likely an explanation? That Tony was killed by some . . . dissatisfied customer, and that the sabotage at Agua Dulce, if it exists, is a totally unrelated scheme organized by—Buddy, maybe—or by someone else? I'm not saying we're wrong, you understand," she continued. "I'm just saying that we have a certain emotional investment in this theory of ours. And you admit you tend to jump to conclusions. So we'd better be damn careful to consider all reasonable alternatives, rule out rival hypotheses—"

"Such as?" said Sam doubtfully.

She paused and looked at him, considering. "Well, such as . . . such as me, for example."

His jaw dropped in amazement.

"Sure," she said. "When you think about it, all Silvia's troubles—the trees, the shed—started *after* I arrived. And I have—ought to have—the knowledge to conceive of the Benyl switch. It's worth investigating."

"And your motive?" Sam inquired sarcastically.

"Well, that would take some further inquiry. Maybe, uh, maybe I was spurned by Tony and was seeking revenge." Not bad, she thought, and not so outlandish a suggestion as Sam, who was convulsed by laughter, might think.

"Well, all right," she conceded, "I'm just making a point here. How about Jim? We know he dislikes the Rodriguezes even more than the norm, and he certainly has the expertise to sabotage their spraying." She was rolling now; she was good at this. "Or how about you?"

"Me?" His face suddenly lost its amused expression, but she didn't notice.

"Sure," she said, beginning to pace again, and gesticulating as if delivering a lecture. "It's a perfectly tenable hypothesis. You've got the expertise, the connections, and as for motive—well, you said yourself that you wanted the Rodriguezes to sell out. Maybe you have some kind of deep-seated psychosis, maybe you identify Carlos and Silvia with your parents, or maybe—maybe something happened between you and Frank when you were kids. Maybe that's what your dream is about. And Tony might have found out about it, whatever it was, and . . . and threatened you or blackmailed you—"

"Stop!"

Sam's voice cut into this intellectual feeding frenzy, and she turned to see him white and stunned. It was like being doused with cold water.

"Just hang on a minute," he continued shakily. "You don't actually believe that . . . that I . . ."

"Sam! No!" she cried. "I didn't mean anything, I was just talking, I was just . . . making a point." Make your point and damn the torpedoes. "Please . . . I'm sorry!"

Never, never, never again would she sacrifice common sense and common decency to a game of logic!

"It's okay," he mumbled after a moment. "Just sort of took me by surprise, that's all." He looked up at her with a faint smile. "Guess I didn't expect anyone in a dress like that to go for the throat like a goddamn Green Beret."

It was Claire's turn to be speechless.

"Let's go to the Rodriguezes," he said.

While Claire agreed in principle that they should visit Carlos and Silvia, sheer social cowardice, which she told herself was delicacy, made her extremely apprehensive about the visit.

"What exactly do they think about Tony's death?" she asked as they turned onto 170. "Do they know it's a murder?"

"Nobody *knows* it's a murder at this point. They think it was an accident—but that it might have been a homicide, probably drug related."

"You going to tell them anything else? I mean, about our suspicions and the Benyl and so on?"

"Hell, no!" he interrupted emphatically. "I know where Frank and Tony got their tempers, and I don't want Carlos taking out somebody with a shotgun!"

Claire gave a little start. "Listen, what was it that Silvia was saying when they took her out of the church this morning?"

"I don't know. I didn't hear."

"It . . . it sounded like *Maté a mi hijo.*"

He raised his eyebrows. "You must have heard it wrong."

"Why?"

"Because that would mean 'I killed my son.' "

They lapsed into silence, trying not to think about this. As they turned up the long dirt road to Agua Dulce, Claire was visited suddenly by a nightmarish premonition of ruin as if somehow the collapse of the Rodriguezes' lives would be manifested in the land itself. But no, the trees still ran in neat geometric rows beside the road; the damaged fruit blushed and ripened on schedule, regardless of its shortcomings as a market commodity; and the small stucco house stood square and complete at the end of the road.

Unafflicted by morbid fantasies, Sam leaped out of the car, squeezed through the half dozen or so cars jamming the driveway, and knocked briskly. In a moment one of the elaborately dressed women Claire had seen at the funeral appeared at the door.

"Sam!" she said warmly. "It's been a long time! It's great to see you!"

"Hi, Liz. Yeah, too bad it has to be under these circumstances."

She shook her head dolefully. "He was such a wild kid." To which Sam made no reply.

Variants on this exchange were repeated as Claire was introduced to Liz and Celia, the older Rodriguez daughters, who now lived in someplace called Pacoima, and to Rosario, the youngest, who had stayed nearby in Poplar. This evidently was the official line on Tony: it was sad that he had been cut down in his youth but then he was a wild kid. Only Rosario uttered the formula with tears in her eyes.

The house of mourning was full of life: the three sisters and their kids, many cousins and their kids, neighbors and *their* kids—every five minutes someone appeared at the door with another enchilada casserole. But the action revolved around a dark center—Silvia, wooden-faced and motionless on the living room couch.

Oh, Christ, thought Claire, *I shouldn't have come. It's going to be just like the funeral.* She wanted to throw her arms around Silvia, to wail, to rend her garments, or at least to sit down and cry. But she just . . . couldn't.

Sam, on the other hand, hardly Mr. Conviviality, seemed to be able to do the right thing. "Hey, *mamacita,*" he said gently and kissed her on the cheek: nothing specially eloquent, just a little physical contact and a murmur of sympathy. But Claire stood awkwardly behind him and said nothing.

Then he moved to Carlos—who, she noted with a flash of resentment, didn't seem to be exactly prostrate with grief—and she retreated to the corner and reverted to observer. A remarkable collection of objects was crammed into the tiny room: china figurines, plastic flowers, real flowers, postcards from Mexico, postcards from Disneyland, scenes from Aztec mythology, scenes from Christian mythology . . . The Virgin of Guadalupe, beatific in her jagged halo of stylized flames, seemed to be everywhere. She gazed demurely from the mantel, where she was flanked by La Familia Rodriguez: lots of little girls in white communion dresses, older girls in white bridal gowns, and a young man in uniform. Frank.

Frank Rodriguez was the center of his own secular shrine. His photograph showed he'd been remarkably like Tony, only broad and robust of feature where Tony was—had been—delicate. To the left were three high-school football trophies; to the right, framed newspaper clippings that described high school athletic exploits and more that brought news from Vietnam: basic training, shipping out, arrival in Vietnam; promoted to PFC, to corporal, to sergeant; awarded a Bronze Star, another Bronze Star, killed in action April 22, 1968.

Awarded the Purple Heart posthumously. Above his portrait were the medals themselves, mounted neatly on silk.

But where in this pictorial family history was Tony? There, at the end of the mantel. He had slicked back his hair and donned jacket and tie for his senior portrait, and was smiling seraphically.

"We can go any time," said a voice behind her. She turned and Sam repeated, "We can go any time. I've expressed my condolences—"

"Sammy, I got to talk to you." Carlos had just walked over to them. "H'lo, Miss Sharples, thanks for coming by," he added politely.

"Oh, I—I wanted to," she stammered. "I—I'll really miss Tony." Lame but sincere.

"Yeah," Carlos replied curtly. She was wrong, she realized; he was upset all right. His eyes were suddenly unnaturally bright and his mouth tight and trembling. But real hombres don't cry.

"Listen, Sam," he continued after a moment, "I need some advice. About selling this place."

The room had become very quiet—quiet enough so that Claire thought she heard a little gasp from the vicinity of the sofa. Silvia was staring fixedly at her husband.

"Hey," Sam said in dismay, "now's not the time to think about that! Give it a few weeks—"

"A few weeks won't make no difference. It'll only be worse."

"Not necessarily. We've . . . ah . . . we've discovered that there's been a problem with your spraying, that's why you've been having such bad fungus problems. So if you sprayed again now you could salvage some of your late-ripening varieties—the Cal Reds, the Flamekists—"

"Sammy," Carlos replied bluntly, "we can't afford to spray again. We can't afford to do nothing but let the damn peaches rot on the damn trees."

"I could lend you a little . . ." Sam began, then trailed off into silence. They all realized the absurdity of this offer.

"Mucha' gracias," Carlos said, "but you know it wouldn't help none, Sam. Besides, you got to think of your future," he added, his eyes flickering to Claire. She suppressed a smile. As if she were going to settle down in this godforsaken hell-hole . . . with Sam, of all people!

"No," Carlos continued, "no. I'm afraid the time has come to face facts. It might be different if I had a son to leave the place to. . . ." His jaw tightened. "But then Silvia was right. Tony wouldn't of made a farmer anyway."

A strange expression crossed Sam's face, and Claire had a sudden insight. Frank wouldn't have made a farmer either; if Carlos had once counted on that he had been fooling himself. But Carlos and Silvia had three daughters. Why were they automatically ruled out as heirs? Celia and Liz seemed like real city girls, sure, but how about Rosario? Rosario who had stayed in the valley?

Well, Carlos's possible patriarchal notions were a moot point. The orchard was going to be sold.

"You talk this over with Silvia?"

"Not yet," Carlos said in a low voice, looking over at her. "She's . . . well, she's kind of crazy right now. Tony was her favorite. *Su niño,* you know."

Maté a mi hijo, thought Claire. Just an extravagant expression of grief. What else could it be?

"Had an offer?" Sam was asking.

"Well, the Hanfords made us an offer about two years ago. Probably should of took it," he said, shaking his head ruefully, "but we said no, absolutely not, forget it. Hope they're still interested."

"Probably," said Sam shortly. "They own everything on four sides of you."

Now what did that remind her of? Sam made their goodbyes and she trailed behind him, trying to remember. Oh, yes. The Sea of Holes and Jim LaSalle's voice saying, "Bill Hanford's going to do something else with the land." The zoning hearing—

The zoning hearing!

"You know," she said diffidently as they backed carefully out of the drive, "this might not be important. But I think some developers are planning a project around here that might include Agua Dulce. I'm not really sure, though."

She described the meeting.

"I wasn't paying that much attention, frankly. I was . . ." What? Admiring Bill Hanford's pretty blue eyes? "I was new to the area, and the geography didn't mean a lot to me. But now that I think about it, the development was just west of the dam—which would put it right about here."

Sam looked thoughtful. "If Carlos and Silvia refused to

sell," he said slowly, "developers might have incentive to give them a little push. Do you remember the name of the company? Or the project?"

"It was Golden Hills Golf Course and Estates," she said, remembering the Buick's bumper sticker. "But if we want to know the details all we have to do is find the minutes from the hearing. Do you know where the zoning commission records are?"

"Vaguely. I think I'll call Tom."

Sam's good friend Tom Martelli, Riverdale's chief of police, was mild of manner, thin of hair, and thick of middle. He met them in front of the county office building in Parkerville, which had the War Memorial architecture of the fifties and a strong institutional smell of floor wax and Lysol. The planning commission records were stored on the third floor in four towering file cabinets, but they ignored the first three and started with October of last year. Claire flipped through folders while Sam and Tom hovered impatiently over her shoulder.

"Here's something!" she exclaimed. "From December—"

Sam ripped the folder from her hand. "It's a proposed zoning change on a hundred acres west of the lake. Looks like part of the Hanford property, all right," he said, thumbing through the documents and reading them aloud. " 'Request for zoning change from A1 to G3. Name and address of applicant: The Venture West Company, a Division of Leisure Concepts, Inc.' "—Claire gave a disgusted cluck—" 'c/o S. Van Horn, 1431 Beverly Boulevard, L.A. . . . Notice of Public Hearing' . . . Look, here's a letter from Van Horn. He says he'll be pleased to attend the hearing on behalf of Venture West and will bring an associate, Donald Chandler."

"Yeah, Stephen Van Horn. He was the guy who spoke," said Claire. "There was somebody with him, sort of a blond surfer type, who passed around literature and set up the projector. Kind of like Vanna White. And Sam, I forgot to tell you—" she paused for drama "—he was at Casey's the night Tony was killed!"

"The surfer?"

"No, Van Horn. And another guy, big and dark."

Martelli meanwhile had grabbed the folder. "Let me see that. Hey, here's a map of the proposed development. Jesus, look at this. 'The Golden Hills Golf and Tennis Club . . . Kaweah Estates, luxury homes on quarter acre lots . . .' There's even a *marina,* for Christ's sake!"

Sam stabbed at the map with a forefinger. "And there's the Rodriguezes' house," he said. "Right over the racquetball court."

Claire, meanwhile, was leafing through the minutes of the County Board of Supervisors meetings, trying to find the hearing itself. Ah, here it was, from February 21. She poked Sam in the ribs and together they scanned the list of speakers: Mr. S. Van Horn, County Supervisors B. Webb, C. Handelmann, and T. Steitler, in favor of the proposal; in opposition, Mrs. W. Baldwin, Dr. L. Fischer.

"Didn't Jim give his usual speech?"

"No. Maybe he was tired. Well, actually, at the time I thought . . . I thought he didn't want to embarrass me," she said. Sam looked at her for a moment, then snapped the folder shut.

"Well, I've seen enough," he declared. "Tom, can you find out something about this Venture West outfit?"

"Sure. Why?"

"Because I think they might have had a strong motive to sabotage the Rodriguezes' crop. And I think it's pretty damn interesting that they were hanging around the night Tony was killed."

As they left the county building Claire asked, "Are we still going to Kavoian's?" hoping devoutly that the answer would be no. It had been a trying day. She wanted to go home, take a cold bath, and lie naked on the bed with the fan pointed straight at her.

Sam glanced at his watch. "It's after five; the crew will have left," he said, and her heart leaped. "But John Martinez will still be there. I can get their names and track 'em down."

"Where?" she said faintly.

"At the bars in West Parkerville. Um, do you want to come?"

"Sure," she said, heaving an internal sigh.

"Well, uh, maybe you should change your clothes. You might attract some unwanted attention . . . you probably will anyway, but the more like a nun you look, the better. I'll run you by your house."

He seemed a little distracted. They headed east toward

Riverdale on 170, but as they were passing the west end of the lake he suddenly swerved off the road and pulled up under a ragged eucalyptus that overlooked the dam. He got out of the car and leaned against the hood. After a moment Claire joined him, and they stood watching the expensive blue water of Lake Prosperity evaporate under the late afternoon sun.

"Those greedy, murderous bastards," he said softly.

"The Army Corps of Engineers?" she asked, bewildered.

"Very funny. Those bozos from Venture West, of course! I might have guessed it would have something to do with developers; they're all scum!"

Venture West. She was gratified that her idea had met with such enthusiasm, but an hour ago he had been absolutely sure that Buddy Hanford was the greedy murderous bastard in question. "Aren't you kind of jumping to conclusions?"

"I've never been so sure of anything in my life," he replied emphatically, and she wondered cynically how many other half-baked theories had received this Sam Cooper seal of approval. She was beginning to think Sam was not emotionally ready for this research—uh, investigation.

"Look," she said patiently, "does it make sense that a company like Venture West would resort to violence to acquire land? They have so many other options."

"Such as?"

"Such as paying a shitload of money for it."

"You heard Carlos. He never would have sold that land if he had any alternative. Everybody knew that."

"Well, maybe. But how about . . . zoning and property taxes and all those other techniques developers use?" she suggested somewhat incoherently. Sam looked at her quizzically.

"I was thinking of the town where I grew up," she said. "In Massachusetts. It was a dairy-farming area when I was a kid, and now it's mostly suburban. And what the developers did there—they call it leapfrogging, I think—was to convince one farmer to sell, make him an offer he couldn't refuse, and put in a housing tract or something. Then they'd buy a little more land, farther out from town, and develop that—and the farms in between would quadruple in value. Suddenly they were being assessed as 'improved' rather than rural land. The farmers couldn't afford to pay the new assessment, they couldn't afford not to sell at the new, inflated prices—voila, no more dairy farms.

"So I'm wondering why Venture West couldn't just hold out," she finished. "Once they started developing the Hanford property, Carlos and Silvia's land would have been reassessed—"

"Two reasons," interrupted Sam. "One, they were in a hurry. Didn't want a bunch of peach trees messing up the eighteenth hole. But the main problem is that we have something in California called the Williamson Act."

The Williamson Act, he explained, was designed to prevent exactly the pattern of urbanization she had described, to protect prime agricultural land. It didn't work too well, but the arrangement was this: farmers made agreements with the county to keep their land in production for a certain period of time, and in return the county agreed to continue to assess the property on the basis of its existing agricultural value, rather than on a "best use"—shopping mall and housing tract—basis.

"Carlos and Silvia have an agreement," he concluded. "Their land can't be reassessed without their consent."

"Does that mean they couldn't sell even if they wanted to?"

"Oh, no, that's one of the problems with the act. There're all these loopholes. For example, if the land all around you is being developed, there's a short 'window' during which you can sell, too, even if your agreement hasn't expired."

He kicked at the camphor-scented eucalyptus buttons at their feet. "Any more objections?"

"Not at the moment, no. As a matter of fact I agree with you; I like these people as villains a lot better than I ever liked Buddy Hanford. But obviously we're both predisposed to dislike developers, and there's absolutely no real evidence that they're involved in this."

"I realize that," he replied, his face troubled. "That's why I called Tom. He's a smart guy. Maybe he can help put this together." He closed his eyes. After a long pause he said, "This time I'm not going to let Carlos and Silvia down. I don't expect you to understand this," he said, still not opening his eyes, "but all my life I've failed people when they needed me. Everybody I cared about. I don't want it to happen again."

She held her breath awaiting more revelations, but he had

clamped his mouth shut like a mail slot. Instead he picked up a eucalyptus button and hurled it, startling a flock of small birds that had settled in the tree. As they rose their shadows slid down the bare hill like loose stones.

CHAPTER 12

Kavoian's Feed and Supply in Parkerville was a huge emporium of chemicals, feed, fertilizer, esoteric machinery, and other paraphernalia of commercial agriculture. Sam nodded to a stocky, dark-haired man standing at the far end of the lot.

"That's Martinez," he said. "I'll ask him who sprayed at Agua Dulce on Friday."

In ten minutes he had returned with three names. " 'Clemente, Armando, Paco,' " he quoted wryly. "He thinks. No last names. They were just a pickup crew he rounded up for that day. Let's see, there are two hundred fifty thousand farm workers in California, so there are probably only five thousand Armandos."

They drove west and crossed the railroad tracks, and all their senses immediately told them they were in Mexican Parkerville: the coloring of the kids in the street, the sound of the language, the smells of dinner. . . .

"I'm hungry," Claire announced.

"It's a little early for the bars, anyway," Sam agreed, and in a few minutes they pulled over in front of a very modest-looking establishment called Rosa's.

Claire carefully waited until he had finished his *machaca* and eggs and two Dos Equises. Then she said, "What did you mean back at the lake? About letting people down?"

Should have waited for the third Dos Equis. "Not much," he said shortly. After a moment he added, reluctantly, "I just have a history of . . . not being there for people."

"Which people?"

"Well, my parents, my wife, my kids, Frank Rodriguez, Tony . . ."

Something made her ignore his obvious reticence and press on. "How did you let your parents down?"

"I could have helped them more. I was completely oblivious to what was happening to them—"

She thought of Boxer in *Animal Farm: I will worker harder.* "And how about Frank?" she interrupted. "You were hundreds of miles away when he died."

"That's just the point." He was sliding his beer around the circle of condensation on the table and she suddenly noticed she was rolling hers across her forehead, a ritual she now performed unthinkingly with all cold drinks. She set it down.

"I should have gone *with* him!" Sam was saying. "That was the plan when we enlisted. Instead I chickened out and went to language school."

"Sounds like a prudent move to me." She was baiting him, she didn't know why.

"Yeah. That's a good word. Prudent." His voice was bitter.

"*Wait* a minute," she cried with exasperation. "Let me get this straight. Your parents' farm failed like thousands of small farms, Frank Rodriguez died in Vietnam like fifty-five thousand other young men—and yet you personally let them down? Who do you think you are, Jesus Christ? You sound like my mother!"

Ah, her mother. Sighing and assuming responsibility for all her children's problems; never their triumphs, mind you, but it came to the same thing: if you couldn't fail on your own you couldn't succeed on your own. Worse, you didn't *dare* fail and add to your poor old gray-haired mother's heavy load. Well, if she was so goddamn responsible, why hadn't she come through when the chips were down, why had she let Claire's father die?

Whoa. Where had *that* come from? Her father had died from Hodgkin's disease, and nobody could have done anything about it.

"—not Jesus Christ," Sam was saying heatedly, "but I was raised to think I ought to be my brother's keeper!"

Claire tried to pull her thoughts together. "That's fine if your brother needs keeping," she said tartly, "and it's pretty patronizing if he doesn't! Or she."

Silence. She had certainly provided stimulating conversation on their first dinner date.

"Well . . . anyway, forget it, it's none of my business," she said. "I just meant—" She took a breath. "Look, you're a scientist. *Use* that training, try to approach the situation at Agua Dulce as objectively and—and unemotionally as possible. That's the way we can do Silvia and Carlos—and Tony, if that makes any sense—the most good."

Damn, was she really saying this? Six hours ago she was excoriating science and all that it stood for, and now she was delivering the MIT commencement address! And talk about patronizing!

"You're right," Sam said. Which made her feel like a *complete* jerk.

Avenue J backed up against the state highway that marked the western border of Parkerville, and Claire knew it pretty well. It was the Street of Failed Businesses, of which the town had others, but Avenue J was the most definitive and the most picturesque. She had photographed several blocks of it one hot, dusty afternoon—the idle auto body shops, the garages that apparently hadn't worked on anything since the Ford Falcon, the quiet machine shops, the hardware stores without inventory and the empty mirror and glass shops—all still, somehow, subsisting, the way barbershops seemed to stay open because it was too much trouble to go out of business.

There was one corner of Avenue J that was, however, flourishing, the block Claire had been too timid to photograph. Where Olive Street crossed and continued west to the next little town, the shops had been converted to Mexican bars—a half dozen lined up one after the other. Even at three in the afternoon their doors had been open, their jukeboxes pumping bass lines onto the sidewalk, and Claire had peered into them from the far side of the street. They were all identical—long bars, pool tables, a sparse assortment of folding chairs. They looked like storefront churches. What distinguished them? Why would you decide to drink at El Morocco rather than Café Numero Uno?

Well, tonight the important thing was where Paco, Clemente, and Armando drank. At eight Sam and Claire walked into El Morocco, its hand-painted sign picked out with dime-sized shards of mirror, a motif echoed by the dime-sized bullet hole in the front window. Sam stepped up to the long bar, where seven or eight men were drinking in silence, and beckoned the bartender.

"You know three guys named Paco, Clemente, and Armando who work for Kavoian's?" he asked, pitching his voice above the blare of the music. Claire sidled up close behind him, looking nervously around, but the customers hardly glanced at her before returning to their beers. They reminded her of something, she couldn't think what. The bartender was impassive behind his Zapata mustache and Sam repeated the question in Spanish. *"¿Conoces a tres hombres que trabajan por Kavoian's? Se llaman Paco, Clemente, y Armando. Solamente quiero hacerles unas preguntas."*

The bartender still gave no indication that he understood.

"Maybe you should try it in Thai," suggested Claire, and Sam grimaced impatiently and scribbled his phone number on a scrap of paper.

"If they should come by that's where they can call me. C'mon," he said to Claire, "let's try the next one."

There *was* a subtle difference in ambience between bars. Whereas the clientele at the Morocco had been apathetic, the customers at the Yucca—a dozen men at the bar and six playing pool—regarded them with outright hostility. Again Sam put his questions to the bartender, who shrugged and turned away to watch a shoving match develop into a genuine fight.

Sam left his number and they proceeded to the Casbah. And then to Café Numero Uno.

By now Claire was beginning to relax a little, and to look around instead of pretending to be invisible. For the most part the patrons were neither the embittered middle-aged men, the broken old men, nor the tough women she had expected—there were no women, despite the signs that promised BAILE! GIRLS!—but young men of about, say, Tony's age. They were lonely and horny and homesick, and the *norteño* music on every jukebox, the oompah of tubas and the mournful voices in close harmony, eased that for a while. These bars were like—like NCO clubs in some godforsaken outpost.

Sam, meanwhile, was getting desperate. "Look," he said urgently, "I'm not from the Migra or anything—*no soy Migra, soy amigo de los Rodriguez. Carlos y Silvia Rodriguez. . . ."* Hopelessly he wrote down his number. The bartender took it, carefully folded it, and placed it in his breast pocket.

"I'd like to help you, man, I really would. But we got a lot of people coming in here, you know?"

They walked out onto the sidewalk.

"This is useless," Sam said. "Nobody's going to talk to us; they don't trust us."

Claire had worked up enough sympathy for all the lonely guys in all the bars of the world that she heard herself say, "Maybe I should try. By myself. I'm nonthreatening."

"But you don't speak Spanish! Anyway, you might get . . . get . . ."

"Get what? Hey, nobody's even looked at me so far. Teach me the sentence. If Bela Lugosi learned his whole part phonetically I can learn one lousy sentence."

"Sure, I can teach you to ask the question, but you won't understand the answer."

"You can watch from the doorway. If somebody starts talking you can come in and interpret." *And rescue me if I get into trouble,* she thought.

"Okay," he said after a moment. "I can think of six reasons why this isn't going to work either, but—repeat after me: *Quiero hablar con Paco, Armando, o Clemente . . ."*

After five minutes of coaching she entered the Lindo Michoacan where, as luck would have it, the jukebox had just run out of quarters. In absolute silence she walked to the bar. Twenty pairs of eyes followed her, twenty pairs of ears heard her recite her halting and possibly unintelligible syllables.

She must have gotten something across because in a moment a voice rang out from behind her. *"¡Oye! Yo soy Armando!"* She whirled hopefully—and another man called, *"¡Y yo, yo soy Paco!" "¡Aqui estoy!" "¡Clemente, soy yo!"* And then the bar was full of Pacos, Clementes, and Armandos, all yelling and laughing and making kissing noises.

Cheeks blazing, she turned back to the bartender.

"Look, do you speak English?" she said, straining to make herself heard over the din.

No answer.

"Well, it's very important I find these people. If they're here, would you tell them to get in touch with this person?"

She handed him Sam's name and sprinted for the door, having learned another important lesson in demystification: just because they were young and lonely and homesick, didn't mean they couldn't behave like assholes.

She scowled at Sam, daring him to make a comment. He didn't even smile, just looked up at the next, and last, sign and read, "El Aguila. *No Se Permite Llevar Navajas.*"

"What?"

"No knives." He pushed open the door—and yelped as a body came hurtling past them and landed hard on the sidewalk.

"Auspicious," she said lightly while Sam jammed his hands back in his jeans pocket; he had thrown an arm across her chest to keep her back and out of the way, just as her mother used to do before seat belts (still did, as a matter of fact.) Her hipbone had smacked against the wall and she rubbed it, to distract herself from the warm band across her front where his arm had been.

El Aguila had a completely different feel from the other bars. *Here* were the embittered middle-aged men and the broken old men and the tough women—hey, somebody had to cater to them. The bartender listened to them attentively and when they were done bellowed, "*¡Oye!* Anybody know a Paco or a Clemente or an Armando that works at Kavoian's?" Everyone shook his or her head in exaggerated fashion, and there was the distinct impression of smothered laughter.

"Sorry," said the barkeeper. "Looks like you struck out. Have a beer." It wasn't an invitation.

They gulped down two Coors Lites as fast as possible and headed for the door. Suddenly a large man stepped into their path. He had a furry torso oozing out of a tank top, a smashed nose, little black eyes, and a homemade tattoo on his right forearm that said MOM.

"You wouldn't be Migra, would you?" he asked conversationally.

"Hell, no!" Sam said emphatically. "We're helping Silvia and Carlos Rodriguez—" pronouncing the name very clearly —"who have an orchard where these guys worked."

Their new friend spat out of the corner of his mouth to indicate skepticism. "Yeah, well . . . look for them someplace else."

Sam raised his hands palms outward in the universal gesture of whatever-you-say-buddy-we-don't-want-no-trouble, they walked carefully around this large obstacle, and in a moment were back on the sidewalk. Automatically they looked toward the curb. The human missile had disappeared, but they hastily moved four or five feet to the side of the door.

"Well!" said Claire. "This evening has been of great sociological interest—"

"But a complete washout otherwise," said Sam. "I know. It was a long shot anyway. Chances are even if we'd found the guys they wouldn't have remembered anything about that day—"

"Momentito, señores."

They both started. A slim figure in long-sleeved white shirt and jeans was standing ten feet away from them, his face in shadow.

"Soy Clemente Gutierrez," he said, and stepped forward.

He had strong Indian features: straight black hair falling across his forehead, high cheekbones, a curving nose over a full mouth. In the ugly neon light his skin was rough and pitted with adolescent acne—or chloracne, thought Claire, depending on what he's been spraying.

"You work for Kavoian's?" demanded Sam.

"A veces. Sometimes."

Sam began to question him in a mixture of Spanish and English, the English for Claire's benefit. "Did you work out at the Rodriguez ranch last Friday? *¿Trabajó al rancho Rodriguez el viernes pasado?"*

He nodded.

"Did you notice anything unusual? *¿Algo raro, extraordinario?"*

Clemente shrugged, and Claire, who had become excited, started to feel hopeless again. This guy must work—what? A different farm every day? He's not going to remember something he did nearly a week ago.

"Nothing?" Sam was saying. *"¿Ninguna cosita? ¿Con las bolsas, o el polvo—"*

"Pues, las bolsas . . ." he said uncertainly.

"¿Las bolsas?" Sam repeated.

"Tal vez no sea importante. Pero fueron sujetadas con armellas. En vez de una cuerda, como siempre."

"Estás seguro?" Sam asked quickly.

"Sí," the young man replied and grinned. *"Porque me rasguñaron la mano."* He held up his hand and pointed to a long red scratch.

Sam smiled broadly. *"Muchas gracias, Clemente. Muchas gracias."* He pressed a ten-dollar bill into his hand.

"You lost me," Claire said urgently. "What did he say? What was that about his hand?"

"He said the bags of Benyl were stapled, not sewn. And the reason he's sure is that he scratched his hand on the staples!"

"Sam! That's perfect!" She paused, then added suddenly, "Where was he drinking?" Sam looked at her quizzically, and then understanding dawned. He called out a question, and Clemente, who was halfway down the block, cupped his hands around his mouth and yelled back.

"Lindo Michoacan."

Claire smirked with satisfaction.

As they drove toward the station so Claire could pick up her car, parked lo these many hours ago, she rehearsed a very simple sentence. "Listen," it went, "why don't you stop by my house for a drink on your way home?" A woman who had successfully obtained information from a . . . an informant in the Lindo Michoacan, a woman who had survived the Aguila, was certainly capable of asking this question.

They pulled into the station parking lot and stopped next to her Toyota. There was a moment of silence, then Claire said, "Listen—"

"I know," Sam broke in. "It's really late, and I have to leave for Berkeley early tomorrow morning. You'll phone Anna Cheng tomorrow afternoon and ask about the assay?"

"Yes."

"Okay. I'll call you Saturday morning. Will you be in the lab?"

"Where else would I be?" she said, slamming his car door violently.

He looked at her peculiarly, but said merely, "Good. Talk to you then."

"When will you be back?"

"Sunday night. Oh, and Claire—thanks for coming tonight. It was a big help."

"Always happy to be of service." She gunned her motor and took off.

Early Friday morning she eagerly trotted downstairs to the lab. Despite her hard line with Sam, she knew what the *Monolinea* plates would look like. Her control group would be thickly encrusted by colorful mold, resembling something out of Edgar Allan Poe, while her treated dishes would remain squeaky clean. Therefore the Benyl would have done its job; therefore whatever Clemente et al. had sprayed on the Rodriguez peach trees couldn't have been Benyl. QED.

She knew something was wrong as soon as she opened the door. The room was too warm; usually a rush of chilled air greeted her in the mornings. Her first thought was that the air conditioner, pushed beyond its limit for the last week, had broken down.

Then she saw the open window.

Three years ago when she had walked into her apartment in Cambridge and found her stereo, her TV, and all her grandmother's jewelry gone, she had felt a physical revulsion, a sense of helplessness and violation, almost as if she had been raped. But now—she was simply enraged. Those damn kids! she thought furiously, as her eyes traveled rapidly across the room. Hubcaps were one thing, but this! The equipment table didn't look quite right; some familiar shapes were missing—and broken glass glistened on the floor. She hurried forward, slipped, caught herself on the corner of the table, took another step, skidded again. Finally she realized that the linoleum was greasy with some Vaselinelike substance, and she bent down for a closer look. Agar. And where there was agar . . . yes, there by her desk was one shallow plastic saucer, and if she looked farther she would probably find others.

With sinking heart she started toward the rack of petri dishes—then whirled at a sound from the storage room at the back of the lab. Was one of the little bastards still in there? Angrily she strode across the lab and pushed the door.

Slowly it yawned open on the small room, pitch-black and cave cool. Her anger gave way to . . . caution, if not actual fear. "Hello?" she said meekly, shuffling forward and waving her hands in the air to connect with the light cord. Then she gasped and froze.

She had touched a nose.

Before she had time to react she was pushed sideways with such force that she sprawled against a stack of boxes, stunned. For an instant she saw a figure silhouetted against the sunlight; then the door closed and clicked, and she was locked in absolute darkness.

"Hey!" she yelled, scrambling to her feet and beating against the door. There were scraping noises outside; he's squeezing through the window, she thought with frustration, and by the time I get out of here he'll be gone. "Hey, goddamn it!"

The cord tapped her lightly on the back of the head, and she reached up, turned on the light, and looked around feverishly at the crates of glassware, boxes of paper, piles of old computer output that no one wanted to take responsibility for chucking, broken machinery. What would get her out of here?

Something protruded from the top of the metal utility shelving, and she pulled it down and blew off the dust. It was a laminated plastic ruler from Hoffmeier's Hardware in Parkerville, with inches along one edge, centimeters along the other, and Historic Flags of Our Country parading down the middle. She flexed it experimentally; it was stiff but thin, like a credit card.

She had actually once seen someone open a door with a credit card, otherwise she might have dismissed the idea as urban folk myth. Impatiently she slipped the ruler between the door and the jamb and slid it upward.

On her eleventh attempt the ruler snagged the latch and the door opened.

Immediately she ran to the window, now wide open, and scanned the landscape from north to south. Yellowing grass, neat rows of orange, lemon, almond trees, the parking lot. No humans.

She sagged against the window ledge as the adrenaline from her encounter began to ebb. Eventually she made an effort to pull herself together. This had to be reported to . . . someone, to Ray at least, and to do that she needed to know exactly what had happened. Once again she turned to her rack of petri dishes.

Six were missing, and it was pretty obvious that what she had nearly broken her neck on a few minutes ago was the *Monolinea rodrigueza* experiment, now mixed into primordial goo in the middle of the floor. But the pattern of vandalism was strange: the top and fourth shelf, which had held the *Monolinea,* had been swept clean, while the second and third shelves were undisturbed. She examined the window again. It had a casement fastening that absolutely could not have been unlatched from outside. And the broken glassware was, as far as she could tell, a couple of cheap beakers; the valuable equipment—admittedly, too specialized to fence, but nevertheless valuable—was intact.

All of which pointed to a half-assed attempt to cover a surgical strike with carpet bombing.

But an attempt by whom? Buddy? Sam had warned her not to underestimate him, but surely this wasn't Buddy's work; to have found, in that whole crowded room, the six objects that pertained to the Rodriguez problem had required genuine expertise. . . .

Well, there was no shortage of experts on the premises. She was surrounded by them. And they all had keys to her office.

Someone at the station, then. But why, with what possible motive? Mechanically she gathered together the shards of glass; the agar would need the mop. As she headed out the door toward the broom closet, the phone rang. It was Jim LaSalle.

"Listen, I'd like to talk to you today about the *Aspergillus* project—that is, if you're not too busy with your other work," he said, unable to conclude without a snide parenthesis.

"Sure," she replied, hung up—and then turned to look once again at the rack of petri dishes.

The undisturbed shelves held the *Aspergillus* that she was managing for Jim.

Jim? Would Jim have trashed her office? Why? And would he have been so obvious as to leave his own work unharmed?

In a profoundly unsettled mood she began to clean up, and by the time she was rinsing the mop in the sink she had decided against reporting the incident to Ray, at least for the moment. Instead she wrote up the *Monolinea* experiment as if it had run to term, and presented him with her summary late in the afternoon.

"This is good news," he said. "Hate to see a Benyl-resistant isolate develop so soon. I guess Jim was right after all; the Rodriguezes just weren't treating their trees properly."

"Actually, Sam thinks there may have been a problem with, uh, with the spraying," Claire interjected, feeling compelled to defend Silvia and Carlos without divulging any details.

"Really? Well, I'm afraid it's academic. I understand the Rodriguezes are going to sell their land." He sighed. "Between the brown rot and Tony getting killed, I guess this year has just been too much for them."

Claire looked depressed. Amazing how fast rumors bounced around this place.

"By the way, Claire," Ray said hesitantly, "this seems as good a time as any to bring this up . . ."

Ominous words, she thought, disconcerted and temporarily distracted from the Rodriguezes. *Am I getting the sack?*

"Perhaps it's a bit premature," he continued, "but I don't know if you'd given any thought to your future here."

"My future?"

"Yes . . . I know this was advertised as a temporary position, but we felt all along that if it seemed to be working out, we'd like to make it permanent. I've—we've really been wanting to get involved in . . . basic research," he said reverently, and Claire repressed a small sigh of resignation. "And although you've only been here four months," he continued, "I think you've made valuable contributions to our work, and . . . well, so far as I'm concerned, the job is yours. If you want it."

Claire stared at him with dismay.

"I realize you can't decide immediately," Ray added hastily. "And if at the end of the year you conclude that you want to return to MIT or to some other academic post, of course we'll understand. . . ."

Some response was required of her. "Ray, I'm—I'm honored, and flattered. And I'll certainly think very seriously about it. But I can't give you an answer yet—"

"Of course not!" he responded too heartily. "I just wanted you to know what your options were."

She nodded glumly. Right now her "options"—returning to Cambridge or remaining in Citrus Cove—seemed as appealing as trial by ice versus trial by fire. Mumbling something she hoped sounded humble and grateful she made her escape, more depressed than ever.

At 4 P.M. she called the Fresno USDA and asked for Anna Cheng. In a moment a soft, slightly accented voice answered, conjuring a vision of delicate Asian beauty. Claire felt a stab of some unidentified emotion and said briskly, "This is Claire Sharples down in Citrus Cove. Sam Cooper left some samples for you to analyze this morning. . . ."

"Oh, yes . . . hold on just a moment, I've got the results right here . . . yes. There were two samples: some white powder in a plastic bag, which Sam said was probably Benyl, and a couple of peaches. Is that right?"

"Right."

"Let's see . . . your white powder was mostly inert matter—lime—with a small percentage of 1-butylcarbamoly-3-benzi-medazole carbamic acid methyl ester. In other words, it was Benyl."

"Good," said Claire. "How about the fruit?"

"Well, Sam said it had been sprayed recently, but all I found was lime hydrate."

"No butylcarbamoly-whatever it was?" asked Claire, suppressing the excitement in her voice.

"No, no active ingredients whatsoever. Only inert material. Is that what you were expecting?"

"Yes, it's exactly what we were expecting. Thank you so much, Ms. Cheng." She hung up the phone.

So that was that. Experiment or no, someone—Venture West? Buddy Hanford?—had dumped sacks of Benyl behind the shack at Amargosa and refilled them with lime hydrate. Clemente Gutierrez and his pals had sprayed the useless stuff on the trees at Agua Duke. And the fungus had thrived.

She stayed at the lab until about eight, then headed for the city's pitiful downtown. Parkerville's broad, shady Main Street with its convenient angled parking and stores for every need—hardware store, department store, shoeshine parlor, movie theater—was now nearly deserted; its shops had winked out one by one, leaving gaps in the neat rows like missing teeth. Only the bars and the squalid old hotel that housed farm workers were still thriving. The east end of Main Street, however, was suffering a doomed attempt at revitalization in the form of a few tourist shops and a mediocre restaurant—Parkerville's finest—all housed in a grand old domed and marbled railway station. It was here she treated herself to dinner.

But the meal did not fulfill, nor did the wine mellow. The destruction in her lab had to be addressed and finally, over soggy chocolate mousse reminiscent of melted Fudgsicle, she turned her attention to the problem.

By now she had convinced herself that only one man could

have been responsible; only one man would have known enough to trash her plates while carefully leaving his own cultures unscathed, and only one man would have made a gloating phone call afterward.

Jim LaSalle.

The problem was: *why?*

Simple malice?

Well, maybe. They certainly didn't get along, but Jim could have found other ways to harass her if that was his only intention. (Let the air out of her tires. Make obscene phone calls.)

But if this were not a sort of prank, directed at her, then it was something more serious: an attempt to disrupt her experiment and obscure the truth about what was happening at the Rodriguezes' orchard. And why would he want to do that?

Because he was behind the sabotage, or knew who was.

Claire backed up for a moment. It was one thing to spin glib theories as she had done yesterday with Sam. But was it really possible that Jim had bulldozed trees or committed arson or ruined Silvia's crop? (She didn't even consider Tony's murder—after all, Jim *was* a colleague and a professional.) Again, *why?* Sure, he "had it in" for the Rodriguezes, as Sam had put it, but that wasn't much of a motive compared to revenge/greed for Buddy and Venture West, respectively. And anyway, it begged the question. Why did he have it in for them?

What had she said to Sam yesterday when she had flippantly accused him of being Tony's murderer? There was something teasing her in one of the hypotheses she had rattled off. Let's see: Sam identifying the Rodriguezes with his parents (a particularly loony Freudianism); something between Frank and Sam—something they had both seen as kids, maybe, or something in Vietnam, except that Sam hadn't been in Vietnam . . . (and except that for all her intellectual games Sam was not a plausible suspect. After all, it was he himself who had identified the *Scirpus validus* and directed her to Amargosa, and in any case the whole notion was absurd, Sam was incapable of harming the Rodriguezes; he was obsessed with his responsibility for others and altogether too protective and gentle—)

Well, never mind that. What about inserting LaSalle into these scenarios? He had lived here all his life, too, was just as likely to have become entangled in some psychological mess with the Rodriguez family. In fact—

In fact, he had served with Frank Rodriguez. Sam had told her, that night at his cabin.

Well, so what? She had seen too many movies. She romanticized the war as much as she did farm workers and strong Third World women. Vietnam was a long time ago.

Still . . .

She couldn't ask Sam about this. If by some miracle of intuition she were onto something, she couldn't ask him to rake up muck about his best, dead, reproachful friend. But other people had served in that unit, and other people knew Kaweah County.

Absently she began to scrape her remaining dessert into a small mound in the middle of her plate, then molded it into a chocolate St. Helen's and stared at it for a moment. Then she found a waiter and was directed to the pay phone.

Tom Martelli had to think for a while before he could answer her question; then he gave her a name which she wrote on a napkin. "Used to be in Mountain View Trailer Park. That's been a few years, though."

She could hear the curiosity in his voice but she merely thanked him, got a number from information, and dialed. There was no answer.

CHAPTER 13

The road home took her past Casey's, and on impulse she pulled into the lot.

Immediately she was visited by a strong sense of déjà vu. No bike, of course (she wondered briefly what would happen to the Harley—auctioned off, probably, which seemed very sad) but otherwise the inventory of vehicles was similar to Friday's: green pickup, white panel truck, long black Lincoln with a plate that read BUDDY H. She regarded this thoughtfully for a moment and walked inside.

Buddy's bulky silhouette was easily discerned; to his right was a familiar looking fellow with a blond handlebar mustache. Claire positioned herself between them and ordered a Coors.

Buddy stared at her offensively for a full minute. In spite of herself she reddened self-consciously.

"A real two!" said Handlebars cryptically, and Buddy turned away and remarked to the world at large, "Looks like a goddamn hippy. Why don't she wear a dress and fix up her hair?"

Claire lost her temper.

"Why don't you lose fifty pounds and shut your mouth!" she snapped, addressing his right shoulder.

There was a moment of shocked silence. Then Buddy began to laugh. He's probably going to say he likes a girl with spirit, she thought with nausea.

"Can't lose the weight," Buddy said. "Too much of this"—he indicated the beer. "Can't seem to keep my mouth shut either." He grinned in what might have been a conciliatory manner, and continued, "You work out at the field station, don't you?" He knew damn well where she worked; he'd seen her there three or four times. "What are you, a secretary or something?"

"I'm a microbiologist," she said levelly. "My specialty is mycology. Fungus and mold."

"Is that right?" he said in a bored voice, turning away. This was not his idea of flirtatious conversation.

"As a matter of fact," she continued, "I just found out something kind of interesting about the fungus problem the Rodriguezes were having. You know, that persistent brown rot—"

"Now that just exactly describes trash like the Rodriguezes," Buddy interrupted. "Persistent brown rot!" He laughed obnoxiously and Claire wished for a sharp object, but she forced herself to continue.

"We were kind of worried up at the station that they'd developed some new, Benyl-resistant strain. But it turned out to be plain old brown rot after all. So I think we've solved their problem," she concluded, watching him closely. He appeared to be utterly indifferent.

"I hear the Rodriguezes are looking to sell their land," remarked Handlebars cautiously, also watching Buddy for his reaction and gratified when he drew a smirk.

"About time," Buddy rumbled. "They've screwed around with it long enough. Give it to somebody who knows what to do with it."

"You gonna buy it back?" Handlebars continued with an air of great daring. But Buddy just grinned as if at some private joke and replied negligently, "I might think about it. If the price was right. Might even let Carlos work for me again—as a field hand!" He slapped some money down on the bar. "So long, Mickey," he said and sauntered out.

Claire watched him go with frustration. He hadn't reacted to her crude hints about brown rot, but something was going on with Buddy Hanford. Maybe she and Sam had underestimated him. He wasn't a buffoon. He did, after all, participate in the management of the billion-dollar Hanford brothers operation, although Claire heretofore had believed this was due solely to consanguinity.

But if Buddy, possibly with his pal, was up to something at Agua Dulce, where did that leave Venture West? Or the new theory she was working on?

She sipped her beer. The jukebox was producing its usual

plaintive noise. Merle Haggard, she thought. He was better than most of them. He had a nice voice, and at least his lyrics were kind of clever, the way they took a colloquialism and turned it around, called attention to it, but the changes were so elementary and repetitive—

Her musical critique was disrupted by a loud voice to her right. "Hey, Mickey, same again!" Handlebars was calling, and the pitch of his voice stirred her memory. Well, well. So Handlebars was the guy who had shouted to Tony on Friday night. What was it—"Buddy here wants to buy you a drink"? He had provoked the fight. She examined him with greater interest.

He was an unremarkable-looking man, his body pear shaped and soft under his plaid shirt, his pudgy face distinguished only by the huge, drooping, sandy-colored mustache that somehow made him resemble a mournful, long-eared spaniel. Mickey had drawn him a beer. With clumsy, slightly drunken movements he fumbled with his wallet, a phony Western affair of elaborately tooled leather, finally pulling out its entire contents and scattering it across the bar: photographs, scraps of paper, tattered business card, credit cards—and a fat wad of crisp hundred-dollar bills. Claire and Mickey looked at this display with awe.

"Damn, Larry," Mickey managed to say, "you knock over a bank?"

"Christmas in July this year," Handlebars—no, Larry—responded with a goofy grin, stuffing the pile back into his wallet. "Ain't you heard?"

Claire regarded him furtively for the next few minutes. Eventually he drained his beer and said reluctantly, "Well, I got to go."

"Sure you won't have one more, just to break another hundred?" Mickey asked sarcastically.

"Naw, I got to get the van back. They lock up the lot at ten. See you."

Claire watched him leave, then turned to Mickey. "Who is that guy? I've seen him around."

"Larry McKeever? He's a delivery man for a big feed and supply outfit—"

"Which outfit?" she asked, knowing the answer.

"Kavoian's. Down in Parkerville."

By the time she reached the parking lot the white panel truck she had noticed earlier was gone.

She stood chewing a knuckle thoughtfully. So Larry worked for Kavoian's. And drove a van. And was flashing a wad. While she didn't for a moment see him as the master saboteur of Agua Dulce, he could be an important link. He was friends with . . . lots of people, anybody who would buy him a drink, but especially with Buddy Hanford; his van could have made the tracks at Amargosa, could have hauled sacks of Benyl and not Benyl, could maybe even have carried Tony's body and the Harley out to the dam that night. Definitely a fascinating character. When Sam called tomorrow she would ask him about Larry McKeever.

On Saturday the station parking lot was nearly empty. Her colleagues came in on the weekends only when the rhythm of some experiment required it; otherwise it was eight to five Monday through Friday, then home to the wife and kids. But Claire couldn't break her academic seven-day-a-week habit, and anyway she didn't have a wife and kids. She at least allowed herself the luxury of arriving at nine o'clock, and then waited for Sam's call.

It came at about ten-thirty. "Hi," he said. "What's going on? What does the *Monolinea* look like?"

"Rainbow Jell-O."

"What?"

She told him what had happened to the lab.

"Damnation! Those fucking kids!"

This was exactly the reaction she'd been hoping for. "Yeah."

"Huh. Maybe Jim's right. Maybe we do need a guard. Anything valuable missing?"

"No. And luckily they waited until yesterday, when it didn't really matter, at least as far as the Benyl went. We knew what the results were going to be. And I called Anna Cheng."

"Ah. Helpful?"

"Yes. The stuff we found on the ground was Benyl, all right, but guess what the Agua Dulce trees had been sprayed with!"

"Lime."

"That's right," she said, mildly disappointed. "Hydrated lime. How did you know?"

"It's cheap, it's available, it looks just like Benyl—in fact it's a major ingredient in Benyl. Just made sense. But you're right; it's pretty convincing confirmation of what we think is going on."

"Yes, I know. And listen, Sam—do you know a guy called Larry McKeever?"

"Works for Kavoian's? Yeah, I know him. Why?"

Claire told him about her field trip to Casey's. There was a short silence at the other end of the line.

"Hello?"

"Yeah, I'm here. I was just thinking. . . . Larry McKeever. Could be . . . but I'm not sure what to do about it. We can't go to Cummings and tell him to check out McKeever without laying out our whole theory, and I'm not quite ready to do that. Let him chase Peruvian coke dealers a little longer. Well, I'll think about it, and we'll talk tomorrow when I get back."

"Okay."

"And Claire—"

"Yes?"

"Um—" He paused uncomfortably. (Another photographic request? she wondered.) "Listen, I appreciate what you found out last night but—take it easy today, okay? Don't go poking around at Amargosa, or . . . or picking fights with Buddy Hanford. . . ."

She laughed.

"No, I mean it," he said insistently. "This isn't just a—a hypothetical situation, you know. Whoever these guys are, they're playing rough. Don't mess with them!"

"All right," she said, surprised. "I'll lock myself in the lab!"

"Good. I'll see you tomorrow." He hung up.

At seven she peered out the back window and read the thermometer. Only ninety-eight. Cooling off; it had peaked at a hundred and six. She thought seriously about spending the night in the lab, but Jim's car was now in the parking lot and that made her feel a little strange. Reluctantly she prepared to step out into the blast furnace of evening, then paused by the phone, fished in her purse, and drew out a crumpled napkin. She dialed the number and a woman answered.

"Could I speak with Manuel Aragon, please?"

Silence. "Yeah, sure. Just a minute."

She could hear retreating footsteps, a faint TV, a clunk and a curse as someone fumbled with the receiver.

"Hello?"

"Mr. Aragon, my name is Claire Sharples. I work at the Citrus Cove Field Station, and I'd like to talk to you"—short pause to gather the wits—"um, to talk to you about Frank Rodriguez," she finally blurted.

The TV babbled, a door slammed, and someone breathed quietly on the other end of the line. Then Manny Aragon, who had served in Vietnam with Frank Rodriguez and Jim LaSalle, very gently hung up the phone.

By the time she reached Riverdale she was sticky and very uncomfortable, and she thought briefly about an air-conditioned booth at Casey's. No. Not tonight. But as she drove by the bar she couldn't help but notice that the white van was once more parked in front. McKeever must stop there every night after work, and then drive back down to Kavoian's to drop off the van and pick up his car.

At home she read on the front porch for two hours while the house cooled, wondered for the tenth time if her Arkie landlady had lied about the wiring ("Now this hyere's an old house, honey, hit won't take no ire-condishner,") then roamed aimlessly about, picking up books and tossing them aside, turning on the TV and turning it off, considering projects and rejecting them. She kept thinking about Mannie Aragon. Should she call him again? And she kept thinking about the white van. What if it contained important clues, like—like grease from the Harley's tires or even a Benyl sack filled with lime? And why was Sam so reluctant to broach their theory to Cummings? Presumably he understood the complex and no doubt sordid politics of Kaweah County better than she did, but she had a sick feeling that valuable data—evidence rather—was slipping away by the minute.

Anyway, the more she thought about it, the more she resented his cautionary tone on the telephone that morning. At the time she had been rather touched by his solicitude, but now she wondered if it hadn't been merely one more attempt to keep her "in her place." Her place happened to be the lab rather than the kitchen, but the effect was the same: rattle those beakers and pans. . . .

For some reason she suddenly remembered that gray day in Cambridge when she had first thought about Citrus Cove, and with a certain sheepishness recalled the highly romantic image of herself as cowgirl that had flitted through her mind. It had been ludicrous; she had known that even then, but still . . . . Here she was, she had done it, she had come west to seek her fortune. And while it was true that the place hadn't exactly lived up to her expectations, resembling as it did the wasteland rather than the Promised Land, what was more to the point was that *she* hadn't lived up to them. She was still the same old Claire, in no way transformed.

Why was it so hard to keep a . . . a sense of adventure about one's life? It was the same with her career: she had begun fired by the romance of "doing science;" now, for the most part, her work was entirely routine, about as romantic as short-order cooking. . . .

At eleven-thirty Claire was staring through the chain link fence that surrounded Kavoian's lot.

In the dim fluorescent light the jumble of tractors, forklifts, and other specialized machinery looked fantastic and nearly unrecognizable. But after several minutes of anxious scanning she saw, nosed up against the fence in the northwest corner of the lot, a white panel truck; saw, in fact, *three* white panel trucks.

Damn. And of course she hadn't noticed the license plate. But it was academic anyway. All three were securely locked behind six feet of chain link and four strands of barbed wire.

Or were they? She checked the gate; it was secured to the fence by a chain and a padlock. But whoever had fastened the chain—Larry, maybe—had been careless: there was enough play in it so that she could push the gate open about ten inches. Plenty of room for a slender and determined person to slip through.

She walked to the vans and laid her hand on the hood of the right-most vehicle. It was cool, as was the second. The third, however, was still warm: maybe this was Larry's truck. But its doors and windows were secured and its interior dark and uninformative.

So now what? She pulled out her Swiss Army knife, with which she had optimistically provided herself, and looked at it. Maybe Magnum could pick a lock with the tweezers or the ivory toothpick, but as far as she was concerned the doors might as well be welded shut. And the van's design—smooth, slightly bulbous, like bubble-form plastic packaging—might have been deliberately created to discourage the accumulation of evidence, sometimes known as "dirt." Systematically she ran her hand along the seamless flank of the vehicle: no nooks or crannies, no grooved running board to harbor, say, silver sand or cigar ash; no spokes to trap bulrushes or other telltale weeds. She rocked back on her heels, feeling frustrated and foolish. This enterprise had not been well thought out—

Wait. What about the grillwork?

Feeling with her knife blade, she scraped each recess and deposited promising detritus onto the back of an envelope. Squashed bugs, more squashed bugs . . . but what about this, just under the cruciform Chevrolet ornament—these brown flakes that looked like tobacco? Surely an odd place for tobacco. She remembered Sam's calloused palm, tenderly cupping the dry spikes of the bulrushes, each spike composed of feathery, rust-colored scales. . . .

Scales that would look a lot like tobacco if they happened to end up crumbled in the front grill of a Chevy van. Using the tweezers from her knife she retrieved the shreds and placed them in the envelope.

She was stuffing the packet back into her breast pocket when suddenly, just outside the fence, a car door slammed.

Claire froze behind the car. Feet approached, crunching on the gravel. She started as a thin beam of light played across the lot, swept toward the vans. *It must be the night watchman,* she thought, heart pounding wildly. *Maybe I should just call out, make some excuse for being here—better than getting caught like a sneak thief.*

Abruptly the light disappeared. With immense relief she heard the footsteps retreat, the door open and close, the engine start. The car pulled away.

She scuttled to the gate and squeezed through. I'm too old for this, she thought as she climbed into the car, I've always been too old for this. Turning on the radio—even a little country music was welcome right now—she waited for her breathing to become normal. Then she started the car, and hesitated for a moment.

Behind her, to the north, was State 170, the main route to Riverdale. But it was Saturday night, which meant that 170 was still jammed with weekenders headed up to the Sierras; she had had to squint against their headlights on her way down, and the mere idea of chugging back up the hill as caboose to a train of Winnebagos chilled the blood.

But there was another, less familiar, way home. A chain of narrow country roads wound due east from Parkerville through the hills, eventually turning north and joining the state highway several miles beyond Riverdale. A picturesque but circuitous route, tonight it might be faster than 170. Claire turned east.

Well, her outing had probably been fruitless, she thought, passing a few lighted farmhouses on her right, but at least it had relieved some of her nervous energy. And maybe Sam could identify those fragments as *Scirpus* scales, though it seemed unlikely that he could pin them down to *Scirpus validus,* and she would have to tell him where she got them, which probably would be a mistake—

Her thoughts were disturbed by an unholy glare, and she glanced with annoyance at her rearview mirror. Some jerk was right on her tail with his brights on, for Christ's sake. Typical. Why didn't he pass her? There was nothing she could do until she found a place to pull over, but this was a real jmaniac, tailgating her at sixty up a winding two-lane road. . . . Ah, there was a bit of a shoulder; she signaled and moved to the right.

Wait a minute—he wasn't passing her, he was pulling off behind her!

Instinctively she hit the accelerator and skidded back onto the road. The other car, an American monster, was right there. With fear rising in her throat, she tried both to pay attention to the road and to understand what was happening, but the blaze of his headlights made it hard to see, much less think.

Was this just some drunk cowboy being cute? Or was it specifically directed at her, was it somebody who had seen her at Kavoian's—Larry or Buddy or someone from Venture West? Or . . . well, somebody else? And whoever it was, did he actually want to force her off the road, like—like Karen Silkwood? Or merely scare her? Or maybe hope she panicked enough to do something stupid like miss a turn, like take a curve too fast—

She wrenched the wheel to the left, barely avoiding a drainage ditch. The road had taken an unexpected sharp bend to the north. Like that, she thought grimly, suddenly calmer, and I'll be goddamned if I'll do the job for him.

She jogged east and north on J-416. He jogged east and north, maintaining a distance of about fifty yards between them. Could this be all in her imagination? she wondered suddenly. Was she just so keyed up from her "adventure" at Kavoian's that she was imputing sinister motives to some poor slob who happened to be going where she was going? But he had followed her when she pulled off the road, and anyway, it was a much more serious error to assume he *wasn't* following her when he actually *was,* than the converse. She had to behave as if it were true.

Driving as fast as she dared, her tires screaming around the tight curves, she desperately tried to think coherently, to develop some strategy. She thought 170 was about . . . six miles ahead, and Riverdale another mile or so west—

Only he would never let her get to Riverdale. Between here and the highway the country was completely deserted: high rangeland through which the road swooped and climbed like a roller coaster. He could outdrive her here—his car was faster, and he was undoubtedly more skillful. In fact, she realized with impotent fury, he could take her any time he wanted to. He was just waiting for the perfect moment.

For miles the road snaked around hills silvered by the bright moon and oaks shadowed black against them; it would have been quite beautiful in other circumstances. Twice his headlights disappeared from her rearview mirror and her heart lightened momentarily: perhaps he had turned off, perhaps the nightmare was over . . . but each time they reappeared around the bend of the hill behind her, steady and relentless.

After what seemed like hours, but was in fact about ten minutes, she glanced at her speedometer and was immediately seized by a new fear: she should be coming to 170 very shortly, but she recognized none of this! What if she had taken the wrong turn somewhere? It would have been easy enough to do; she had only been on this route two or three times and all these little back roads looked exactly alike—maybe that's why he hadn't made his move, maybe he was gloating, knowing she was winding her way deeper and deeper into the lonely hills.

They were descending now into a little valley, heavily wooded. Claire could see a small road coming in at a sharp angle from the left. The road seemed somehow familiar. Surely—surely she knew this intersection! But she had approached it from the other direction, from the smaller road, from the west, from . . .

Abruptly, she hit the throttle and spun the wheel hard to the left. The car swerved and fishtailed crazily, but somehow she held on—her reflexes had been honed on icy Massachusetts roads—and in a few seconds she was speeding westward again, along the narrow dirt road that disappeared into the trees.

Her sudden maneuver caught him by surprise, and the big car hurtled by the turnoff. Immediately she heard the squeal of tires; he was correcting his mistake, but for the moment she was out of his sight. She turned right, then left again, feverishly searching the darkness for the turnoff. There, up on the right . . . she pulled into a grove of oak that partially hid the car and ran across the road and up the long driveway to Sam's house.

The cabin was dark, of course—Sam wouldn't be back until tomorrow—and the front door was undoubtedly locked, but she had seen a window last Saturday, around the side. . . . Yes, thank god, it was still open. She scrambled through and tried futilely to close it behind her, then she felt her way across the room until her hands touched what they were seeking: the cool steel barrel of the shotgun.

She fumbled for the box of shells, silently thanking her big brother for a few impatient lessons in the woods of western Massachusetts. The luminous face of her watch read 12:32; it had been ten minutes since she had left the car. Either she had lost him, or—suddenly she heard the faint whine of an engine climbing the hill. Oh Christ . . . with unsteady hands she managed to crack open the barrel, load two shells, and snap it closed. Then she waited. The car was very close now—it had actually turned up the driveway when she remembered the safety catch. Shit, where was it? A car door slammed as she felt for the catch and snicked it open. Steps on the porch . . . he would try the front door, then walk around until he found the window. . . .

In one horrible instant the door opened wide and the room was flooded with light, illuminating her standing white-faced, the shotgun trembling but level—

"What's going on?" Sam said mildly.

CHAPTER 14

Claire sat with a large glass of scotch and began her narrative. As soon as she told him she had broken into Kavoian's lot, he exploded.

"You did *what?"* he said incredulously. "Of all the—"

"Stupid, childish, ill-conceived things to do," she concluded miserably. "I know. Believe me, I know."

"But *why?!"* he exclaimed. "I even warned you, I told you to stay in the lab—"

That's why, you jerk, she thought bitterly, but what she said was, "I guess I was tired of being the effete intellectual. I wanted to do something . . . heroic."

He looked at her incredulously. "Go on," he said after a moment.

She fumbled for her envelope of brown dust, which he examined and sniffed. "Tobacco," he pronounced, and her face fell.

"Are you sure?"

"No," he said, humoring her. "Go on," and she began to describe her wild ride through the hills.

"Who was it following you?" interrupted Sam. "Was it McKeever?"

"The headlights blinded me. I couldn't see the driver."

"Well, what kind of a car was it?" Sam pressed.

She shrugged helplessly. "Some kind of big American car, I don't know—"

"What do you mean? A Ford? An Oldsmobile?"

"I *don't know!"* she shouted. "Jesus Christ! I could barely keep it together to stay on the road, much less identify the damn car—" She set down her glass with shaking hands.

There was a short pause.

"Okay," Sam said quietly. "Sorry. What happened then?"

"I managed to lose him on the way up here. I climbed through your window and found the shotgun."

"You could have used the front door," he remarked. "I never bother to lock it."

"So I gathered," she said wryly, "when you walked in and took ten years off my life. . . ."

"*Your* life!" Sam looked pointedly at the shotgun. "And where did you learn to use that thing?"

"I—my brother taught me, a long time ago. I don't even know if I loaded it properly," she said sheepishly.

"Oh, it's loaded." He looked at her thoughtfully. Finally he said, "Well, you didn't handle yourself too badly, for an effete intellectual. Except for the initial outrageous error in judgment. But McKeever, or somebody else from Venture West, sure as hell knows what we're up to now."

Claire cleared her throat, and then, with great reluctance, said, "Sam, I don't know that it was either one. I don't know that this was connected with Tony at all. I mean, at the time I assumed it was, but in fact it could have been a random drunk—"

Now he was really angry. "What the hell is the matter with you?" he said, smacking the coffee table with the flat of his hand. "You have to read something in the *Annals of Microbiology* before you believe it? This isn't the goddamn laboratory, Claire, this is what we call life! And in life," he continued with heavy sarcasm, "we sometimes have to act on insufficient data—on our feelings, our instincts! Otherwise, we may get wasted by some homicidal maniac!"

Only it turns out I don't have any instincts for life, she thought unhappily, staring at the floor. *I don't even have any for science. No instincts at all.*

There was a long silence, then, "I'll talk to Cummings in the morning and tell him all about McKeever and the Benyl and everything else, I guess," Sam said, rising. "In the meantime I think you'd better stay here, just in case. You can sleep in the bedroom. I'll stay on the couch."

"Sort of like Claudette Colbert and Clark Gable," she said faintly, following him to the bedroom. She was feeling a bit giddy.

"Who?" He switched on the light. "Look, there's a quilt in the closet if you need it and, well, I'll see you tomorrow." He shut the door.

* * *

Claire lay on the narrow bed, weary but strangely alert. Her terror and subsequent chagrin had given way to a kind of euphoria. She tried to remember when she had been so frightened: not since early childhood, surely. So this was the attraction of rock climbing and sky diving and other insanely dangerous pursuits: this calm after the storm, catharsis after fear. Some kind of atavistic reaction, no doubt.

She thought about the fragments of . . . whatever, in her pocket. Despite Sam's ex cathedra pronouncement, she was sending them to whatever his name was in Berkeley for identification, by god. She thought about the gun. Could she really have shot anyone? she wondered. And Sam, Jesus, what if she had hurt him! Sam. It was amazing how he had walked in at the very instant she had been expecting the bogeyman. He had been anxious to get back, he had explained, and had decided not to wait until morning. But really it was amazing, almost as if . . . as if . . .

As if he had been her pursuer. There. She had said it, and it was absurd. My god, she had been through this before; it was logically implausible and—and psychologically impossible, for Sam to be involved in any of this. And anyway the car following her had been much larger than his Valiant. Much larger. Of course, it was hard to judge size in the dark.

Dammit! She was doing it again! Why did she keep coming back to this idea? It was like a little kid trying to scare herself with ghost stories: what if that pile of clothes over there in the corner were really a monster? What if your Mommy were really a . . . an evil witch? What if the man you love—

Ah. The man you love.

It was so obvious that even she had finally recognized it.

The minutes ticked by, and she thought about Sam. It was very strange to remember that only a few weeks ago she had been absolutely appalled by her stirrings of feeling for him, had considered him a wildly unworthy object of her affection and her desire. And now . . .

Oh, now, she thought impatiently, now she was completely loopy about the guy. But what had happened? Had she changed? Had Sam changed? Or had she just acknowledged her true emotions?

All of the above, of course; it was always the answer to her own rhetorical questions. She had indeed realized some—

mostly unpleasant—truths about herself. And Sam . . . well, Sam seemed to be the kind of person who shone in a crisis. Probably not as amusing a dinner companion as Phil, but—she tried to imagine how Phil might have behaved during the events of the past week. Phil, fishing out the body of a friend from the lake. Phil, breaking the news to the bereaved parents. Phil, reading tire tracks in the dirt, stalking a killer—it was no use. In fact, she could hardly imagine Phil at all.

Still, god and the superpowers willing, she wouldn't always be in the midst of a crisis. And when this one was over, what then? Would she again find Sam's shirts (she hadn't noticed his shirts in days) and his enthusiasms—his music and his *Scirpus validus*—unbearable? It all sounded so petty—

Petty and completely irrelevant. Because Claire loved Sam, and Sam regarded Claire with professional respect colored, at present, by mild contempt.

At four A.M., resigned to a sleepless night, she got up, pushed open the bedroom door and tiptoed into the living room.

The full moon was high and a shaft of silver light fell across the couch. Reminded obscurely, perhaps, of Cupid and Psyche, she tried to avoid looking at Sam as she walked past. But of course she failed: he was sleeping quietly, one bare arm flung across his face so that only the tip of his nose and his mouth were visible. She stood there for a moment, then slipped outside.

The air was cool and fragrant. Below her the land sloped away toward town and the river. The hills to the east were dark against the bright sky, the mountains beyond invisible but omnipresent: a lonely prospect, but in her exalted mood, exhilarating. She sat down on the steps.

"Hey." A voice called softly behind her. Sam stepped onto the porch.

"I couldn't sleep," she said.

"I'm not surprised," he remarked dryly, sitting beside her.

She could feel the warmth radiating from him. Suddenly, angrily, she thought, This is ridiculous. I nearly died tonight, and I'll be damned if I spend one more second of my life behaving like a moony teenager. Act on your instincts, he'd said. . . .

She reached up and pulled him toward her.

He jerked back as if scorched. And then, abruptly and mi-raculously, his arms were around her and he was holding her very tightly.

After all the weeks of fantasy the simple fact of his . . . his *solidity,* was just astonishing: the sharp ridge of collarbone pressed against her cheek, the strong heartbeat under the soft T-shirt, were almost more than she could take.

"That was so easy!" she gasped.

He mumbled something inaudible, his voice muffled by her hair. Then he began to kiss her.

Eventually she said, "Could we go inside? I think I just got a splinter."

So they spread a sleeping bag on the floor of the living room, beneath the fixed smiles of little Shannon and Terry.

Sunlight filled the room when Claire awoke. It was ten o'clock, and Sam was gone; but on the table by the photographs was a tersely worded note which she read with a mixture of amusement and annoyance. "Gone to P'ville to talk to Cummings," it said. "Will call. Stay put.—S."

"Stay put." What a message to leave for someone with whom you had just spent a night, or several hours anyway, of ardor; Sam carried this Western taciturnity a little far. If that was all it was . . . A vague uneasiness stirred in the neighborhood of her solar plexus. She stood up and walked restlessly around the room.

Last night—well, this morning, technically—had been wonderful. Hadn't it? For a moment she was overwhelmed by a flood of memory so intense it left her weak. Oh yes, it had been wonderful. Then why this niggling doubt, this insecurity?

She had initiated the action. Was that the problem? But hell, somebody had to make the first move, and Sam had certainly responded, my god . . .

But he hadn't said anything. He hadn't said, "I love you," or "you're beautiful," or, "I've been waiting months for this moment" . . . and Claire was a person who liked things to be said. Written and published, if possible; to her the phrase "nonverbal communication" was a meaningless oxymoron. Of course, she hadn't said much either: both of them had been so tired they had just sort of collapsed into each other's arms, egos blown to bits by exhaustion. And she couldn't have been mistaken about Sam's reaction. He had wanted her, too.

She wandered into the kitchen and opened the refrigerator. Two six-packs, half a loaf of Wonder Bread, a slimy, crumpled package of some anonymous Band-Aid-colored lunch meat . . . well, sure he had wanted her, she thought, closing the door hastily and looking for the coffee instead. Given the circumstances—warm night, full moon, reasonably attractive, reasonably young woman lunging at him—what was he going to do?

The question was, what was he feeling now? Stirrings of desire? Revulsion? Nothing? And goddamn it, why wasn't he here so she could ask him?

This was grossly unfair, she knew. Right now Sam was probably abasing himself before James T. Cummings . . . poor Sam. And poor Claire. The percolator wheezed and groaned to a climax, she poured herself a cup of coffee, and tried to read.

At two the jangle of the phone sent her racing from the living room. She picked up the receiver before the second ring.

"Claire." Sam's voice sounded thin and remote. "Listen, you need to come down to the sheriff's office right away. In Parkerville. You know where it is?"

"Sure, but why—"

He interrupted curtly. "McKeever's car was found a couple of hours ago, and Cummings wants to see if you can identify it as the one that followed you last night."

"McKeever's *car?* What about McKeever?"

There was a long pause. The answer came very slowly.

"McKeever was in the car." Silence. "In the trunk."

Several seconds passed before Claire comprehended this statement. "Jesus Christ," she whispered finally, but Sam was talking again.

"I don't have time to explain right now," he was saying, "just get down here as fast as you can." And with that he hung up.

Two hours later Claire was pacing the gray linoleum of the Kaweah County sheriff's office, waiting for Sam and Cummings to finish conferring, or rather, for Cummings to finish haranguing Sam out in the corridor.

Under the sheriff's impatient eye she had dutifully examined the brown Plymouth Duster parked in the lot outside, viewed it from every angle, taken in its curlicued customized detailing and its bumper sticker that read COWBOYS STAY ON LONGER—knowing all the while it was a hopeless task. And inevitably she had been unable to recognize the relentless and terrifying juggernaut of the previous night in this slightly battered, unremarkable vehicle.

Unremarkable except for its trunk, of course. Like the camera in a Hitchcock film, her gaze had focused hypnotically on that sinister trunk, noting how generous, how—how obscenely capacious it was. Obviously too enormous for the spare, the family luggage, or the groceries, it evidently had been just big enough for one medium-sized man, compactly folded, hands tied behind back.

And in spite of her inability to identify the car she was now convinced that it had been McKeever who had pursued her last night. Why else had he been murdered? Even her carefully cultivated skepticism couldn't embrace that coincidence. No, he had tried to kill her, he had probably killed Tony Rodriguez, and she was not sorry he was dead. Nevertheless the brutal efficiency of his dispatch was horrifying and frightening, and she had looked to Sam to find, and to offer, reassurance.

But Sam was no comfort. As they had stood in the parking lot below he had relayed the grisly details of the discovery of the body in a rapid monotone, all the while staring at the asphalt, his watch, his feet—anywhere but at her. When she had begun to speculate about what McKeever's death might mean, he had grunted and walked off to speak with Cummings. And that had been their sole interchange of the day. Her earlier mild uneasiness about his emotional state was now a fully mature anxiety.

Well, there was one redeeming feature of today's events, she thought sourly, checking out the FBI's Most Wanted individuals for the third time. McKeever had been found at nine A.M., at which time, the police judged, he had been dead for about four hours—and she knew exactly, but *exactly,* where Sam had been at five that morning. So that particular nightmare of unreason was laid to rest.

She looked up at the clock—four twenty-four. And the murmur of voices continued in the hall—Cummings's blustery bass alternating with Sam's beleaguered tenor. Tom Martelli was there, too. Evidently the remote spot where McKeever had been found was technically in the city of Riverdale, so

Martelli was "on the case"—a very good thing, given Sam's assessment of Cummings's integrity and competence. But weren't they ever going to finish? If she didn't get a chance to speak with Sam soon she was going to be ill.

She wandered over to the old-fashioned mahogany desk and sat on the corner, idly glancing at the officious brass nameplate of Sheriff James T. Cummings, the stacks of forms, the Kiwanis Club Honorary Man of the Month paperweight, the metal tray containing assorted keys, loose change, tooled leather wallet—

Wait. She had seen that wallet before. It had been lying on the bar at Casey's, bulging with hundred-dollar bills. So these must be Larry McKeever's what do you call it, his effects. Fired by morbid curiosity, she gingerly picked up the wallet and flipped it open.

The bill compartment was empty. Someone had disposed of the hundreds: the sheriff or Larry himself or his . . . his executioner, she thought grimly, and probed further. Her breath hissed sharply as a familiar mustachioed face suddenly glowered at her. Oh. Driver's license. Mobil, Chevron, Sears credit cards; Kavoian's employee ID; greasy photograph of nude woman. . . . She frowned in dissatisfaction and repeated the inventory. No, that was all.

Something about the wallet bothered her. She closed her eyes and visualized its contents spilled across the glossy wood of the bar—

The handle of the office door turned. Hastily she dropped the wallet into the tray and stood up just as Sam walked in.

Without a glance in her direction he collapsed into a hard wooden chair by the door and propped his head wearily on his hand. A wave of protective tenderness swept over her and she moved toward him.

"Sam . . ." she began tentatively.

"What?" He looked up, it seemed to her, with the closed face of a stranger. She halted uncertainly.

"Tell me what happened today," she said finally, sitting down again.

Head leaning back against the wall, eyes closed, he began a terse narrative. "Got to Cummings's house about nine-thirty," he said. "He was mowing the lawn. I told him I thought McKeever might be connected with Tony's death. I described Larry's sudden and mysterious affluence, and I said you thought he had tried to run you off the road last night, but I didn't mention the Benyl or McKeever's connection with Kavoian's because that would have led to Venture West. And I didn't want to bring them up yet.

"So as a result the whole story sounded mighty thin, and Cummings was looking forward to an afternoon of beer and the tube, so he wasn't exactly receptive anyway." He paused for a moment.

"But I managed to persuade him to drive over to McKeever's." A slight hardening of his voice hinted at heroic efforts of tact and humility. "Unfortunately McKeever's place was deserted. Which put Cummings in an even fouler mood. I guess he figured he'd missed *Gilligan's Island* for nothing.

"And then, on the way back to Parkerville, a report from the highway patrol came over the radio. Some tourists driving up to the mountains had spotted a car in a ravine, off 170. A brown Duster. The CHP had traced the plate, and it was registered to Lawrence McKeever.

"So we head for 170 hell bent for leather, sirens blaring, lights flashing—Cummings likes that kind of thing—and about ten miles beyond Riverdale we see the CHP parked by a hairpin curve. They had already hauled up the car and were opening the trunk." He stopped abruptly.

A number of cogent questions occurred to Claire. Why exactly had McKeever been killed? Had Buddy killed him? Venture West? Had Sam talked to Martelli about Venture West? What did Tom think?

"Did you have anything to eat?" she asked.

Startled, Sam finally looked at her. "I bought a candy bar from the machine downstairs," he answered after a moment, "but I've still got it. Want it?" He stood up and fished in his pocket.

"Yes," she said, walking over to him and holding out her hand. Their eyes met for an instant; then he turned away.

"Let's go," he mumbled.

CHAPTER 15

Claire followed the blue Valiant up into the hills, incoherent with unhappiness. Larry McKeever formed a sort of grim substrate, but most of it was sheer misery over Sam.

She understood exactly what that sick anxiety in the pit of her stomach meant; she had known all day and had refused to acknowledge it. She of all people knew what rejection felt like.

Why, why had she done it? If ever a man had made clear that he just wasn't interested, it was Sam; if ever a woman should have learned not to act on impulse, it was Claire. And now she had screwed up everything. They could never even be friends again: both would be self-conscious and embarrassed; she, humiliated; he, ashamed that he had responded to her.

In fact, if he didn't want her he shouldn't have responded. But she couldn't blame him; men were just helpless pawns of their testosterone sometimes, and anyway, even if he had turned her down, their relationship would have been ruined. At least this way she had gotten a few blissful hours.

She turned into his driveway and pulled up beside the Valiant. Why, she wondered, had he even wanted her to follow him? and immediately answered her own question. He wants to get it over with, she realized with sad clarity. He wasn't Phil, who had strung her along for months; there would be a swift, clean, cauterized cut. "Claire," he would say, "about last night . . ."

Slowly she got out of her car and walked up the steps.

Sam was standing in the middle of the living room, hands in pockets. She regarded him stonily, and an expression of pain passed briefly over his face. "Claire," he said immediately, "there's something I have to—"

He halted abruptly and Claire waited stolidly for the inexorable phrase. Ah, here it was: "About last night . . ." he began again; then he trailed off uncertainly.

There was a long silence. Finally, taking pity on them both, Claire said in a low voice, "I guess I made a mistake, huh."

"Yeah," Sam muttered, "a mistake." He walked to the window.

After a moment he added, with obvious effort, "Look, it was my fault. I knew you were . . . overwrought, that you didn't really know what you were doing—"

"Don't patronize me," she snapped, then, controlling herself, "I'm sorry, but—but I knew exactly what I was doing. I realize you're trying to be kind, to protect me, but I'd rather you didn't—"

"Don't tell me who I'm protecting!" he interrupted fiercely, whirling to face her. As Claire attempted to digest this remark he continued, "And what the hell do you mean, you knew what you were doing? You just said you made a mistake!"

Claire stared at him. The tinny bells of dramatic irony were clanging faintly in her ears. "I meant," she said warily, "that I was mistaken about . . . about your feelings."

"*My* feelings!"

"Yes, goddamn it!" she exclaimed, throwing caution to the winds. "*My* feelings have been perfectly clear for some time; I mean, I've been in a state of sexual hysteria for weeks! I just finally worked up the courage to do something about it!"

"You expect me to believe that? Hell, I didn't even think you *liked* me!"

She opened her mouth for an angry retort—and began to laugh instead.

"Listen," she said, "you have to read it in the *Annals of Microbiology* or what?"

He looked at her suspiciously. Presently a reluctant grin spread slowly across his face. "No," he said, "no. I'm open to persuasion." After what seemed like a very long time he walked toward her, then halted.

"Sexual hysteria?" he repeated in a pleased voice. "Really?" And he pulled her gently into his arms.

"I'm completely confused," murmured Claire after a moment.

"Me too," replied Sam, sliding his hands under her shirt. "How about if we figure it out later?"

Later, when Sam appeared to be taking a little nap, Claire propped herself up on one elbow and with the guilty delight of a voyeur—voyeuse—admired the planes of his face—really extraordinarily beautiful, how had she failed to notice before? —and the long contours of his body. A phrase popped into her head: "It was there all the time . . ." What was that? Oh, yes, the water, that reservoir of sweet water under a dry, forbidding surface . . .

Sam opened his eyes. "I'm hungry," he declared. "Really hungry."

Claire remembered the refrigerator and shuddered.

"We could go to Casey's," she offered.

He frowned. "Why Casey's?"

"Why not? It's cheap, and close—"

He sat up. "You know," he said uncomfortably, "showing up together at Casey's is like—like publishing a formal announcement in the *Riverdale Courier.*"

Well, exactly! "Ashamed to be seen with me?"

"No! No, it's not that at all! It's just that, well, growing up here, I learned long ago that if I wanted any privacy at all I had to be very, very . . . discreet."

"Ah." There was a short pause.

"Yes, maybe I overdo it," he said with a smile. "Okay, Casey's it is." But he didn't move. Instead he stared vacantly at the foot of the bed, and Claire knew exactly what he was thinking about. Larry McKeever's death, of course; any moment now he would ask a question about it, she would reply, he would offer a speculation, and there they'd be, caught up once more in the whole sad, sordid mess.

Claire rebelled. Now was not the time for tales of greed and brutality; now was the time for the story of Sam and Claire: how they met, quarreled, parted, reunited; how their feelings for each other grew; how mutual misunderstandings developed and were resolved; how all previous loves paled beside the shining perfection of the present, et cetera, et cetera. Time, in short, for the mysteries of Jane Austen, not Mickey Spillane. Dammit, it was traditional, she wasn't going to be cheated out of it.

Sam opened his mouth to speak. "Sam—" she said rapidly

and somewhat wildly "—tell me . . . uh, tell me how long you've been interested in me."

His startled expression confirmed her suspicions that he had been about to embark on another topic, but he recovered quickly. "What makes you think I'm interested in you?" he asked, kissing her knee.

"I accept it as a working hypothesis. But let me tell you, it comes as a complete, if delightful surprise—especially after this afternoon in Cummings's office. You wouldn't even look at me!"

He was slightly chagrined. "I *was* pretty dazed," he admitted. "But I'd been so sure for so long that you didn't care about me that I couldn't seem to make the transition. And then seeing McKeever like that sort of drove everything else out of my head. . . ." His eyes started to lose their focus again, and Claire, single-minded as an eight year old, acted quickly.

"Yes," she said insistently, "but when did you first start to like me?"

Sam put his hands behind his head and regarded her with mock resignation. "Okay," he said, "but it's gonna be the short form. I'm starving."

"Fine!" she agreed with eager egocentrism, and Sam's voice took on a reminiscent tone.

"I thought you were kind of cute, right from the beginning," he said, "when you came out in January for the interview. Only I have a rule against getting involved with people from work—not that the issue has come up before—and I didn't really trust you. I still don't trust you," he added somewhat defiantly, "and you were arrogant and cold—"

"Me!" interjected Claire indignantly.

But Sam raised his hand warningly, said, "No itemized deductions on the short form," and continued. "And anyway, I would have bet my pension you weren't remotely interested in me. That was the main thing. Although a couple of times . . . well, in any case, that day we went out to the marshes you told me about some guy, what's his name?"

"Phil."

"Yeah. Phil. I said to myself, well, that's it, buddy. Give it up. She's carrying a torch for this Phil character, that's why she left MIT."

"Was it that obvious?" she asked.

"To a man on the brink of the precipice, sure. Especially since I never bought the official explanation for your move out here—that crap about political and intellectual scruples. Sorry," he added hastily, seeing her expression, "it's not that I doubted the sincerity of your convictions. I just don't believe that people make major decisions for such abstract reasons. Was I wrong?"

"I'm not sure. Probably not. Go on."

"Where was I?"

"In the marshes, on the brink."

"Oh, yeah . . . well, like I say, I figured you for a lost cause. So I repressed my animal urges, with some success—"

"Complete success, from my point of view," said Claire dryly.

"Some success," repeated Sam with a grin. "It took a lot of cold showers"—*and Darlene,* thought Claire; *I'll have to ask him about Darlene sometime*—"but I did have myself under control, more or less, until last week. . . ."

There was a short pause. "A lot of things happened last week," he said finally, "and somewhere in the midst of them you just . . . sort of . . . overwhelmed me." For a moment he looked at her in a way that made her feel dizzy.

"Finish the story," she managed to say.

"Right. Well, I guess the moment I knew I was a goner—" He paused, and Claire waited breathlessly. What had been the decisive factor? Her brilliant exposition of the theory of the phony Benyl? Her . . . her plucky confrontation of Buddy at Casey's? The clever way she had eluded Larry McKeever?

"Was when you walked into St. Xavier's in that black dress," he concluded.

As Claire stared at him in amazement, he covered his face with his hands. "I mean, there I am at the funeral of this kid who was like my brother," he continued in a muffled voice, "who's been brutally murdered, whose parents are sobbing in the pew next to me . . . and all I could think of was you, under that dress!" He laughed helplessly.

"Of course," he remarked after a moment, "Tony would have understood perfectly. Blood may be thicker than water, but some things are thicker than blood." He rolled over and grabbed her.

Incredible, just incredible, she thought, suppressing a

snicker and rubbing his head. Sam had fallen for a slinky black dress. What about integrity, resourcefulness, wit, all the other qualities she had attempted to cultivate in the last few weeks? How could her *clothes* be so important—?

The phone rang.

He sighed. "I guess I better answer that. Don't move."

When he returned in a few minutes his amorous mood had evaporated. "That was Tom Martelli," he said somberly. "Seems those unidentified fingerprints on the Harley are Larry McKeever's. And they found traces of blood and oil in the delivery van. So we're batting a thousand there," he concluded, sounding thoroughly depressed.

Blood and oil. Welcome back, Mickey Spillane.

"Oh, and one other thing. Nobody's seen Buddy Hanford since last night."

"Let's eat," she said.

Heads indeed turned when they walked into Casey's fifteen minutes later. Claire was by now inured to furtive barroom stares, but Sam, she noted with sympathy and a trace of amusement, was extremely self-conscious. (And this was the man who had nonchalantly stuffed a .45 into the glove compartment upon leaving the cabin. "Can't be too careful," he had explained cheerfully.)

"Might as well relax and enjoy it," she remarked as they located a table. He shot a hostile glare in her direction, and then grinned suddenly.

"You're absolutely right. A burger and a Bud for you?" He walked to the bar to order.

"Howdy, Sam," Mickey said loudly, then dropped his voice, made a few comments, and guffawed.

Sam was smiling as he returned to the table. "He wished me luck," he replied to her questioning glance. "Said I'd need it." He rummaged in his pocket for change and headed for the jukebox. "Any requests?"

"John Coltrane."

"Must be an East Coast singer, never heard of him. How about Reba McIntyre?" And soon a sweet female voice drifted through the bar.

What did he see, or rather, hear in this stuff? she wondered as she watched him walk back to the table. She toyed with the idea of interrogating him on the subject, but instead waited patiently while he sat down across from her, propped his elbows on the table, and said without preamble, “Okay. Who killed Larry McKeever?”

She was ready for this. “Why was he killed?” she rejoined. “If we knew that we’d know who killed him.”

“We know why he was killed.”

“We do?” She stared down at her beer. Sam was looking at her, she knew, and presently she lifted her eyes to meet his. “Because of me,” she said reluctantly.

Sam settled back in his chair. “You were just the last straw,” he said comfortingly, and shook his head.

“Ah, Larry,” he sighed. “I remember him as a fat, dumb little kid. He just moved right into fat, dumb adulthood without any sort of . . . grace period. Never had a chance. It was hard not to feel sorry for him and it was hard not to be disgusted by him. He used to drink here every night and pester people to play this, uh, game, sixpack, with him.”

“Sixpack?”

Sam grinned. “It’s very complex,” he said. “He must have made it up himself. See, you watch all the women who walk in—you really check ’em out; I think maybe he had a six-point scale or something—and when you see one who meets your high standards you say ‘sixpack’ real loud. I mean, he would do this for *hours!*”

Claire stared at him open-mouthed, remembering that loud “two!” when she had walked into the bar Friday. Why hadn’t he just shouted out her bra size (34B)? “That’s pathetic,” she stated after a moment.

“That’s what I’m telling you,” he replied emphatically, leaning forward. “And this is the guy selected as the crux of a secret operation! Of course he screwed it up! First, by killing Tony so ineptly—”

“Why ‘ineptly’?” she interrupted. “If you hadn’t noticed the *Scirpus* on the bike—”

“Hell, it was completely botched,” he said impatiently. “If Cummings was even close to competent he would have identified those fingerprints a week ago. And then, trying to run you off the road . . . I mean, it was a stupid idea to begin with, but at least he should have carried it through—”

“Thanks,” she said acidly.

“But as it was,” he continued, pausing only to grab her hand and hold it firmly, “if you’d been able to identify his car, well . . . I think Larry's employer got a little tired of having a loose cannon rolling around Kaweah County. Anyway, spraying's over for the season."

Claire considered this cryptic remark for a few seconds, then responded, "You mean Larry was expendable."

"Right. He'd done his job: taken the sacks of Benyl from Kavoian's, filled them with lime out at Amargosa, and delivered them to the work crew at Agua Dulce. Why let him continue to shoot off his mouth, attack people, and otherwise call attention to himself? These guys decided to eliminate him."

"These guys," she echoed. "You mean Venture West."

He shifted uneasily in his seat. "Yeah. I suppose so." After a moment he added, "One thing I know—Buddy didn't kill him."

"Why?"

He didn't answer directly. Instead he said, "I sure don't have any sympathy for Larry, but for what it's worth I think he killed Tony out of panic and sheer stupidity, same as he did everything in his life. But the way he died . . . well, *you* don't think Buddy's smart enough to have imagined this plot, and *I* don't think he's cold enough to have killed Larry like that, like a—a butcher; to have just tied his hands behind him, made him crawl into the trunk, and slit his throat. There was blood—everywhere."

He looked gray, and Claire swallowed hard. No wonder he had been distracted that afternoon. And he was right; it sounded a little savage for Buddy or for . . . anyone. Especially Jim LaSalle, right? Still . . . "Anybody could have hired Larry," she said.

"Sure. Those developers might even have met him right here in Casey's. God knows he was a fixture. We're supposed to meet Tom for breakfast at Katy's tomorrow; he's been doing some research on Venture West."

But Claire hadn't been thinking about Venture West.

"Burgers are ready," called Mickey.

"I'll get them," she said, walking to the bar and laying down a twenty dollar bill.

"You got to watch out for Sam Cooper, now," Mickey told her knowingly as he made change. "Them quiet types is dangerous." *Sexual mores in America,* she thought idly. *I get warned and Sam gets a pat on the back.* The music had changed to a familiar tune: "If we make it through December—" and Claire stared at the bills lying on the polished wood. She frowned. Something had stirred briefly in her memory . . . something she had been trying to remember earlier in Cummings's office . . . No, it was gone. She shrugged. It would come to her.

CHAPTER 16

Katy's Koffee Kup was a favorite breakfast spot for the working men and women of Riverdale. A small pine-paneled room, it featured a counter and a dozen tables, four clocks and three calendars, two old tinted photographs of a ghoulish-looking child (Katy's son Bobby, now a hefty fifty-year-old), lots of charm, and wretched food. Really awful. Especially the coffee: the chef seemed to believe in starting with a watery brew and allowing it to ripen during the day. Possibly Katy's koffee passed through a moment of perfection at some point in its life cycle, but Claire always caught it at the dishwater or thirty-weight stage.

Tom Martelli was steadily working his way through a Hi-Lipid Breakfast Special when they arrived at eight on Monday morning.

"Sorry to pull you away from home, Tom," said Sam, as they sat and ordered coffee.

"It's okay," he replied, balancing a wedge of fat pancakes on his fork. "Actually it's kind of a relief. The baby's kept us up for the last two nights—this is the first peace and quiet I've had in days. First decent meal, too, and I need strength to tackle this McKeever thing. Now what can I do for you?"

What indeed? wondered Claire, surveying him skeptically. With his mild blue eyes, gentle voice, and talk of babies he was a great deal more like a Unitarian minister than like Kojak. She took a mouthful of coffee and grimaced: oven cleaner.

"What have you found out about Venture West?" Sam asked, and Tom opened a manila folder.

"Nothing real exciting. They're a legit contracting-developing corporation. Based in LA, but they've done some projects up here: a condo complex in Bakersfield, a shopping mall in Fresno. . . . Here's some photos the LAPD faxed up."

Claire immediately recognized the curly-haired Van Horn and his surfer blond associate. "These are the men who were at the zoning hearing, all right, and Van Horn was at Casey's, too, as I said—Wait a minute, why would the LAPD have pictures of them on file?"

Tom was smiling beatifically, the professor whose student has just asked the tricky question. Claire began to regard him with a little more suspicion than heretofore.

"Well, one of the things this outfit has been involved with down south is toxic waste disposal. And it seems that a couple of years ago there was some question about just *where* they were disposing of their loads." A threatened lawsuit just sort of fizzled out for lack of evidence, Tom explained; no charges were brought, but that accounted for the police data. And the pictures.

Martelli shoved a third photo under their noses.

" 'Jesus Cardenas,' " Sam read, pronouncing it "Hay-soos."

"Otherwise known as Jay. He may or may not have threatened some witnesses in that waste disposal case. Like I say, nothing was ever proved. But LA seemed to think he's somebody we might want to watch out for."

"That's the guy who was at Casey's with Van Horn." Claire studied the dark, broad face, imagined she read brutality there, and then chastised herself for latent racism.

"Now let me get this straight," Tom was saying. "The theory is that somebody, either a) Buddy Hanford or b) these guys from Venture West, hired McKeever to sabotage the Rodriguezes' orchard and when he started screwing up they, uh, terminated his employment. Screwing up being trying to run Claire here off the road, after killing Tony Rodriguez." He stopped suddenly. "Why would they care that he killed Tony?" he asked. "Seems like that just strengthened their hand if they wanted Agua Dulce."

Good point, thought Claire, but Sam remained unflustered. "It wasn't the fact that he killed Tony, it was the sloppy way he did it."

"Unprofessional," offered Martelli, apparently satisfied. "All right. You figure he followed the Rodriguez kid from Casey's to Amargosa that night, saw him examining these sacks of phony what do you call it—Benyl—and hit him over the head. Something like that?"

Sam nodded and Claire added eagerly, "Tony was talking to me about Benyl earlier that evening, at Casey's. And McKeever was there. I think he must have heard him and realized he suspected something."

"Well, if you're right about any of this, Tony's murder really upped the ante on a neat, low-profile operation," Martelli remarked in a neutral voice, looking at Sam. "Kind of a stupid thing to do."

In a moment of insight Claire realized that this terse statement was an expression of sympathy over Tony's death. These two had known each other—how long? since first grade, Sam had said—and still they maintained a relentlessly cool tough-guy facade with each other. With exasperation she thought, I'll never understand These People, this being a loose but useful category that for the moment included Sam and Tom, men in general, all Kaweah County residents, traditional white culture, and the patrons of Katy's Koffee Kup.

"Signed his own death warrant," replied Sam shortly.

"Maybe so," said Tom noncommittally. "Maybe so." After a moment he turned to Claire. "McKeever was killed a few hours after he followed you from Kavoian's, right?" he asked with a hint of challenge. "So these guys would have had to act mighty fast."

"I've been thinking about that," Sam answered. "I think that after McKeever lost her he contacted Venture West *immediately*—he might have called from Riverdale—to tell them about what he'd done. To brag about it, probably. They must have decided on the spot to get rid of him, and made some excuse to meet him up in the mountains."

"Okay, that's a possibility," Tom conceded. "If so, it means these Venture West people were staying in the area that night, and we should check the motels in Riverdale and Parkerville. I'll get my staff—" he grinned sardonically; his staff consisted of a secretary and one half-time deputy "—on it right away. Might enlist you two for some legwork."

"What do we do then? How do we go about making a . . . a case against these guys?" Sam asked.

"Whoa—hold on. Aren't you forgetting an important person here?"

Sam was stubbornly mute, and Tom shrugged in annoyance. "Buddy Hanford!" he said. "I mean, I know you dislike developers on principle, Sam—occupational hazard, I guess—and this particular outfit doesn't seem like a group of real nice guys, but if you're right about the connection between this and the Rodriguezes' troubles, you can't ignore Buddy. Everybody knows how he felt about them. And he's missing! That looks mighty peculiar."

"What it looks like is that he was killed the same time as Larry," Sam muttered grumpily, "and we just haven't found the body."

"Maybe. Or maybe he's lying low at the Hanford condo at Tahoe, or in Costa Rica. Now, I understand *you*"—turning to Claire—"had a conversation with Buddy and McKeever at Casey's the other day."

"Yes. And while I personally agree with Sam that . . . uh, that *Buddy's* not behind this," she said, stressing the name so that Tom looked at her peculiarly, "I definitely got the impression he and Larry shared some sort of secret."

"Mmm. Could be anything, with those two. Could be they were just running a number on you." He sighed. "See, I have a problem with Buddy as a suspect, too. I mean, Larry you could rent for a roll of hundreds, sure, but Buddy—he doesn't need money. The only reason he'd get involved in this would be pure spite, and that's weak compared to, say, greed. Greed, lust, fear, and anger, those are your serious motives."

"Right," Sam interjected eagerly, "so let's get back to greed. And Venture West."

"Okay," Tom acquiesced, "though I don't rule out Buddy. Not until we know what happened to him. Now as for the so-called case against Venture West, it's completely in your head at this point, Sam. Even Cummings's drug-smuggling theory looks a hell of a lot stronger."

"Well, what do we do about that?" pressed Sam, undaunted. "What's our strategy?"

Martelli considered for a moment. "Let's look at what we actually know so far," he said. "One." He held up his thumb. "Lawrence McKeever killed Antonio Rodriguez on the night of June sixteenth. Two"—his index finger—"the stuff Carlos and Silvia were having sprayed on their trees wasn't what they thought it was. Three"—middle finger—"a company called Venture West wanted to buy the Rodriguezes' land."

He paused and they all looked expectantly at his hand, waiting for the next finger to pop up. It didn't.

"That's it," said Tom. "Those are the facts, folks. We've got *this,"* he explained, regarding his own splayed fingers with detachment, "when what we need is *this!"* Abruptly the hand closed into a fist and smashed violently down on the table, rattling the crockery. Claire jumped and eyed her Unitarian minister warily.

"It would be nice to have some hard physical evidence, and this was a clean, professional job," he continued peacefully. "No footprints, no fingerprints, no cigar ash, no scalpel or whatever was used to slice the throat. So we build up a circumstantial argument. We know Venture West had a motive to interfere with the Rodriguezes, we know McKeever killed Tony, so if we can show that Venture West had dealings with McKeever, then we're on our way. But that's the real weak link: the connection between McKeever and Venture West. There's no indication that they knew each other."

"Maybe we could find some witnesses who saw them together," Claire suggested. "They *must* have met at some time to put this together."

"Casey's," Sam said. "I'll bet Mickey could tell us something. In fact, I'll bet this whole plan was probably hatched at Casey's."

"Okay, that's a start," Tom agreed. "I'll take the photos up there. And if we find out where they stayed when they were in town, maybe you two could help me out one night. Lately my evenings are sort of taken up with changing and bathing babies," he explained a little sheepishly. "Marie says if I don't pull my weight with this one she'll blow my head off. Figure of speech."

Sam went to pay the bill and began chatting with the cashier. Martelli immediately leaned over to Claire and asked curiously, "Did you get hold of Manny Aragon?"

"Yes. But he wouldn't talk to me. I'll try one more time."

He shook his head. "Not sure what you're up to, but I think you're barking up the wrong tree."

"Oh, probably. But in any case I'd appreciate it if you didn't say anything to Sam—" She ended hastily, as Sam returned and they all stood.

"I'll call you if I need you," Tom said. "Meanwhile let's hope

Buddy shows up. That would simplify things. So long, Cathy," he called to their waitress.

"So long, Tom. Keep the rubber side down."

Scrupulous about such things, Claire had to admit that her suspicions about Jim rested on very little—and if they were true, she certainly didn't want to communicate them. So she struggled to maintain a normal working relationship, and thus spent most of the afternoon in the station's almond grove with him working on their experiment to determine the relationship between insect damage and infection by *Apergillus flavus.*

This was a continuing project that they had begun in May, when they had selected representative pairs of nuts and covered them with small paper bags. In early June they had randomized these clusters into four groups—two to be infested and two to serve as controls—and had inoculated the treatment groups. Today, a few weeks before harvest, they were repeating the inoculation. Into each bag Jim placed five navel worm eggs on a piece of paper, and Claire blew the dry "conidia," or spores, from a culture of *Aspergillus* she had grown.

This was fun for the first two hours, but by two o'clock it was 107 degrees. She certainly wasn't going to be the first to suggest taking a break, however, and LaSalle kept working stolidly. As a result of this macho competition, by the time they finished, Jim's face, neck, and arms were flaming scarlet and Claire was sick to her stomach. When she walked in, Bonnie, their motherly receptionist, took one look at her and made her sit down and drink a quart of Gatorade, kept on hand for just such occasions.

"Bet you miss your New England weather right about now," Bonnie said.

"Well, Massachusetts gets hot—" Claire replied, then stopped. It didn't get *this* hot. Anyway, at home she worked in her air-conditioned lab all day, not out under the merciless sun like a damn fool.

When Sam walked into the lab she was stretched out on a bench.

"Hi," she said, not opening her eyes.

"Hi. Bonnie just said you were a bit shaky from the heat."

"I was out in the almond grove for six hours straight," she

snapped, sorry for herself but perversely annoyed at having become yet another of Sam's responsibilities.

"Why didn't you take a break?" he asked reasonably.

"Jim seemed to want to keep on working."

"Jim's used to this weather. Anyway, he's a show-off."

"So am I."

He laughed. She opened her eyes and sat up, ignoring his proffered hand.

Sam was positively chatty as they drove to Riverdale. He embarked on a rambling anecdote of adolescent mischief involving himself, Martelli, and Frank Rodriguez, to which Claire only half listened. The rows of orange trees flicked by. In the distance they crawled over the hill like fat green caterpillars; here by the road they resolved into identical spherical trees, each casting its perfectly round shadow on the perfectly bare earth below—an ordered landscape that soothed her chaotic brain.

She seemed to have blown a fuse this afternoon. She couldn't put together a coherent thought. All she could feel was a dim sort of anger at . . . somebody, something, for allowing events to crash headlong into each other like cars piling up on the freeway. It was so unfair; she had barely digested the fact of Tony's death when she had to accept that it was a murder, and then that someone had tried to kill her, and then that she was apparently involved with this total stranger who looked like Ichabod Crane and seemed to be assuming that they would spend the night together.

Inevitably she focused not on the most distressing happening, but on the one over which she had some control.

"Sam," she blurted, interrupting his story, "I want to go home."

He looked at her oddly. "We are going home."

"No, I mean—" She hesitated. What did she mean? The lab at MIT, her apartment in Cambridge, her mother's lap? Kansas? "I mean to . . . to *my* home, my house," she stammered. "I think I need to be alone for a while."

He stared straight ahead at the road. "Of course," he said politely, sounding hurt. Naturally he was hurt: forty-eight hours into the relationship and already she "needed to be alone?" She made an effort to explain.

"I'm a little shell-shocked," she said apologetically. "Too much happening too fast. I'm just an effete academic, remember." Self-deprecating humor evoked no response, and she examined the Toyota's floor mats.

But after a moment he replied, "Sure, I understand. Just drop me off at my place."

No reproach, no sulkiness. She looked at him with surprised gratitude. "Sam, you're a peach. A—a Flamekist."

"Late ripening, huh?" He laughed humorlessly. "Yeah, well, I'm bucking for sainthood. As you yourself pointed out."

"Yeah, well, I'm a pain in the ass. As I myself point out."

This time the laugh was genuine. "You are," he agreed as they pulled into his drive. "But you have some redeeming features." He kissed her hard on the mouth and strode up the path.

Contrary to expectations the furniture in her living room was not white with cobwebs nor the food in the refrigerator moldy and desiccated. She had only been gone two days, after all. (Two days?) There was a new issue of *Science* in the mailbox, and she flopped down on her bed and read it cover to cover, even the articles by astrophysicists and geologists, which she never understood. At about seven-thirty she flipped on the radio and picked up a ball game.

It was exactly what she needed. The dry, distinctly American voice of the announcer, the faint crack of a base hit, the friendly buzz of the crowd on a warm summer evening were timeless and immensely reassuring. They should play this stuff in the psych wards, she thought drowsily, and fell asleep in the bottom of the fourth with the bases loaded.

The lake was cold and deep and its still surface mirrored the trees along its margin—maple, spruce, birch: Vermont trees, the lake was in Vermont. At its center was a small island, also densely wooded, and it was toward this that Claire was swimming, splitting the clear green water and sweeping it around and behind her. Steadily the shore receded and the island neared, and now she was pulling herself out of the water, stepping carefully on the sharp gray rocks, making her way inland. Only now the brush was so thick that she had to crouch, then crawl on hands and knees, then stretch out flat on her belly, and now a heavy dark tree limb had fallen across her so that she was trapped, she struggled helplessly under its weight. . . .

* * *

She woke to find that the sheet had tangled around her and was anchoring her to the bed. Groggily she unwound herself, sweating in the hot, airless room; maybe she should have slept up at Sam's after all . . .

At the thought of Sam the claustrophobic panic of her dream surged through her again, and she sat upright, now fully awake.

Doc, I keep having these crazy dreams.

Ja, vell, this one is child's play; you feel trapped by this man Sam.

But, Doc, last week you said my dreams meant I had an unacknowledged sexual passion for Sam!

Ja, vell, nobody said this vould be easy. . . .

But she did love Sam. At least, as far as she could tell she loved him. That is, she felt for him that combination of lust, tenderness, and anxiety associated with the early stages of love, or perhaps infatuation—well, hell, she loved him.

But it wasn't too late to change that. A quick, clean break—it would hurt, sure, but the amount of hurt was proportional to the length of the relationship, at a ratio of about twenty to one, she had once figured. So better now than later.

Because it was damned inconvenient loving Sam. It tied her to Kaweah County, to a job without glamor, to this ugly, frightening murder case, and to—let's face it—a totally unsuitable man. Really, other than strong mutual attraction . . . here she lost her train of thought for a moment . . . strong mutual attraction, what did she and Sam have in common?

And there was another problem. After the catastrophe of Phil she had sworn never again to become involved with a coworker, because nothing lasts forever and falling apart under the sympathetic and secretly gratified gazes of her colleagues had made those months complete hell. Scientists were terrible gossips.

After all, Sam deserved a simpler, warmer woman, and she needed someone more sophisticated, more verbal, someone who would, well, fit in with her life and her friends.

Her glibness suddenly nauseated her and she stomped across the room, turned on the fan, and stomped back to bed. She couldn't possibly figure this or anything else out now; the world would just have to wait.

It waited about an hour. At ten o'clock the telephone rang

and Claire, programmed to respond without question, leapt up out of a deep sleep, ran across the living room, and answered it before she knew what was happening.

"Miss Sharp?" It was a man's voice.

She thought for a moment. "Uh, yes, Sharples, this is Claire Sharples. Who is this?"

"Manny Aragon. I want to talk to you about that—that subject you mentioned."

"Oh. Oh! That's wonderful, Mr. Aragon! When would you like to get together?"

"Now."

"Now?"

"Yeah. If I wait till I'm sober I won't want to do it."

Great. "O-okay, fine. You're in Mountain View Trailer Park?"

"Yeah, space seventeen."

"I'll be there in twenty minutes."

Mountain View Trailer Park was right on State 170 between Riverdale and Parkerville, and the easternmost row of trailers might, indeed, get an occasional view of the mountains, smog permitting. For everyone else scenic opportunities were distinctly limited, but "Lots of Other Trailers View," or "Your Neighbor's Satellite Dish View" wouldn't have attracted prospective residents. Claire made her way through the warren of single-wides, double-wides, and the odd Airstream, until she came to space seventeen. This contained a white double-wide trailer, not new but well cared for. Geraniums lined the short walk and a fuchsia hung beside the door. A kid's tricycle lay on its side in the bathmat-sized front yard.

Timidly she tapped at the door. She could hear the TV blaring and knew she hadn't been heard. She rang the bell, which didn't seem to work, and was winding up for a killer knock when a voice came from close beside her: "Over here."

She jumped, and peered into the darkness. A diminutive covered patio jutted out from the trailer, and someone was sitting there. As she approached she caught a strong smell of beer, and something earthier—fertilizer, maybe.

Aluminum scraped over flagstone; she reached for the webbed chair pushed toward her and sat. The other figure was still only a dark silhouette. He spoke, and she recognized the voice from the telephone: beer-blurred, strong lilt of a Mexican-American accent. "It's quieter here."

They were surrounded on all sides by roaring air conditioners, but white noise has to pass for quiet in crowded quarters. "You're Manny Aragon?"

"Yeah. Want a beer?" Before she could answer a cold can was pressed against her palm. "You said you wanted to talk about Frank Rodriguez. What exactly did you have in mind?"

"I want to know about him and Jim LaSalle," she said, and held her breath. Would Aragon understand what she meant, or was she out in left field after all?

"That's what I figured," he said, and she exhaled. "But I don't much like talking about it."

"All I can say is that the story won't go beyond me." Sort of.

Amazingly, the assurance was good enough. "Okay," he said, "I been wantin' to get this off my chest for a long time, anyway. I told a priest, once. Just pretend you're my confessor."

And Claire listened.

Manuel Aragon had grown up in a little town about fifteen miles south of Parkerville. On the day he had graduated from high school—having fulfilled this promise to his parents—he'd driven into town and enlisted. He'd done his basic training in Texas and had arrived at a firebase on the Mekong just in time for the Tet Offensive.

A roll of the dice had assigned him to a company with two other boys from Kaweah County. One was a freckled private from north of Parkerville, almost as green as himself, named Jim LaSalle. The other he'd already known by reputation: Parkerville High's phenomenal halfback Frank Rodriguez. By February 1968 Frank was a sergeant already nearing the end of his second tour of duty.

But Manny's hopes for a little homeboy camaraderie in this alien, terrifying place had soon faded. LaSalle was aloof and superior—even ten thousand miles from home, Anglos didn't mix with "Mexicans." ("Fucking Okie," Aragon now snarled resentfully, "if I was a Mexican, how come I was in 'Nam askin' to get my tail blown off?") And Frank—well, if Manny hadn't already been in awe of Frank, he would have become so very quickly. Frank was a little scary. Reckless by nature, addicted to his own adrenaline, and high on Thai stick half the time, Frank had begun to seek out dangerous situations, putting himself and the men with him in mortal peril and then coming through on audacity, instinct, and sheer luck.

"It got to the point," Manny said to Claire, "where if a lieutenant needed somebody to do something stupid and dangerous they would automatically pick Frank. 'Sergeant, take a few men and cross that completely unprotected rice paddy to draw off enemy fire.' 'Yessir!' 'Sergeant, run along that ridge and make a target of yourself.' 'Yessir!' "

And every time he'd pulled something off, his conviction of his own invulnerability grew.

Frank had ridden Manny pretty hard, believing, evidently, that every Latino soldier had to be twice as good as any Anglo soldier, but it had been worse for LaSalle. Because LaSalle had been afraid—oh, everyone was afraid, but Jim had never been able to forget about it, could never lose himself for a moment in the dope or the liquor or the slim black-haired girls.

And if LaSalle didn't like Chicanos, he sure as hell didn't like Chicanos who outranked him. So Frank, noting the prejudice and sensing fear as only a bully can, had made LaSalle's life miserable. Especially after that day in late February.

They had been crossing a rice paddy in single file. It was noon, and incredibly hot—not dry and hot like home, but wet and hot and stifling. You couldn't draw air into your lungs, just mosquitos.

Suddenly they'd started taking enemy fire. It'd been the first time for many of them, and Manny had found himself not scared so much as numb as the whole line started running toward a dike fifty yards ahead, with Frank Rodriguez bringing up the rear, cursing and driving them on. "C'mon, you motherfuckers, c'mon!" Panting and shaking, they'd reached the shelter of the wall without casualties.

Suddenly someone had called, "Hey, Sarge—*look!*"

They'd all looked. There, in the middle of the paddie, stiff and blinking like a scared rabbit, was Jim LaSalle.

"LaSalle!" bawled Rodriguez. "What are you doing? Get over here, goddamn it!"

LaSalle had stared at him, uncomprehending. He was in a stupor of terror.

It had been like a shooting gallery out there, with LaSalle as the helpless target. Bullets had whined past him but mi-raculously left him unscathed—maybe the guys couldn't shoot. (A lot of them couldn't, Manny said; they'd fire from the hip like cowboys instead of taking aim.) Or maybe they'd been playing a game, like circus knife throwers, trying to see how close they could come without actually hitting him.

Rodriguez had hesitated a moment, then taken off, running the most brilliant broken-field pattern of his career. As the unit watched in excitement and fear he got to Jim, grabbed him by the arm, and pulled him toward the wall. "Run, *conejo!*" he screamed. "Run, you little rabbit!" LaSalle began to stumble toward the wall with Rodriguez behind him, pushing and screaming in his ear and the fire raining all around them.

Frank had gotten a medal for that and LaSalle a name. Rabbit. Everyone had called him Rabbit from then on, and made childish, cruel jokes at his expense—Frank because he couldn't imagine such fear, the other men because they could. But it had been hard to get a rise out of Jim; he would sit and blink at you with his bulging blue eyes, much like his namesake, and soon lots of other crazy, scary, bloody stuff had happened and the incident had sort of been forgotten. After a while people had barely remembered how he'd gotten his name—except that Frank would always remind them.

Two kilometers upriver from the base a canal carried water to the rice paddies to irrigate them, and five kilometers up the canal was a little village of farmers. All this was familiar to the boys from Kaweah County, but somehow it hadn't made the villagers any more human. They were all, possibly, VC; to Manny they all looked alike and they all looked like death.

In early April the enemy had taken to making nocturnal forays into the village, coming across the canal from the jungle. They'd murder a few important residents, recruit a few others, and intimidate the rest, and take food and other supplies. Manny's platoon had started making nightly patrols along the canal. It was a completely exposed situation: a bare strip about forty yards wide passing through dense cover—and Manny always felt like part of a line of fat ducks waddling along in the dark, quacking with alarm at the noises around them.

On the night of April 22, Frank, Manny, LaSalle, and seven other men had completed an uneventful patrol and were returning to base. It had rained during the day and the sky was still overcast, occasionally clearing to reveal a watery quarter moon and the pale wavering walls of bamboo on either side of them. They'd been nearing the village when a shot rang out from the grass on the far side of the canal.

They'd dropped to their bellies. "Should we try and get to cover on this side?" Manny had whispered to Frank, hoping the unsteadiness of his voice wasn't audible.

"No," Frank had said, "into the ditch," and they'd scrambled down into the canal.

The water was only knee-high and at least it was warm: certainly no worse than the trenches of Flanders. *And* they were equipped with very expensive state-of-the-art star scopes, which enabled them to see their attackers even in the dark. They'd all inched to the top of the ditch and looked through their star scopes.

"I can't see a goddamn thing." "Fucking piece of shit." "Why don't they ever give us something that works?"

The plaintive voices had been interrupted by another burst of fire, which they returned for a minute or two until Frank had barked, "Cease firing."

"Think we run 'em off," somebody had whispered, and as if in answer another shot exploded.

"Shit!"

"Shut up!" Frank had snapped and thought for a minute. "Okay," he said almost soundlessly, "we'll try to outflank 'em."

He'd motioned for three men to take off to the left; he and LaSalle and Aragon would come around from the right, while the remaining men stayed behind and kept up a cover fire—a simple maneuver, one they had all executed many times.

Simple or not, Manny'd been scared. He hated the tall grass even worse than the exposed canal; it pressed in against him from all sides and wrapped around his legs with malevolent intelligence, making him stumble and thrash as he'd desperately tried to keep up with LaSalle. They didn't even try to keep up with Frank, who as usual was well ahead of them both, moving quickly and surely, instinctively finding a trail through the bamboo. Soon they could no longer see him, though they could still hear him, between bursts of automatic fire, somewhere beyond them.

Suddenly LaSalle had stopped dead and raised his hand.

Manny had nearly run into him, stopped, and looked wildly around him.

The clouds had parted momentarily. A ray of moonlight fell on a small clearing to their left and something glinted there. Manny squinted and saw . . . a helmet and the barrel of a rifle.

Slowly, almost dreamily in the moonlight, the rifle had lifted and aimed: not at them, but beyond them, about twenty yards down the trail. It aimed at Frank Rodriguez.

The words had formed in his throat—*Sarge, look out!*—but LaSalle had put a hand on his arm as if to silence him, and Manny had hesitated for a moment. His mind raced. Jim had been there three months to his two—did he know something Manny didn't? Was this one of their own guys from the other flank? If so he was a hundred yards out of his way. And the helmet was wrong. And—

The figure in the clearing squeezed the trigger.

"Then everything happens at once," Manny said. "LaSalle takes aim, cool as can be, and picks off this guy in the clearing. Our guys on the other side are in position and they start firing. I'm running up ahead to where I figure Frank should be, yelling and crying." He stopped.

"I never was no good at running through that stuff," he continued after a moment. "I fell right over him. He had took the hit in his throat. He might of been alive when I first found him, I don't know, but by the time the medic got there he was gone."

He reached back and switched on a light.

In the darkness, lulled by a fluent narrative that had the immediacy of something deeply felt, Claire had imagined herself sitting across from the young kid who had gone off to war. Now when she saw Aragon's black hair streaked with gray and his lined face she felt the panic of disorientation. He's *old!* she thought, as if he had aged before her eyes like a skewered vampire. It took her a moment to remember that it all had happened almost twenty years ago. Manny might have a son as old as he was that night on patrol.

A cricket had found its way into this tin and concrete maze and was chirping heroically to make itself heard above the air conditioners. Aragon crumpled his beer can and tossed it on the growing pile.

"To this day I don't know why LaSalle stopped me from shouting to Frank," he said. "I been over it a thousand times in my head. Did he think the VC in the clearing was one of our men? Did he freeze, like he did that time in the rice paddy? Did *I* freeze? I mean, maybe I just imagined he was shutting me up! I don't know; we never talked about it. I couldn't. All I know is if I had yelled, Frank Rodriguez might be alive today."

He stood unsteadily and detached another beer from its plastic mesh. She caught another pungent whiff of earth stench.

"You work over at Poplar at the meat packing plant, don't you?" she asked with sudden inspiration.

"Yeah," he answered dully. His tragic brown eyes and weary, heart-shaped face were teasingly familiar. "Martelli tell you?"

"Yeah."

There didn't seem to be any more to say. She rose, thanked him for his story, repeated that it wouldn't go beyond her.

"I don't give a shit," he answered, looking directly at her for the first time that evening. (Ah, she had it: Chavez. He looked like Cesar Chavez.) "I was nineteen. Nineteen years old. You make a decision—no, you *hesitate* about a decision for three seconds—and your life is changed forever. And somebody else's ends. It ain't fair."

And so you pay penance at the packing plant. "No. It isn't."

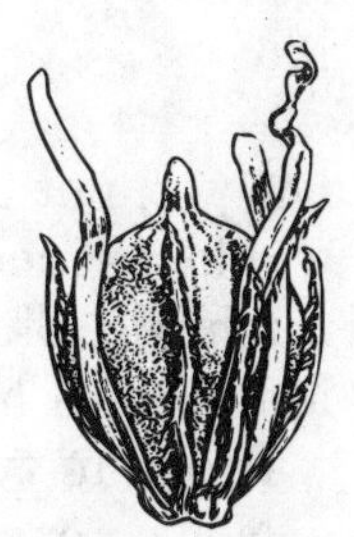

CHAPTER 17

Manny Aragon's story was too tragic for Claire to feel the triumph of vindication, but neither did it surprise her. If Aragon was confused, *she* had no trouble understanding what had happened that night so long ago: Jim LaSalle had murdered Frank Rodriguez.

Okay, he was only twenty (easy to imagine; he must have looked exactly as he did now), and maybe he hadn't actually pulled the trigger and maybe it hadn't been premeditated, but essentially—morally—it was murder. He hadn't panicked or frozen, he had merely acted on instinct. And what instincts! Knowing that Aragon would follow his lead, he had with one apparently innocent gesture wiped out the man who had persecuted and humiliated him—and, incidentally, had once saved his life.

LaSalle's guilt had come later, and then the rationalizations, transmuted into anger, generalized to the whole Rodriguez family. *That's* why he hadn't spoken his usual piece at the zoning meeting, she realized as she pulled into her driveway—he *wanted* Silvia and Carlos to lose Agua Dulce!

But how much did he want it? Enough to hire Larry McKeever to sabotage the spraying? And why now, after *twenty years?* That was a hell of a grudge.

Well . . . that tight jaw held secrets, that was for sure. And Manny Aragon had just now felt ready to talk about Frank Rodriguez. Maybe these war experiences had a long incubation period; maybe things floated very slowly to the surface, like debris from a town flooded by a dam: year by year, tree limbs, street signs, bodies—

That reminded her of Sam's dream about Frank. And *that* brought up the problem of Sam.

Problem one: was she going to tell him about LaSalle? No,

not yet; not unless she had to, in fact. The news about Frank would be incredibly painful, and there was no telling what he might do. She would have to handle this herself, or with Tom Martelli, if he was willing to help.

Problem two: was she going to break off the relationship?

Not so easy. An hour ago—she looked at her watch; make that four hours ago—she had had the chain of logic clear in her head. But right now life seemed short and brutal and treacherous, and love, though imperfect, very precious.

After six hours of sleep she had reverted to normal, and on Tuesday morning headed for the station fully intending to break up with Sam before things went any further. Half intending. Well, determined to keep the relationship a complete secret forever. But when she drove into her parking space Sam was leaning against his old Valiant waiting for her, and two minutes later when Ray Copeland came in they were locked in a torrid embrace.

She tried to pull away in embarrassment but Sam hung on. " 'Might as well relax and enjoy it,' " he quoted in her ear. "In fact, let's give him time to spread the news."

When they walked in together twenty minutes later Bonnie beamed at them, and Ray shot her a significant look as she passed his office. Her face felt hot and she thought sourly, sure, he's happy, he figures he's got himself a new microbiologist. But she couldn't repress a smile.

"About time you two got together," she heard him chortle behind her. She did what any mature adult would do: pretended she didn't hear and bolted down the stairs.

At ten she called Martelli and told him about her conversation with Manny Aragon. There was silence at the other end. Then, "Can't say I'm totally surprised," said Tom.

"Really? Why?" Maybe this was going to be easier than she had thought.

"Oh, I don't know. Jim always struck me as somebody who might be . . . untrustworthy, under fire. Wouldn't want him behind me in a tight situation, that's all."

"Were you in the war?" she asked, suddenly curious.

"Marines. Three years."

"Oh." Huh. Who would have thought it? "Well, he certainly knows all about plant pathology, and he could have arranged for McKeever to switch the Benyl—"

"Wait a minute, wait a minute—you're talking about LaSalle as a suspect in the *Rodriguez* case?"

"Yes! That's the whole point! Don't you see, *that's* why he didn't say anything at the zoning hearing when the subject of the Rodriguezes' land came up—"

"I'm afraid I find that a little farfetched. This Frank Rodriguez thing, that happened almost twenty years ago."

"Don't you have memories from the war that still haunt you?" she asked melodramatically.

"Sure. That's beside the point. Why would he conspire against Frank's parents? Seems like it would go the other way 'round."

"They didn't know about it. Nobody knew, except Aragon. Unless Tony had found out . . ." She was considering the implications of this when Tom's next statement startled her.

"So you figure LaSalle killed McKeever."

"What?" Oh, of course. Whoever hired him had killed him. But Jim "Rabbit" LaSalle overpowering Larry McKeever, trussing him like a sacrificial sheep, and ripping open his throat?

He *had* killed that sniper.

But that had been in the heat of battle and at long distance—and surely if Jim, gun freak that he was, were to kill someone, he would shoot him. . . .

This was not the kind of question she was qualified to answer, and Martelli was waiting. "Well, no, I—"

"No." Martelli sounded tired. "That's what I thought. Look, I'm meeting with this Stephen Van Horn from Venture West in my office tonight at eight. You and Sam should probably be there."

"Wait, Tom," she said, "Jim broke into my lab—"

But he had hung up.

Claire felt extremely foolish. Sam was getting to her, she thought; she had borrowed a page from the Cooper Manual of Bad Science and adopted a theory without thinking it through. Jim LaSalle's sordid past was a serendipitous discovery and a motive for . . . for *something,* but Tom was right: she couldn't imagine him slaughtering McKeever. And if he hadn't killed McKeever he hadn't hired him, and if he hadn't hired him he hadn't supervised the sabotage of the Rodriguezes' peaches.

But damn! she hated to let go of a good theory just because of a few incorrigible facts.

Of course, Jim could have hired someone to do the actual killing. Someone like—like Larry McKeever, if only he hadn't been the victim (which appeared to present an insurmountable objection to that line of thought), or like Jesus Cardenas, Van Horn's muscle. She'd bring this up with Martelli, she thought, brightening.

At Sam's they ate a silent dinner. Claire was afraid to talk for fear of spilling the beans about Jim, and Sam, normally quiet, seemed especially preoccupied. She assumed he was nervous about meeting Van Horn, the putative *éminence grise* behind Tony's death. What would he say if she told him he had worked for years beside the man who had killed Frank?

Don't think about that. "Feels almost cool right now."

"Mmmm."

"Maybe the heat's finally broken."

"Mmmm."

"Or maybe I'm getting used to it."

Sam's standards of discourse required the exchange of hard information—except on rare ceremonial occasions, such as funerals—so he now walked into the kitchen and switched on the radio, tuned, as always to the Fresno country station.

Aha! Her topic had presented itself. "What is it exactly that you like about this kind of music?" she demanded.

He looked at her, surprised into a reply. "I never thought about it," he answered. "I'm sort of accustomed to it, I guess."

When it became clear that no more was forthcoming, she prodded, "What else?" Sam was going to talk about Art if it killed him. He had just enrolled in Small Talk 101.

"Well," he said helplessly, "I like to sing along with it while I'm driving, and—and it's kind of adult," he added, with sudden inspiration. "I mean, the singers sound like they're older than sixteen, and the songs are about real things, like divorce, and . . . and the economy. . . ."

"What about the ideology?"

"The what?"

"You know, the whole mythology: cowboys, outlaws, the simple godfearing country life—"

"Oh, that," he said dismissively. "Well, hell, if some poor

sucker wants to pretend he's an outlaw—some Toyota mechanic, or . . . or . . ."

"Agronomist," suggested Claire, and got a grin.

"Look," he said, "we all fool ourselves a little to get through life. It's harmless."

"I don't know," she replied. "Some myths are dangerous, and this one seems pretty reactionary. The good old days when white folks ran things, before the niggers and the wetbacks came along—"

"Hey, what about Charlie Pride? What about Freddy Fender and Johnny Rodriguez?"

"Who? Never mind," she said hastily, seeing his attention start to wander. Maybe that was enough for one session. "We'd better go on down to Riverdale."

"Well, that's quite a story," said Stephen Van Horn, grinning engagingly. They were gathered in Martelli's office. Sam had wedged himself into a corner where he could keep Van Horn under narrow-eyed surveillance. Claire, beside him, was jiggling her foot and squirming. Martelli was wiggling a pencil between thumb and forefinger. Only Van Horn, leaning back in his chair, seemed perfectly relaxed. His fingers interlocked and his palms passed smoothly over his head, coming to rest behind his neck. Probably checking his hair weave, thought Claire nastily. Just because he was innocent didn't mean she had to like him.

But she had to admire his technique. He had entered a room full of hostile people, and in twenty minutes had managed to wrest control of the so-called interrogation from Tom so that at present *he* was passing judgment on Martelli's statements.

"Quite a fabrication," he repeated. "Of course, it's ridiculous." He brought his hands down, rested his elbows on Tom's desk and his chin on his hands. He was wearing an ornate class ring from—Claire squinted—USC, wherever that was. "I work for a legitimate multimillion-dollar business concern. We would never become involved in a petty criminal scheme such as the one you've described."

"Petty" seemed to be the operative word here. Martelli opened his mouth and Van Horn said quickly, "You may have heard some rumors about . . . certain activities. Just remember they are only that—rumors. We have never been indicted," he added proudly, as if this were the company slogan.

"Secondly, I don't know a peach tree from a—a carrot. I could never have invented this sabotage. I still barely understand what you're talking about."

"But plenty of people up here could have done it for you," Sam interjected. "Like Larry McKeever."

"Now, let me see if I've got this straight. He's the fellow who killed the Rodriguez boy—what was his name—"

"Tony," said Claire.

"Right. Well, I know the Rodriguezes by name, of course. It's quite true we were interested in a parcel of land that included their orchard. And you say this McKeever fellow then was killed himself?"

They all nodded.

"Well, I certainly didn't know either him or the boy—Wait a minute." With composed, deliberate movements he reached for his briefcase, opened it, removed a Filofax date book, and consulted it. Claire watched, fascinated in spite of herself by the way his typical lawyer's self-importance was overlayed with an air of friendly informality that was purely Californian and purely spurious.

"Mmm-hmm. Yeah. The Rodriguez boy was killed late on the evening of Friday, June sixteenth, you said?"

"Early Saturday morning, actually," Tom said.

"Whatever. We certainly would have had no motive there. Because on Friday afternoon—I'm talking about that same day, June sixteen—Bill Hanford called down to LA to say that Mrs. Rodriguez had agreed to sell her land."

There was a moment of dead silence. Then, *"What?"* Sam and Claire exclaimed simultaneously. "I don't believe it," Sam added. Only Tom asked the right question.

"Why would Bill Hanford call you?"

Van Horn waggled a finger. "Ah-ah—haven't done your homework, sheriff!"

"Chief."

"Chief. That was the deal. We weren't negotiating for the land directly; Hanford was supposed to deliver it to us, and if he couldn't guarantee the whole parcel, the sale was off. He owned, oh, eighty percent of the acreage already. All but this place, Agua Dulce, and he'd been trying to persuade the

Rodriguezes to sell for two years. We were just about to look elsewhere, when bingo! the old lady changes her mind."

Sam looked at him murderously and Tom interceded hurriedly. "And this was Friday afternoon—*before* Tony was killed."

"That's right. Call came through about four P.M. Hey," he said, looking at the hostile faces around him, "talk to Bill Hanford. He'll corroborate the information."

"I'll certainly do that," Tom replied. "I'd like to speak with Buddy Hanford, too."

Was it her imagination, or did Van Horn's amiable face turn blank for an instant?

"Buddy Hanford," he mused. "Don't believe I know him."

"Bill's younger brother. He seems to be missing," Tom said, rising. "Will you be staying in the Parkerville area, Mr. Van Horn?"

"No, I'm going to drive back down to LA. You know how to get hold of me."

"Right. Thanks for your time."

There was a moment of silence after the door slammed, then an explosion of conversation.

"I can't believe Silvia was going to sell that land. I just can't believe it." Sam shook his head.

"They were pretty strapped," Claire said. "Silvia even made a joke about it when I was there Thursday afternoon! Asked if I wanted to buy an orchard. At least I thought it was a joke." She thought for a moment. "But could she sell without Carlos's consent?"

"No, it's common property. But if she'd made up her mind, she could probably convince him. She's the power in that family."

"Well, it's certainly easy enough to check—why don't you ask her?" Tom said. "I've got some asking to do myself. Think I'll pay Bill Hanford a visit tomorrow."

"You know," Sam remarked after a minute, "even if Silvia did agree to sell, that doesn't remove suspicion from Van Horn and his pals."

Tom nodded.

"Because," he went on, "if Tony was snooping around, Venture West still would have had an interest in preventing him from discovering what they'd been up to at Agua Dulce. And we've already agreed that Tony's death was unplanned, that McKeever panicked."

"Hell," said Tom after a moment, "we don't even know if McKeever got the news! If Hanford didn't talk to them until four, he may not even have known."

"That's right." A pause. "Did you see the way Van Horn looked when you mentioned Buddy?"

"Yeah."

To Claire, a detached observer, this was the conversation of two men trying desperately to convince themselves of something—a process she understood very well.

"You're going to talk to the Rodriguezes?" Tom was saying.

"Yeah—it's a little late now, but I'll go in the morning."

"Okay. And why don't you come out to Hanford's with me tomorrow afternoon?"

As they drove up to Sam's, Claire suddenly remembered that this morning she had been about to end this relationship. Right now she couldn't recall exactly why, and certainly the prospect of a cool house, a warm body, and a good night's sleep overrode more exotic criteria.

The house *was* cool. And so was the sex: Sam was perfunctory and hasty. Afterward he began to stroke her, willing as ever to fulfill his obligations, but she pushed his hands away, her desire doused.

"Sorry," he mumbled. "I feel like we're closing in on these guys and I'm afraid they might weasel out somehow. It's all I can think about."

"I understand," she lied.

"Good," he said gratefully, and turned over.

Some hours later she thought, If he's so obsessed, why is he lying there snoring while I'm staring at the ceiling? By two-thirty she finally drifted off to sleep, and immediately thereafter the alarm rang. She picked up her watch from the floor and blinked at it incredulously: Five-thirty.

"What are you doing?" she croaked, as Sam rolled out of bed and headed for the kitchen.

"Phoning Carlos and Silvia. They're farmers; they get up early."

In a few minutes he returned and began dressing. "I'm going on in to work. Silvia said to be there at twelve. Want to come?"

"Maybe. Let me get a few more hours of sleep and see how I feel."

Oh, babe, are you feeling bad? Sorry I woke you so early. Let me rub your head while you go back to sleep . . . Claire silently supplied this tender dialogue while Sam said cheerfully, "Okay," and banged out of the bedroom.

At eight she gave up, got up, and went in to work. The first thing she had to do was to talk to Jim LaSalle. She had managed to avoid him yesterday, but unpleasant or not, relations had to be maintained. He might just possibly have hired someone to kill McKeever, and he certainly might have engineered the petty harassment of the Rodriguezes—the shed, the trees—and if Venture West didn't pan out she would suggest this very humbly to Tom. And in the meantime she had to work with the guy and she didn't want to make him suspicious.

She stuck her head in his office. "Hi," she said brightly, startling him so that he spilled his coffee. He gave her a thin, begrudged smile.

"Morning."

He *does* look like a rabbit, she thought, and stifled an explosive snicker. A pink rabbit. "How's the sunburn?"

He shrugged. "Fine. Heard you fainted in the lobby."

"No, not exactly, I—"

"Matter of fact, you don't look so good right now. Havin' trouble sleeping?" Nudge nudge wink wink.

"Well, actually, it's been so hot—"

"Hot! Yeah, I guess your nights been real hot lately!" Nudge nudge wink wink knowwhatImean.

For whatever reason, Jim seemed bent on being particularly offensive. Could he be jealous? And if so, of whom—her or Sam? She had, of course, speculated about Jim's sexuality before, and couldn't picture him hetero-, homo-, bi-, pan-, or anything but a-. Her best guess was that he slept with his guns. But people could fool you.

She kept smiling. "Let me know when the graphs are done. I'll go over them with you," she said, and left in a hurry.

Sam had his legs up on his desk, his hands behind his head, and was staring at absolutely nothing. He gave a sort of protonod when she entered and continued to stare.

She yawned ostentatiously a few times and finally he stirred and said, "Tired?"

"Well, yeah. I only got three hours of sleep."

"Three hours?"

"Mmm-hmm. I couldn't fall asleep." And then, against every instinct of human decency, "I was sort of keyed up."

He reddened and finally looked directly at her. "Hey, I would have been happy to—"

"Fulfill your conjugal duties, I know. You're very responsib—"

". . . Would have been happy to make you feel good, goddamn it!" His legs and hands came slamming down, and they eyed each other across fifty acres of desk. Sam was the first to lower his gaze.

"I don't understand," she said. "If you were lusting after me during Tony's actual funeral, why are you suddenly so easy to distract?"

"Because his murder was just an abstraction before. Because now the killer has a face! And now I feel—" he hesitated, then pronounced the word defiantly "—responsible. I'm responsible for seeing that the truth comes out!"

"And you won't rest until you bring the outlaws to justice. I was right—too much of that music warps your judgment. Sam, this ain't the old West! Justice could take years—or forever! First somebody has to be convinced to issue a warrant, and then there's the hearing and the preparation and the jury selection and the continuances and the trials and mistrials and the appeals. . . . He—they—could get off on a technicality! It's all very well to deny *yourself* pleasure until your alleged obligation is fulfilled, but what about me?" she finished plaintively.

He laughed as she knew he would, but all he said was, "Well, let's hope it's over soon." She was unnaturally aware of his mouth and his hands and his lean body under the green shirt. Polyester. Who the hell cared what clothes he wore, anyway? She would just rip them off, and then they would roll around right here on the cold linoleum . . . all ambivalence had vanished; nothing is as seductive as indifference.

Love heats faster under pressure, she thought, *just like water.* Already their relationship seemed to have gone through about two years' worth of misunderstandings, emotional turmoil, and shifts of power.

"I think I should go to Amargosa again," Sam was saying.

"Now?"

"No, no—now we have to go to Agua Dulce and then out to Bill Hanford's. Tomorrow morning, probably."

Why? she started to ask, but was distracted by a noise in the hall. She turned, saw that she had left the door open, and had the feeling that someone had been listening—probably hoping for some hot stuff. Fat chance.

The heat *had* broken, a little—it was only about ninety-three as they drove the dirt road to Agua Dulce—but it felt no cooler. The humidity had risen, and the air was clear but heavy and blue—the sky a dull, thudding blue, the ridge of the mountains a dark purple blue, like whales on the horizon. Beyond them white thunderclouds boiled up and poured rain on the High Sierras and the desert, but here there would be no rain. Just this stifling humidity and heat.

Claire didn't remark on the weather. In fact, she had vowed not to initiate any extraneous conversation until Sam was a little more responsive, or until she burst.

In the driveway sat Carlos's truck, an old white Ford with a homemade wooden railing around the bed, but there was no answer when they knocked on the front door. Sam circled the house and came back alone.

"Could they have forgotten?" Claire asked.

"I don't see how—"

"¡Hola!" someone called, and they saw Silvia bobbing toward them, swinging a short length of pipe in one hand.

"Got a flat," she said, nodding toward the truck, "and the damn lug nuts are rusted on. I was just looking for some extra muscle." She shook the pipe.

Sam grinned. "Well, here I am, lady. Where's Carlos?" he asked, as he pushed on the end of the cruciform lug wrench.

"He took the car into town," she said. "Should be back any minute."

Four nuts unscrewed with relative ease, but the fifth was stubborn. Silvia handed Sam the pipe and he fitted it over the end of the wrench and resumed pushing.

Meanwhile Claire examined Silvia. She looked okay; better than at the funeral certainly, and her hair hadn't turned snow white overnight or anything. But the beautiful girl, the lively girl, the girl for whom Alfredo Ruiz had washed exactly half his car—Claire couldn't find her.

"Silvia," said Sam between clenched teeth, yanking mightily on the pipe, "did you tell Bill Hanford you would sell him Agua Dulce? Ah!" he exclaimed, as the nut began to turn.

She helped him wrestle the tire off and began to inspect it. "Probably a nail," she muttered, running her hand over the tread.

"Silvia?"

In the silence they heard a car coming down the drive and in a moment a battered light blue Chevy Nova had skidded to an abrupt stop.

Before he had even stepped out of the car, Carlos began waving his hands and shouting. His face, his unfortunately comic face, was bright red and he was incomprehensible in two languages.

"What is it?" Sam asked. "Calm down, Carlos, and tell us what happened!"

"That sheriff, that Cummings—he says Tony's death wasn't an accident! That he was murdered because he was selling drugs! Son of a bitch!"

It was hard to tell whether this epithet applied to Cummings, to Tony, or was merely an expression of rage.

Claire and Sam exchanged glances, then Sam said, "Carlos. Forget what Cummings said. Tony's death had nothing to do with drugs—"

"No!" A strong voice interrupted them and they looked at Silvia, who was still holding the tire. "It had nothing to do with drugs! It was me, *me* that killed him!"

CHAPTER 18

Silvia laid down the tire carefully, crossed her arms, and turned toward Sam.

"You asked me if I agreed to sell the land to the Hanfords. Yes. I did."

At this Carlos erupted again, but she held up a hand like an Old Testament prophet—or, since the Old Testament was woefully lacking in female prophets, like Cassandra. Or Medea. "Old man," she said without rancor, "if it wasn't for me you'd still be picking grapes at a dollar an hour. So shut up and listen."

It had happened Thursday, the day Claire had visited the orchard. After the argument between Tony and his father, which had ended as usual with Tony tearing off at a hundred miles an hour on his Harley and Carlos stomping back to work, Buddy Hanford had shown up to ask once more about the land—

"Buddy Hanford?" interrupted Sam.

Yes, she said; it was Buddy who had nagged her for two years to sell Agua Dulce. All day Friday, as she went about her chores, as Tony and his father screamed at each other whenever their paths crossed, she had thought about it, and when Tony once again took off on his bike toward the mountains she had called Buddy to capitulate. After that she had made dinner, served Carlos and his cousins, washed up, all the time planning how she would approach Carlos with the news.

"You could of approached me with a machete," Carlos broke in, "it wouldn't of made no difference. Not then. Not before . . ." He halted, his voice choked with grief.

Silvia looked at him impassively. "You should of told him you loved him, old man." And she resumed her story.

She had sat on the front step until past eleven, smoking a cigarette and waiting for Tony, who she knew was drinking at Casey's. With every minute that passed her anxiety had increased; she lived in terror that he would kill himself on that motorcycle. Finally, with immense relief, she had heard the engine roaring up the road.

She had smiled at him warmly, conspiratorially. They were alike, almost like sister and brother, she and her youngest son. But this time Tony didn't respond; he was angry and incoherent, and maybe a little drunk. Something was wrong with the orchard and the spraying, he raved, and somebody was out to get them, and he was going to find out who. Silvia hardly heard him; he had a bruise on his cheek and a cut under his right eye, and she had reached up to touch his face. But he had shrugged off her hand.

Angry and hurt herself, she had thought, I'm right, this is no place for him—he's growing up rough and hard and stupid, just like his brother. She had thought, I made the right decision. And she had blurted out what she had done.

"Don't you see, *hijo,* we can move to LA, you can study music, go to college . . . no more working in the fields!"

"And what about Papa?" he had asked, using the childish term for the first time in years.

She couldn't read his mood; he was calmer, but his face was set and cold.

"I'll persuade him," she had said eagerly. "You know I always can. And with all the trouble we've been having it won't be hard—"

Then he had exploded. "Yeah, you'll persuade him, you selfish fucking bitch," he had yelled, "and break his heart!" And he had roared off, his bike slicing the road and churning up gravel like foam. Stunned, she had watched him go, tears rolling down her cheeks.

"I knew," she said now, "I *knew* this time he'd have an accident." She turned to Carlos. *"Entiendes,* old man, I killed him. But he died for love of you. He loved you and I don't know why. He loved you and you never gave him nothin'. To you he was just the kid who wasn't Frank," she said, snapping each word like a bullwhip, until he threw his arms up in front of his face.

"Silvia," Sam said helplessly, stepping between them,

"Silvia, Tony's death was not an accident and it had nothing to do with you! It was going to happen anyway!"

He might as well have been glass. She continued to look with hatred and contempt at the man she had lived with for forty-five years.

Next stop: Bill Hanford. Claire tossed the car keys to Sam, claiming she didn't know the way. Actually she just didn't want to drive; she was trembling from the intensity of the scene they had just witnessed—and also relieved. *That's* what Silvia had meant at the funeral; that and nothing more horrible.

Well, of course—Christ, of *course* Silvia hadn't murdered her son! What had Claire been thinking? She was becoming completely unhinged. This business of clues, of what, out of all the information in the world, constituted a clue, was a paranoid endeavor. It occurred to her that Sherlock Holmes hadn't differed that much from people who received personal messages from God from license plates and billboards and radio broadcasts.

Sam was quiet, thinking—whatever it was Sam thought; she hadn't the faintest idea. At one point he muttered something.

"What?"

"Buddy," he said, and was silent again.

Tom met them at the gate to Bill Hanford's property. They piled into his funky black-and-white ("City's buying me a Blazer next year," he announced confidently), and as they drove through a mile of orange grove Sam told him what had happened at Agua Dulce.

"Buddy." He grunted. "Wonder what that means? And where the hell is he?"

Ahead of them a new Lincoln was stopped on the side of the road.

"That ain't no field hand," Tom remarked, and pulled off behind it. Bill Hanford was kneeling by a water line, conferring with his foreman. When he saw them he stood, dusted his hands on his trousers, and walked toward them with his lean-hipped, elastic stride.

"Running a little late. Sorry, gentlemen, lady," he said, favoring Claire with an especially dazzling smile. His blue knit sport shirt exactly matched his eyes. "Do you want to drive up to the house . . . ?"

"Naw, let's just park ourselves under a tree," answered Tom. "This won't take long."

In the grove it was cool and pleasant and the aroma of a few late blossoms still lingered. It was like a real orchard from home—except that, as usual, between the trees the ground was perfectly bare.

Sam couldn't contain himself. "You use 2,4,D?" he inquired.

"Nope. Dinoseb."

Sam's eyebrows lifted but all he said was, "You ever think about trying a few rows without herbicide?"

"You mean"—there was a brief, fastidious pause—"just letting the weeds grow?"

"Yeah. Not as neat, but actually the weeds provide a habitat for some beneficial insects. They've done trials up at Kearney—" He halted when he saw Tom standing patiently. "Well, we'll talk about it some other time."

Tom squatted on his haunches, and Bill and Sam followed suit.

"I'd like to talk to you about Venture West," he said. Hanford looked surprised, and maybe a little apprehensive, but not guilty. Maybe those clear features couldn't express guilt. "We've already spoken with Stephen Van Horn," Tom added.

"Well, if you've talked to Van Horn, you know all there is to know."

Tom waited, and eventually Hanford continued. "Venture West approached us about two and a half years ago. They were interested in some property along the river just below the dam, most of which was ours."

"But not all."

"No. There's a small peach orchard there that belongs to a former employee of mine," he said dryly. "And Venture West was interested in the whole parcel or none at all."

"So what did you tell them?"

"I told them I'd do my best to guarantee the sale by their deadline, which is August of this year."

"And what steps did you take to do that?"

"Well, I . . . I made the owners—"

"Silvia and Carlos Rodriguez—"

"Right, Silvia and Carlos, an exploratory offer, which they

turned down. And then I turned the whole matter over to someone else to handle."

"Who?"

"My younger brother, Wallace. Buddy."

They thought about that for a minute. "What did Buddy do?" Tom asked. "To persuade the Rodriguezes to sell, I mean."

"Tom, I have no idea. This is a huge operation, and the whole point of delegating tasks"—(Is to have an alibi when the shit hits the fan, Claire finished silently) "is to not have to worry about them."

"Why did you delegate this one to Buddy?" Sam asked suddenly.

"What?"

Sam looked at Martelli, who nodded as if to say, take it, and Sam continued, "There must have been a tidy sum riding on this deal with Venture West. Why entrust such important . . . negotiations, to Buddy, when you have lawyers and accountants and real estate people on your payroll?"

Hanford smiled winningly. "Sometimes it's hard to find a job that's suited to Buddy's capabilities."

"Such as beating up babies and grandmas?" Sam retorted. "C'mon, Bill, didn't it occur to you that Buddy might do something violent, not to mention illegal?"

"Certainly not!" Hanford said indignantly, and Martelli raised a pacifying hand.

"Sam, Bill, there'll be plenty of time to talk about this later." Hanford turned a little pale under his Tahoe tan. "I think I've found out what I wanted to know. My only other question is, has Buddy shown up?"

Hanford shook his head.

"You filed that missing persons report with Cummings?"

"Not yet. I keep thinking he'll come back."

"You oughta do that, Bill—not that it matters, actually. We've got every deputy in the county looking for him anyway."

Sam was grinning when they climbed back into Tom's car. He looked over at Claire and said, "That felt good."

She nodded. "For the toilets."

Martelli, misunderstanding, said, "Yeah, he's a scumbag, all right."

Tom wouldn't let them leave until they had accepted a

folder with photos of Van Horn and associates, and one of Larry McKeever. "Help me out here," he begged. "I gotta stay home tonight, but somebody needs to take these over to the Wagon Wheel Motel in Parkerville and see if he was there Friday night. He claims he wasn't. Even if that's true, he might have met with McKeever at some point. Ask around."

"Sure. You want to come?" Sam asked Claire, who grimaced. She was feeling distinctly unappreciated of late, and she toyed with the idea of simply retreating to her little house until Sam decided that she was as interesting as Stephen Van Horn. But common sense whispered that Sam's cabin was at two thousand feet and that you lost three degrees for every thousand-foot gain in altitude.

However, she did need fresh underwear and clothes, and another pair of earrings. "I need to stop by my place first."

"No problem," Tom replied. "It's only five. The night crew doesn't come on till nine."

She picked up her car at the station and headed north toward Highway 170.

The highway passed through zones of odors like warm and cool currents in a lake: alfalfa. DDT, or something damn near like it. Feedlot, not unpleasant at this distance. More alfalfa, or some other grass, sweetly suburban. Every thirty seconds Claire's eyes flicked to her rearview mirror; since the night she had been pursued by Larry McKeever she had begun to do this obsessively. Directly behind her was a light-colored pickup truck, and then a big American land yacht. There wasn't much traffic; by now the daily slight coagulation of cars known locally as "rush hour" had dispersed. When she glanced up again in a few moments, a Winnebago had trundled onto the road, blocking her view and the vehicles behind it. As she watched, the frustrated driver of the pickup emerged from behind the camper and attempted to pass it.

His timing was bad. At that moment a southbound tour bus, carrying, apparently, Hector Nuñez y Su Banda Tropical, was barreling toward them, and the white pickup narrowly squeaked back in behind her just as the Banda Tropical thundered past. She pursed her lips at his reckless move, wondering why he had been so hell-bent on staying close to her, and she noted that he turned east on 170 when she did.

Nothing in that; but when he followed her off the highway and onto Riverdale's Main Street she started to worry a little.

Maybe she was being paranoid. But rather than dismiss her fears altogether she struck a compromise: she didn't drive straight to the police station, nor did she ignore him. Instead she executed a rudimentary evasive maneuver and turned down Willow Court, one street before her own; everything on this side of the highway dead-ended at the river, and she knew she could walk up the river path until she reached home. With relief and a certain amount of pride in her own resourcefulness she saw him whiz past on Main. She must be becoming a naturalized Californian; she was getting good at car chases!

She parked at the end of Willow and walked downhill, pausing as always to admire the last house on the street. "Wonderland," she called it: at its core a modest white trailer now smothered under a tea cozy of bric-a-brac, wrought iron, and gingerbread. Plants and wind chimes and hummingbird feeders dripped from the eaves; Disneyesque statuary sprouted from the Astroturf lawn, along with wooden ducks that whirled in the wind, birdbaths, concrete deer, and a sign that said THE PRESLEY'S (the elderly residents' name, not a tribute to the King). It was a fantastic achievement, and someday she would think of a pretense to get inside. She took brief inventory—there seemed to be a new string of lights around the door—then turned and stepped into the forest.

Immediately the temperature dropped five degrees and the river enclosed her and flooded her senses. Aroma of damp earth, delicate clematis, and bay trees, sharp and medicinal; vines and thick brush, crowding her path and plucking at her clothes; quiet that made her listen hard to the faint gurgle of running water and the crunch of her own footsteps. Soon the trees hid the lights of Willow Court and the path veered toward the river and she walked faster. By day she loved the lush green coolness and the big button willows and cottonwoods netted by wild cucumber and grape, but now she remembered Manny Aragon's malevolent jungle, and her own dream of strangling underbrush. Every so often dry leaves crackled off to her left—birds and squirrels, no doubt, but her nervousness amplified them to the size of bears. Or men. She tried not to think about Van Horn's pal, Jay Cardenas, with his flat, brutal face, or about Larry McKeever's gaping throat.

She walked faster, then broke into a trot. Had she missed the end of her street? Could it possibly take this long to walk a quarter mile?

By now the twilight had faded to the point where she could barely make out shapes, but the sycamores' peeled white trunks still were incandescent in the dark, like candles. In fact, if he hadn't been standing in front of a sycamore she wouldn't have seen him at all.

But she did see him. A dark figure, motionless, thirty feet ahead of her on the trail.

She stifled a scream, which would have been feeble anyway —she wasn't much of a screamer—and, characteristically, thought instead. She thought, *It's just another evening stroller, but maybe it would be prudent to turn back anyway.* She thought, *It's certainly a man, I can tell from the shoulders, but—there's something wrong with the figure. . . .*

Then, suddenly, she thought: *his face. Why can't I see his face?*

As a photographer Claire had a trained awareness of the behavior of light. And right now she knew that this person's face should reflect what light was left, should shine out at her like a pale moon or like the sycamores. But . . . pants, shirt, face, all were equally dark against the tree. Even if he were black, and there were no black people in Kaweah County, she should have been able to see his eyes. Unless he had something over his face.

Like a ski mask.

She was backing up as she thought all of this. Still believing himself to be invisible, he moved, shifting something from his left hand to his right. In transit it gleamed for a moment, dim but unmistakable. *No knives,* she thought hysterically, turned around, and started to run back up the trail.

If it had doubled in length on her way upriver, now it was a marathon. The man was slow in starting—he hadn't realized he'd been spotted—but then he was crashing behind her, slowly closing the gap. Her heart boomed in her ears like a car stereo and her lungs burned and she ran, praying that no little viny tendril snaked across the path to snag her ankle. Crash, crash behind her. . . . Moronically she arched her back, as if to put it a little farther out of reach of that horrible slicing blade. The lights of Wonderland flickered through the trees, but he was gaining, gaining. . . .

Suddenly the crashing became wilder and there was a loud *whump!* and then an instant of silence. He's fallen! she thought joyfully, sprinted like a rabbit, and was out of the woods.

"Help me! Help me!" she cried, smacking Wonderland's aluminum screen door with the flat of her hand and ringing the fake Liberty Bell. "There's someone after me!" Fearfully she looked down toward the river. "Please—let me in!"

Finally a response. She heard shuffling behind the door, and a whispered discussion. Oh Christ, she thought in an agony of terror and impatience, hurry up; she'd be the Kitty Genovese of Riverdale, they'd find a Snow White corpse on the Astroturf, wedged between Sneezy and Grumpy. "I'm a neighbor!"

This seemed to work. The door opened a crack and she inserted a foot. "I've never seen you," someone quavered.

"A man is following me. I have to phone the police," she said firmly, and scooted inside.

Inside Wonderland, and she couldn't even appreciate it. Two gnomelike white-haired presences in frayed Pendleton bathrobes watched suspiciously while she phoned Tom Martelli, relaxing only when they saw she *was* calling the police, and this wasn't a ploy to steal their Hummel collection.

"Dora and Leroy Presley's place?" said Tom. "I'll be right over. Don't leave!"

Not bloody likely, thought Claire, and phoned Sam.

"Did you get a good look at him?" Tom asked. He and Claire and Sam were drinking coffee in the Presleys', um, kitsch-en, each from a cup inscribed with the map of a state and its motto. IDAHO—FAMOUS POTATOES, said Claire's. According to the Presleys' clock—a urethaned redwood plaque featuring an airbrushed vision of Jesus feeding the masses—only fifteen minutes had passed since she had forced her way in to safety. Sam was holding her hand.

"Well, I . . . I thought it might be that guy from Venture West whose picture you showed us. You know, Jesus Cardenas."

Sam dropped her hand, and Martelli looked very alert.

"Cardenas? Really? Could you identify him?"

"No, I didn't actually see his face—"

Blank stares.

"But something about this guy reminded me of him," she finished decisively.

Tom snorted and began to interrogate her. It soon became clear that she couldn't describe her pursuer at all, that her only reason for believing him to be Cardenas was purest voodoo: she had been thinking about him, in particular about him murdering Larry McKeever, and voila! she had conjured him out of the air. You shouldn't think bad thoughts in the woods at night.

"We'll do a standard investigation," Tom said, "and I'll find out where Cardenas was tonight—though why he should be after *you* in any case is beyond me. And you didn't happen to get the license of that white pickup? No, I didn't think so," he said, making Claire feel that the whole episode had been her personal failure.

Go ahead, blame the victim, she thought with a faint attempt at plucky humor. Actually she was pretty shaky and was grateful for Sam's apparent solicitude as he hustled her into his car. But even he seemed more interested in the idea that Cardenas might have been her attacker than that she had been attacked.

"Is there any reason why he would want to kill you? Did you see or hear something that might implicate him—something that Tom and I didn't see?"

"Not that I know of. Oh, Sam, it probably wasn't Cardenas. Look, I'm kind of upset. Could we just go home?"

There was an uncomfortable silence. Sam cleared his throat.

"We're not going home," she stated after a minute.

"Um, well, remember, Tom wanted me to go down to the Wagon Wheel Motel in Parkerville, to talk to the night crew about Van Horn, and I'd really like to get that information—"

"I really would rather not be alone right now," she snapped, partly resentful and partly genuinely afraid. "What if that guy—"

"No, no, no, of course I won't leave you alone," he interrupted, and she relaxed a little. She knew it was wrong, she knew it was a weakness, but on rare occasions she did sort of want to be taken care of and it was good to know that Sam would take care of her—

"We'll go together!" he said.

CHAPTER 19

The Wagon Wheel Motel was a long pink stucco barracks identified to students of semiotics as Western by certain signs and symbols: a huge metal wheel embedded in gravel and two neon spurs, which advertised the Wagon Wheel Lounge. They walked up the drive and into the lobby. Here they found the night manager, who in keeping with the motif was an Indian. An Indian Indian, in a turban: B. SINGH, said his nameplate.

He glanced at the photographs of Van Horn and Chandler "Oh, yes, these men have stayed here on several occasions," he told them in his liquid accent. "I don't remember this fellow"—tapping the picture of Cardenas.

They flipped through the file of registration cards, starting with today's date and working backward. "Here," Sam said suddenly. "S. Van Horn. Room two hundred two. Checked in at eleven P.M. on June twenty-four—no, the twenty-third, the date's crossed out."

"The twenty-third would have been Friday," said Claire. "Did he stay the next night, too?" Because on Saturday, June 24, someone had ripped open Larry McKeever's throat.

Singh studied the card, muttering. "These kids we get as night clerks . . . you'd think they would at least know the date." Finally he shook his head. "I'm sorry, I just can't tell. You might ask in the lounge; maybe these fellows like to drink and someone saw them there."

The bar was nearly deserted. They sat down at a booth and in a moment a waitress in fringed ersatz cowgirl skirt and high-heeled boots approached them. Claire just had time to receive a vague impression of bouffant blonde hair and heavy makeup when she felt Sam stiffen beside her.

"Holy shit," he muttered, as the woman stopped before their table.

"Hi, Sam," she said coolly.

Darlene!

"Howdy, Linda," he replied weakly. *(Linda??* Claire stared in disbelief at the nameplate perched perkily above the woman's left breast; LINDA, it read.)

"When did you start working here?" Sam was saying.

"About a month ago. I told you last time I saw you. Guess you weren't paying attention," she said, turning an expressionless face to Claire.

"Oh, uh, this is Claire, Claire Sharples, she works at the sta—"

"I remember her from the picnic," stated Linda.

Silence.

"Well, how . . . how're you doing?" asked Sam.

"Fine."

"How're the kids?"

"Fine. What'll you have?" she said, a question heavy with significance.

"Oh, well, a couple of Buds, I guess," he replied feebly, and Linda walked superbly away, leaving behind two people in a state of complete social paralysis. Finally Claire managed to remark, "I think I'll go wash this Scarlet *A* off my forehead," and headed for a door marked COWGIRLS.

The bathroom was dark and reeked of bubble-gum scented disinfectant. Claire automatically examined herself in the dimly lit mirror. Her hair was stringy, her face bony and plain; there were deep circles under her eyes and a livid scratch along her right cheek. Definitely not at her best after having been chased through the woods by a crazed knife-wielding maniac. And her best was not that spectacular anyway; interesting, maybe, but not exactly Christie Brinkley.

Whereas Darl—Linda was really a very pretty woman. Under that somewhat garish makeup were regular, delicate features, she decided judiciously, recalling with difficulty the face seen through a haze of embarrassment . . . embarrassment! How about Linda, having to *wait* on both of them! Of course that had given her a distinct moral edge which she hadn't been reluctant to exploit. And speaking of moral edge, Sam had mentioned kids; wonder how many she had. She must work here to support them. Her husband had probably left her—and now Sam had done the same, the bastard. Oh, no, that was unfair, Claire hadn't heard his side of the story, but he had looked so guilty. . . .

And just what made her think Sam *had* left Linda?

She pulled up short. This noblesse oblige, this sisterly solidarity was all very commendable, but maybe *Linda* was the love of Sam's life. After all, she fit the profile of perfect mate for Sam that Claire herself had devised the other night. Maybe Claire Sharples, PhD, smart as a whip and almost as cute, was merely—an interesting experiment. A brief dalliance. After last night she could almost believe it, and the idea made her feel sick. She ran her fingers through her eternally messy hair. Maybe—up? She fished through her pockets and found a rubber band. There—that was better. But wasn't it a bit obvious? Run to bathroom, return with whole new hairdo . . . she took it down again, rattier than ever, splashed some cold water on her face, and tried to regain her emotional equilibrium. After ten minutes she reentered the bar.

Linda had sat down across from Sam and they were engaged in earnest conversation, heads close together. The photographs were pushed negligently to the far end of the table. As Claire approached, Linda rose abruptly and strode swiftly away, fringe bobbing vigorously.

Sam glanced up unhappily. "Let's get out of here."

In uneasy silence they walked through the empty lobby and out to the parking lot. Claire tried out several sentences in her head, but when they reached the car all she said was, "Did Linda recognize the photographs?"

"Aw, she was too pissed off to even look at them," Sam replied, moodily kicking a front tire. "Damn! I just flat out forgot that she'd started working here! She says she told me at the picnic—the Memorial Day picnic, you know; she came with—"

"I remember her."

"Oh."

They were leaning side by side against the car; the neon spurs flickered crazily in Sam's glasses. "Let me tell you about Linda," he said. Having explained Claire to Linda, he would now explain Linda to Claire.

"She's an old friend of Debbie's—my wife's. She and her husband split up about the time Deb and I did, and we've been seeing each other off and on ever since—and I mean off and on," he repeated emphatically, looking hard at Claire. "It was real casual. Neither of us took it seriously."

Claire felt faint with relief. This didn't sound like a man in love with Linda. "Maybe she took it a little more seriously than you did," she said, achieving a tone of mild feminist reproof.

He considered for a moment, then shook his head. "Maybe," he said doubtfully, "but—hell! She's seen other guys, plenty of times; I would have sworn I was just somebody to fall back on. Sometimes I didn't even think she liked me! I mean, I really wasn't her type. She was always trying to get me to wear those Western shirts, you know, the kind with snaps—what's wrong?"

Claire was laughing. "Nothing," she said, brushing his cheek, "but you seem to have a hard time believing that women like you." *(And have a universal female aversion to your shirts,* she thought.)

"It's true"—reaching out and pulling her against him—"I find it incomprehensible." After a moment he said, "I don't know. I sure feel like a cockroach right now, so maybe I was fooling myself about what was going on with her. Because it was so . . . convenient. And Debbie used to tell me," he said, squinting at the sky, "that I withdraw and become insensitive to the people around me. You might have noticed it on occasion."

"Um, yes, you're a bit obsessive."

"Oh." A pause. "Is that bad?"

"I don't know. I'm used to it. Most scientists are like that." *Or learn to fake it,* she thought privately. "Go on about Linda."

"Yeah. Anyway, I was going to tell her about you, but with one thing and another I hadn't got around to it yet. But the worst part," he continued, with touching compassion, "is that I really blew this thing with the photographs. Martelli will have to send somebody else down here, and even then I don't know what she'll—"

"Sam."

A soft voice interrupted him, and they looked up to see Linda standing about ten yards away. Her hair glowed like radium under the fluorescent light. "Could I talk to you for a minute?" she said. "Inside?"

"Sure," he replied apprehensively, standing up.

"Bring your pictures," said Linda; then, looking back over her shoulder at Claire, added, "She can come too."

So they trooped back into the Wagon Wheel Lounge and spread out the photographs on a table. Linda glanced at them and said immediately, "Sure, they've been here a couple of times. This one"—indicating Van Horn—"and the cute blond, and once they met this guy"—indicating Cardenas. "This one" —Van Horn—"always tells me to stop by his room when I get off. One of these nights I might take him up on it." She laughed, looking at Sam with a hint of defiance.

"I wouldn't advise it," he replied seriously. "How about him?"—producing the last photo.

"Isn't that Larry McKeever? Oh, yeah, Larry comes—came —in here once in a while. But not with them."

Sam nodded. "When was the last time Van Horn was here?"

She scrunched up her face, thinking. Even that was cute. "Last weekend, I think."

"The weekend of the twenty-fourth."

"Yeah—at least, I don't know about Friday, I don't work then, but they were here either Saturday or Sunday, I can't remember which. These two"—indicating Van Horn and Cardenas.

"Saturday?" Sam suggested eagerly; Saturday was the night McKeever was killed. The night Sam and Claire had consummated their . . . whatever it was.

"Maybe . . ." she said, sounding very uncertain.

"And they were here in the lounge. . . ." Sam prompted.

"Yes, till about one o'clock. Then the phone rang for—Van Horn, is that his name?—and he and the mean-looking guy left."

"A phone call!" Sam interrupted excitedly. "From who? Do you know?"

She shook her head. "Just some guy asking for Mr. Van Horn. I didn't recognize the voice."

"Could it have been Larry McKeever?"

She wrinkled her perfect nose in distaste. "Poor old Larry," she said. "You know, it might have been. I couldn't swear to it, though." She paused. "Yeah, it really might have been. Because when Van Horn hung up, he sort of muttered under his breath, 'stupid son of a bitch.' So it might have been Larry. Anyway, after the call he and the other guy sort of argued, and finally they left in a hurry. Didn't even leave me a tip, and he always leaves a big tip."

Sam posed a few more questions. Then he gathered up the photographs, after which there was an awkward silence.

"I'll go on out to the car," offered Claire, rising. Then, making a supreme effort, she turned to Linda. "Good-bye," she said. "It was . . . it was nice to meet you again."

Somehow uttering these weak banalities was as hard as waiting in the dark with a loaded shotgun for someone to burst through the door. For the first time Linda lifted her very blue eyes and looked fully at Claire. "Same here," she replied politely with the ghost of a smile.

Sam showed up five minutes later looking haggard. "Everything's all right, I think," he said rapidly. "She said it was just kind of a shock when we walked in, but when she thought about it she realized she didn't have any claims on me, and we were still friends, and she hoped I'd be very happy. Jesus, what a week," he ended abruptly. After a moment he continued in a businesslike tone, "Okay. What have we got?"

"Well," replied Claire, "nothing definite, really. Van Horn and hit man *might* have been here the night McKeever was killed. They got a phone call from somebody who *may* have been McKeever—

"Who might have been calling to say he'd chased you and you'd gotten away—"

"Who *might* have been calling to collect on a bet, and then they argued, and left."

"Possibly to kill McKeever."

"Possibly to get a burger. Sam, there's a lot of 'mights' and 'could haves' and otherwise speculative language here."

"Yeah." He looked at his watch. "It's only ten-thirty. Let's go see Tom."

Claire cleared her throat. "Oh, Sam, um, by the way . . . does Linda have some other name? I mean, a middle name or a—a nickname, that she goes by sometimes?"

"Not that I know of," he replied, bewildered. "Linda, that's her name. Linda Nelson."

* * *

"Linda *Nelson?*" interrupted Tom Martelli, his eyebrows climbing. They were sitting in the Martellis' living room where they had roused Tom a few minutes ago (actually, they had roused more than Tom; Claire could hear the angry squalls of a newborn baby upstairs).

"Yeah," Sam said sheepishly, and he and Tom suddenly grinned at each other in a moment of pure locker-room bonding.

"Thought she was working over at Cheryl's," Tom remarked, shoving his hands into the pockets of his worn blue bathrobe, "but anyway, go on."

Sam recounted Linda's story. Martelli interjected a question from time to time, but for the most part he listened in silence.

"Does she think it was McKeever that called?" he asked.

"She says that it *might* have been," Claire interjected, "and that after he hung up Van Horn said 'stupid son of a bitch,' which I doubt qualifies as positive ID."

"It's suggestive, though," added Sam, and they all had a laugh at the expense of poor Larry, who was past caring anyway.

"She did say," Claire went on, "that McKeever drank there sometimes. She'd just never seen them together."

"But somebody might have," finished Tom. "Okay, we'll follow that up." He paused. "And frankly, I don't know what to do after that, except to hope that Buddy Hanford shows up. Alive or dead."

At that moment the phone rang and Tom went lumbering off in the direction of the ring, muttering about late night callers and the general difficulty of his life.

"Probably a cat in a fucking tree," he said bitterly. But when he returned he looked strangely serene.

"That was Linda Nelson," he said. "She called to say that you had just asked her some questions about McKeever and Van Horn, and she thought I might like to know that she'd remembered. It was *Sunday* night that Van Horn and Cardenas were drinking in the bar and got the phone call."

"Sunday?" Sam said, dismayed. "Is she sure?"

"Positive."

"But—but McKeever was killed on *Saturday!*"

"Welcome to the wild wacky world of police work."

"Well, what do we do now?"

"We could," said Claire carefully, looking meaningfully at Tom, "uh, pursue other avenues of investigation."

"Like what?" said Sam.

"Not yet," said Tom.

CHAPTER 20

"I get the feeling that what's going on is sort of . . . asymptotic, you know?" Sam was saying as they drove home. "Like no matter how close we get we'll never actually get our hands on Van Horn, never be able to prove anything. But I know exactly what happened to Agua Dulce, to Tony, to Larry McKeever—it's so damn frustrating!"

"Is that a white pickup?" Claire was looking in the side mirror.

"I don't see it," Sam said after a moment, and now she couldn't spot it either.

"Oh." Maybe she had imagined it. Certainly she was wrung out enough to imagine anything, but . . . who had a white pickup? Carlos, but that was an old junker; Jim's was powder blue, which might look white at night, but it was one of those super-wide models, with an extra set of wheels. This looked more like a Japanese import.

She crawled into bed, expecting insomnia interpolated by menacing dreams, and immediately sank into a coma. Around five in the morning she realized that Sam was not in bed and padded out to the kitchen, where she found him at the table. He was surrounded by desiccated bits of greenery and his *California Flora,* a twelve-pound tome, was open before him.

"How long have you been here? What are you doing?"

"Trying to key these out. I got up around four."

"Did you just go out and collect this stuff?" she asked incredulously. "In the middle of the night?"

"No, they were in the refrigerator. I collect specimens I can't identify and store them in a plastic bag till I have time to check 'em out." He finally looked at her, his face pale and drawn. "It's kind of soothing. Absorbing."

Resignedly she made a pot of coffee while Sam discarded the specimens he had named and carefully replaced the others in the refrigerator. He walked outside and perched on the lowest step, elbows propped on knees. In a moment Claire followed and sat behind him on the porch, watching the clouds appear in the eastern sky. Sam's hair stood up in tufts like shredded wheat and automatically she reached down to smooth it, thought again, clasped her arms across her body, and leaned forward.

"You still going to Amargosa today?"

"Yeah," he replied wearily. "Eventually. Don't ask me what I hope to find there, either. First I'm gonna talk to Tom, though, and see if he's got any good ideas on what to do next."

"You think this is too much for him to handle."

"Well, I hope not, because he's the best hope we've got. And Tom's a smart guy. But he's never had to deal with anything this complicated, and these Venture West people—they're real pros. They're from LA, after all."

Invisible birds warbled around them, quickened by the promise of light and warmth. Suddenly a tiny green bird shot up in front of them—twenty yards straight up, as if buoyed on a jet of water—then dropped again.

"Ana's hummingbird," Sam said tonelessly, like a park ranger. "Each species has its own unique flight pattern."

"Seems to be characteristic of the male of the species. Flight, I mean," she heard herself say.

Surprisingly, he knew what she meant. "You've done your share of fleeing in this relationship." He was still looking out at the hills.

"Not now."

"No, because now *I'm* retreating. I retreat, you advance; you retreat, I advance."

Lightly she rested her palm on his spiky hair. "Couldn't we leave our armies behind for a while? Maybe meet in the middle for a parley?"

After a moment he twisted around and looked up at her; then he turned completely so that he knelt on the step, facing her. He tugged at the sash of her bathrobe, stopped to shrug impatiently out of yesterday's green shirt, then opened her robe and pushed it back around her shoulders. Gently he pressed her down until she was lying on the porch and he was on top of her.

"Afraid of splinters?" he whispered.

"No."

Soon, however, she yelped and rubbed her back and he scraped his knee and they headed inside to soft mattresses and cool sheets.

And later still Claire put her hands under her head and watched the ceiling. Sam was lying facedown and inert, and she wondered why the men she had known were always, well, *drained,* after sex, while she was often invigorated, renewed, and clearheaded. She did some of her best thinking after making love.

The radio was playing country music at an almost subliminal level, but somehow she didn't mind it in these circumstances. It reminded her of an old Dylan song, about a loft in Soho where the heat pipes just coughed and the country music station played soft . . . the song was so evocative it was like a memory, and if she had made a few different choices in her life it might have been *her* memory, and she might be somewhere very different. But she hadn't, and she was here, and when she looked at Sam she felt helpless to change that. Infatuation she could ride out, but this . . . this was something else. He seemed so vulnerable, with his lingering Hardshell Baptist guilt and his obsessions, nerdy and noble. She wanted to protect him from the truth about Jim LaSalle and Frank Rodriguez, to tell him that . . . oh, that life let people down no matter how responsibly he personally behaved, that there was no way he could make things all right for Carlos and Silvia, or for himself, ever again, that solving the mystery of Tony's murder wouldn't "solve" their grief . . .

She was dozing off when the irony hit. She felt *responsible* for him!

Sometime later the sound of the shower woke her. Sam emerged, clad for battle in semiclean Dacron, kissed her on the forehead, and left for Martelli's/Amargosa/Places Unknown. She lay in bed contemplating her own characteristic flight patterns.

For example: Jim LaSalle. Had she rationalized herself out of confronting him? Sure, she had told herself it would be better to wait until the case against Buddy and/or Venture West was at a complete standstill before revealing what she knew. Why rake up old memories—hurting Sam and Silvia and Carlos in the process—unnecessarily?

But the investigation of Venture West could go on for month after indecisive month. If Van Horn et al. were completely peripheral to the crime, if Buddy never reappeared, why waste that time—a time during which, incidentally, Sam might continue to be distant and distracted—when a conversation with Jim might establish whether there was a case against him?

At eight-fifteen Claire knocked on Jim LaSalle's office door, her guts churning from coffee and anxiety.

No answer. Jim *always* arrived by eight and left for his field calls by eight-thirty, but a phone call from the lab at eight-twenty still brought no response.

She walked upstairs and again knocked on his door to be sure, then stopped by Ray's office.

"Is Jim out? I wanted to talk to him."

"Yeah, he called early this morning and said he had to go up to Fresno to the Cal State library. Anything I can help you with?"

"Oh . . . no, it can wait."

Her relief was tempered by the knowledge that she would merely have to gear herself up all over again tomorrow.

At noon, resisting the desire to track Sam down, she nevertheless drove all the way home for lunch—something she never did—and on her way through Riverdale casually checked Tom's office for his car. Not there.

Though her larder was suffering from the fact that its owner didn't know where she lived at the moment, she managed to put together some slightly moldy quesadillas and returned to the lab a little after one. A pink telephone message lay on her desk.

"12:45," it said. "From: Sam. Message: meet me at 2:00 at Amargosa. Important."

"Bonnie," she said, breathing hard after a dash up the stairs, "are you sure about—Where's Bonnie?"

A blonde teenager was sitting at the main desk studying *The ABCs of Accounting*. "Bonnie's on vacation this week. In Las Vegas. I'm the temp."

"Oh—right. Well, uh—"

"Chris."

"Chris, did you take this message?"

"Yep."

"And you're sure that was the name of the place? Amargosa?"

"Uh-huh. I made him spell it. He sounded sort of funny—like he was excited."

"I'll be gone all afternoon," she called, making for the door.

She tore out of the parking lot in considerable mental uproar, which would have shortened her drive except that she kept feeling she was being followed. But she never quite managed to prove it to herself, and before she expected it she had traveled the last dirt road and rounded the last turn and come to Amargosa.

Sam's Valiant didn't seem to be there; maybe he had not yet returned from wherever he had gone to call her, or maybe he had left the car somewhere. Out of a similar caution she pulled off the road and hid her car in a tall stand of tules. Then she walked slowly past the ruins, heading for the shack.

"Sam?" she called tentatively. Once again she felt the suffocating, ominous spell of the place. She did her best to shrug it off. After all, last time she had felt watched here someone was indeed watching her—a real live (at the time) human. No Ghost of Okies Past, no lonesome Joads, haunted Amargosa; how corny could you get? With phony jauntiness she kicked at a scrap of plywood, and began to think about why Sam had called her.

What could he have found that they had missed before? Something that pointed to Venture West? Or to someone else —someone like Jim? That was an enticing idea; if there were independent evidence marking him as a suspect she wouldn't have to march into his office and intone *"J'accuse!"* She examined the ground, once again trying to decide what constituted litter and what a clue. Something bright caught her eye and she squatted and fished it out of the dirt: it was the corner of a hard pack of cigarettes, dull red. Marlboros, maybe. Buddy smoked Marlboros, she remembered. Now, was that a clue?

She stooped to gather it up, wondering where the hell Sam was. She straightened slowly and headed for the back of the shed, calling nervously. Then she stopped and listened intently. A car was rumbling up the dirt road.

Sam! she thought with relief. Finally!

But it didn't sound like the Valiant: no crescendo and pause of a stick shift, just that constant monotonous whine, coming closer and closer. . . .

Something made her step back and crouch in the rushes, just as a long black stretch limousine swept past in the swirling dust and pulled up at the end of the road. Doors slammed; footsteps crunched for a few yards and stopped. Cautiously Claire peered through the tule.

Twenty yards away, in the clearing between the debris of the camp and the storage shed, stood two men. One, dark and Hispanic, looked remarkably like the man who dogged her nightmares, and maybe her steps: Jesus Cardenas. The other was Stephen Van Horn.

"Hey," Van Horn called in his easy Southern California voice. "Anybody here?"

No response. "Hello?" he called again, scanning the perimeter of the clearing, for a moment looking directly at Claire behind her bulrush curtain, and then moving on. Something —a sound, maybe, or an intuition—drew his attention to the shed, because he turned toward it and called again. "Hey, friend, it's okay. Come on out." He gestured to his companion, who stepped to the side of the door and leaned back against the shed. Then, with a motion Claire had seen a hundred times on television, Cardenas reached into his jacket with his right hand and stood poised, waiting. That means a shoulder holster, she thought. And that means bad news for whoever's in the shed.

The door swung open with the creak that had scared the daylights out of her on that first trip to Amargosa, and someone stepped into the clearing. Hairier, dirtier, maybe even thinner, but still unmistakable—it was Buddy Hanford.

Claire was stupefied.

"Where have you been, Hanford?" Van Horn was saying. "A lot of people have been looking for you."

"Yeah, I bet." Buddy moved closer to Van Horn and squeaked, "I just bet they have! Look, Van Horn, I didn't sign up to get involved in no murder!"

There was a pause. "That's *my* line," Van Horn said, sounding a little puzzled.

"What the fuck's that supposed to mean?"

"I mean, Mr. Hanford, that we made a very simple deal for some land. How you went about it obtaining it was your business—except that if you start killing people, you have to be discreet and professional. Otherwise you're a liability, and my company divests itself of liabilities."

"Killing people?" Buddy sounded genuinely bewildered. "Hell, I never killed nobody! Sure, I torched a building and ran down some trees—but *you* paid McKeever to waste the Rodriguez kid, and then you murdered McKeever, and I don't want nothin' to do with it! That's why I been hidin' out here since Sunday!"

Claire was too afraid of Jay and Jay's gun to try to move, and anyway she was fascinated. She knew Buddy was devious and his apparent bewilderment meant nothing; on the other hand, she was inclined to believe him.

"You're wrong, Hanford," Van Horn said. "I never heard of this McKeever until you called me at the motel the other night."

So it was *Buddy* who had made that call on Sunday night!

"Then your local yokel police chief asked me about him," Van Horn continued. "Listen, Hanford, we didn't murder anyone; this project wasn't worth it to us—and we certainly would have been a lot more competent if we had." He was silent for a moment.

"Either you're lying," he said finally, "or there's another player in this game." That casual manner had tightened like a damp tennis racket. "And since I don't know which, I'm going to take you down to LA to talk to some people who have a little more expertise in these matters. Jay?"

Buddy glanced to his right and saw Cardenas for the first time. He took an involuntary step backward, but Jay caught his elbow and guided him toward the car, and when he tried to pull away Cardenas grabbed his ear with his left hand. With his right he propped the gun against the base of Buddy's skull.

Buddy emitted a sort of sob and allowed himself to be pushed toward the limousine. He clambered in ahead of Cardenas, Van Horn started the engine and turned the wheel. And stopped. And backed. And stopped. And turned, and stopped, and backed again—the long car inched around like the *Queen Mary* in the Charles River. Finally they had rotated 180 degrees, and with a spin of tires in gravel they were gone.

Claire stood up slowly, trying to make sense of this. Was Buddy lying? Was Van Horn's denial merely a ploy to make

Buddy tractable and get him into the car? Or was he telling the truth—was there another "player," as he had said? If so, who? Her hand hurt, and she looked down to see that the sharp corners of the Marlboro box, which she had clenched in her fist, were cutting into her palm. She began to tuck the box into her breast pocket, but something was in the way and she extracted it. It was one of her business cards, with the State of California seal, the field station logo, and her name in one corner—

Something clicked.

Suddenly she was back at Casey's. Larry McKeever was dumping the contents of his wallet on the bar and she was staring at the wad of hundreds, the credit cards, the business cards . . .

A card. Larry had been carrying a business card from the field station that day. And when she went through his wallet at the sheriff's office, it was gone.

Maybe he had just thrown it away. Or maybe someone had removed it to protect himself.

It hadn't been her card, of course; another name was printed at the bottom. She squinted, trying to recall the pattern of those letters, concentrating, hearing the small, eerie noises around her: the reeds rustling, a bird crying overhead, a sigh—

A sigh. A small, terrifying sigh—as though someone had exhaled close behind her.

The panic she had suppressed finally exploded and she whirled, heart pumping, telling herself, it's nothing, it's nothing. . . .

But it wasn't nothing. Ten feet away someone stood watching her, hands resting on his belt, tight little smile on his eight-year-old's face. It was Jim LaSalle.

V. James LaSalle. That had been the name at the bottom of the card.

CHAPTER 21

She took a quick, harsh breath, the air rushing in as if filling a vacuum. Jim! The last person she had expected to see! And there was no reason for him to be here—no reason except one.

Jim was the other player. And Jim had the instincts of a killer: he had let Frank Rodriguez die long ago, and now she knew he had killed Lawrence McKeever last Saturday night.

Her throat tightened and all she could do was stare at him like a cat in the headlights. Dimly she registered the presence of a gun—his beloved Colt, no doubt—on his hip, in a holster. He was still smiling.

"Glad those bozos finally took off," he said, and then, smugly, "I knew that little gal wouldn't recognize my voice."

It took her a moment to produce a response. "That was you who left the message," she said numbly. "Not Sam."

"Yep."

A pause, while he eyed her speculatively. Then he said, "Manny Aragon called me two nights ago. And ever since I've been trying to figure what I should do about you."

Her terror had subsided a little, and her mind was clearing. It was just possible, she realized, that Jim didn't know that she had made the connection between Vietnam, his sabotage of the Rodriguezes' crop, and his murder of McKeever. Therefore it was just possible that he had lured her out here merely to scare her into keeping quiet about Frank Rodriguez and not to kill her. Surely that old story in itself, however shaming, wasn't worth murder. At least if he were behaving rationally.

Well, she had to assume he was behaving rationally, and she had to keep his focus on what happened on April 22, 1968, without hinting at more recent ramifications.

"Believe me, Jim," she began, as earnest as if her life depended on it, "I have no interest in stirring up old troubles. It was a long time ago, and a lot of people would be hurt by the truth about Frank—"

"The truth?" he interrupted, eyebrows contracting in anger. *Shit. Bad word choice.* "I'll tell you the 'truth' about Frank Rodriguez. The son of a bitch was too stupid to be scared!"

Grinding his fist into his thigh, he continued. "He never did have any judgment. His father's exactly the same. Just jump right in; never take time to plan. If it had just been his neck on the line, hell, nobody would have cared, but he was responsible for the men under his command—his *command,"* he repeated incredulously. "That shit-for-brains had about as much business leading men as a beef burrito! He was incapable of learning from his mistakes. And anybody who's studied military history will tell you that that is the prime requisite for a good commanding officer!"

Clearly he had nearly forgotten Claire and was caught in this private debate in which the positions were known by heart and the judgment was always the same: vindication. Temporary. Until the next round. She wondered briefly if she should make a break for the car and decided she didn't have the nerve. Instead she arranged her features in an expression of warmth and sympathy in case he should happen to look her way.

Jim marched on. "But, boy, didn't he love to rub our noses in it! Yesterday just another dumb beaner from the valley, today up from the ranks . . ." He gazed off across the marshes and the white plains shimmering beyond them, and gave a violent shake of his head. "Manny and I followed him that night," he said. "We did our jobs!"

Sure. Except you didn't warn Frank about the man in the clearing. Or wasn't that part of your job? She couldn't bring herself to utter the soothing words of approval that were required of her.

He looked up sharply, pricked by her silence. Then he asked abruptly, "You ever been scared?"

He moved a step closer. "I mean, *really* scared, every second of every minute of every hour, day after day, except maybe when you're drunk. . . . You constantly make yourself imagine the details of your worst fears—the bullet in your brain, the metal in your belly—so it won't be such a shock when it comes. Christ, you wish it *would* come, anything would be better than the waiting. You listen harder than you've ever listened in your life, and all you can hear is the breathing of the guy behind you and your own heart pounding like a goddamn jackhammer. . . ."

By now he was only a foot away, which was alarming in itself; she liked a decent buffer between herself and the rest of the world. Through a haze of fear all she could see was his face, unnaturally clear, like the foothills on a hot, desert-dry day, and—yes, by god, those were little lines around his eyes! And a faint sandpapery quality to his cheeks . . . Jim shaved!

Certainly he couldn't have chosen a better place or moment for a lesson in the physiology of terror. She could hear the rasp of his breath and her blood roaring in her ears . . . a roar that seemed to come from outside her head. It took her a moment to realize that it *was* outside her head: a vehicle was coming up the road.

The noise released tension rather than heightened it, and Claire felt a tremendous rush of adrenaline. Jim was right: anything was better than suspense. He seemed to be distracted, listening, and she bolted toward the road.

In an instant he had recovered, lunged toward her, and grabbed her arm. She tried to twist away, but it is one of nature's many injustices that even a spindly male possesses by birthright about twice the upper-arm strength of an average female. Jim pulled her around and caught her other wrist, and they stood panting, facing each other. His eyes glittered and she wondered with revulsion if he was excited by this. Just her luck to have finally discovered the secret of Jim's sexual preferences.

Nearby, a car door slammed.

Sam! she thought joyfully, and started to cry out—and then her relief changed to confusion. No, Sam hadn't called. Sam didn't know she was here. It was Jim who had called . . . but Sam *had* planned to come out here today, which Jim, that inveterate eavesdropper, must have overheard and made use of. . . . Meanwhile, Jim was dragging her back to the wall of tules and forcing her to crouch beside him, hidden in the dense growth. He must be planning to ambush Sam, if it was Sam. She would wait, quiescent, and then scream, if she could scream. And throw herself sideways against Jim's arm as he took aim.

She tensed herself for these maneuvers. Footsteps crunched toward them, then squelched, as they hit marshy ground—and then stopped.

A figure was looking down at them, backlit by the sun so that his face was in shadow. Not Sam, too broad for Sam, but he reminded her of someone—

"Hey, *conejo,"* Manny Aragon said. "What's happenin'?"

Jim's hand tightened convulsively on her forearm, then dropped to his side. "Manny . . . uh, what are you doing here?" he asked nervously.

Yeah, you ought to be nervous, you son of a bitch, thought Claire, rubbing her arm. She was beginning to relax.

"Thought you might need a little help, *conejo.* Again. You know how helpful I am."

Help? thought Claire, vaguely disturbed. *What kind of help?* Aragon's face was still in shadow, and as he shifted something from hand to hand, she realized who he reminded her of.

The man in the ski mask.

He stepped forward and grinned pleasantly. He still looked a lot like Cesar Chavez, and for a moment she thought she had made a mistake. Then the wicked butcher's blade in his right hand glinted, and she realized what Manny did at the meat packing plant.

They were frozen in tableau: she and Jim still squatting. Manny facing them about ten yards away, the rushes swaying around them. And in that moment a car came rattling up the road.

Grand Central fucking Station, Claire thought wildly, but she recognized those rattles and squeaks. Sam had finally arrived.

She felt an instant of surging hope which drained at once. Sam was no cavalry, no deus ex machina. How was he supposed to save her? He would walk into this completely unprepared, and would be shot himself or sliced. She had a horrible vision of him lying with his throat cut, dark blood pulsing out into the white sand. So the question was, how would *she* save *him?*

Out of desperation she acted.

Some time ago she had noticed subconsciously that another migrant had found a home in Amargosa—about ten inches to the left of Jim's thigh, to be exact. Round, dull green, and about twenty inches high, *Salsolis kali* had long ago made its way from the steppes of Russia to the great central valley of California. In seedlinghood it was succulent, tender, and anonymous; in middle age it acquired nasty spines along each branch and was often called Russian thistle; and in death its spiny skeleton became bare and brittle, detaching itself from the earth to blow picturesquely across rangeland and highway, and pile up against fences.

In short, Jim was crouching next to a tumbleweed.

This particular specimen seemed to be in its scratchy prime. Claire gave Jim a firm push with her left hand and grabbed his revolver with her right. While he yelped in pain and Manny lurched toward her she tried to remember what her brother had taught her about handguns, realized he hadn't taught her about handguns, pointed the .45 at the sky, hoped for the best, hoped it was loaded, and pulled the trigger.

The recoil dumped her on her ass, and their soldiers' reflexes dropped the two men to their bellies, heads well down. Immediately she was up and scrambling through the tule and toward the road. Someone else hadn't wasted any time either; she heard thrashing behind her, and then cursing. A line from Manny's story ran through her head: "I never was no good at running through that stuff." And he had fallen when he chased her that night along the river. So Manny was clumsy. And that might save her life.

Thirty seconds and she was out of the reeds. Crouching low, she darted across the road, then crept along behind a line of woman-high bulrushes for about fifty yards. She passed Sam's Valiant (but where was Sam?) and came to Jim's pickup. It was parked in a shallow ditch, well camouflaged by cattails and rushes, which was why she hadn't seen it when she drove in. Directly across from it was a white Isuzu pickup. Manny's truck.

Breathing hard, she leaned against the tailgate of Jim's truck and made another unpleasant discovery: the back window of the cab was empty. The .22 was gone from the gunrack. Jim *always* carried that gun! Could someone have gotten here before her?

Not for the first time that afternoon fear crept along the back of her neck. She whirled, convinced she was being stalked. Were those tules waving in their private wind, or was someone moving in the rushes . . . ?

"Hey," said a soft voice a foot behind her.

Once again she jumped, turned—but sluggishly now, her adrenaline spent—and found herself facing Sam. He was hefting Jim's .22, and next to him stood . . . Jim! Shaky looking but with a certain . . . resolve or resignation, it was hard to tell—on his face.

Now she was thoroughly confused. "Sam, look out!" she whispered hysterically. "Jim tried to ki–"

Sam put a finger to his lips.

"But Manny Aragon, he's got a knife—" she gabbled.

He was nodding rapidly. "It's okay," he said soundlessly. "I know. It's okay."

Oh. It was okay. She couldn't figure out *how* it was okay, she just gratefully handed the situation, and Jim's revolver, to Sam, who held out the keys to the pickup and indicated that she should get in and start the engine.

"Gun it," he mouthed, before fading into the rushes beside Jim.

She had dutifully obeyed, quietly opening the door and sliding across to the driver's seat, when she realized with a certain detachment that this was a trap, and she was the bait. But as long as she kept the doors locked, she should be safe from even the sharpest of knives. She turned the key in the ignition and floored the accelerator several times, producing a deafening roar.

Nothing happened. She raced the engine again, twice. *Okay, this was a bust; how about Plan B,* she thought, anxiously searching the reeds to her left.

When she turned back Manny was in the middle of the road, ten feet beyond the hood of the pickup. His soulful face was expressionless. His feet were set wide in a marksman's stance, and he was aiming a gun straight at her head.

She gasped, squeezed her eyes shut, flung herself sideways on the seat. It had never occurred to her that Manny might have a *gun!* The truck idled roughly, missed, caught again. Oh god, where were they, what were they waiting for? How could she have put her life in the hands of Jim LaSalle?

She lay there, muscles taut as piano wire, for what seemed like forever. Then a strange thing happened: the light changed. Even through her closed eyelids she could sense it;

it was like a total eclipse, and Claire felt a superstitious terror. Trembling, she turned her head toward the passenger's side and slowly opened her eyes. . . .

Manny Aragon's grinning face filled the whole window, like a jack-o'-lantern. The barrel of his gun, big as the Lincoln Tunnel, was flush against the glass.

She tried to scream and produced only a strangled gurgle, but *somebody* yelled, and there was a shot—a high, sharp explosion—and with one galvanic jolt she jumped like a pithed frog, and was still.

CHAPTER 22

The first thing she noticed when she cautiously opened her eyes was that there was no hole in the window. Only then did she touch her forehead, and then gingerly explore the rest of her skull, checking for stickiness and splinters of bone; she had read somewhere that people who had been shot in the head didn't always immediately realize it. But she appeared to be intact.

The second thing she saw was that the figure of Manny had disappeared. When she craned her neck and peered over the door she could just make out a foot lying inert in the dust beside the truck.

Then Sam and Jim came running in from opposite sides, weapons ready.

"Good shot, Cooper," yelled Jim, as if they had just bagged a twelve-point buck.

"Careful," Sam called, "a twenty-two might not put him out of commission."

Jim knelt beside the sprawling form. "This one did. It's in his heart."

Sam walked to the dead man and looked down at him. "Oh, Jesus," he said in a quavering voice.

"He was going to kill me," Claire said. By now she had eased her way out of the truck and was standing behind him. She pressed her hand against the small of his back, which was soaked with sweat.

"Yeah, but I just meant to stop him. . . ."

"And you stopped him," Jim said, suddenly the Voice of Command. "What were you going to do, shoot the gun out of his hand? This isn't the movies, Cooper, this is combat!"

Claire stared at him incredulously and he flushed under his freckles. He stood, and then stooped again to pick

Manny's gun out of the dust. ".357 Magnum with a silencer," he muttered. "Nice."

"Martelli's on his way," Sam said.

"How does he know . . . ?" Claire began, and then stopped, woozy with confusion. For example: by consensus they had moved to the back of Jim's truck and were sitting on the tailgate, leaving Manny where he had fallen. She had been careful to put Sam between her and Jim. But what was she supposed to think about Jim? She noticed that Sam had collected all the guns, including Jim's, and put them under the front seat, so he must not know what to think either. Or maybe he *did* know.

Sam explained that he'd become suspicious when the secretary had told him about "his" call to her, and before heading out himself had told Tom to show up at Amargosa at four, just in case. Claire nodded, carefully, as if her head might come off.

"So I guess," she said, "I *guess* neither Buddy nor Van Horn killed McKeever. I *guess* Manny did." She paused. "But why? *Why?"* she repeated fiercely, suddenly jumping down and whirling to face LaSalle. "Why did he kill him? Why did you lure me here? Why did you scare me? Were you going to hurt me? What did Manny mean, did you need help 'again'? And why did he want to kill *me?"* By now she was shrieking with fury and frustration and delayed shock, and she actually stamped her foot in the dust. *"Why?"*

Sam slid off the tailgate behind her and put his arms around her. She was shaking and panting. "Yeah, Jim," he said quietly. "Why?"

Jim seemed to have shrunk a little, and a very unchildlike furrow appeared between his eyebrows. He cleared his throat.

"Well," he began haltingly, "you know what happened in Vietnam. With Frank Rodriguez."

"I know," said Claire, feeling Sam's arms suddenly tighten around her, "what Manny told me that night." Her voice was hoarse from screaming. "That the three of you were out on patrol, and you stopped Manny from warning Frank about the sniper who killed him—"

"He told you *that?"* Jim interrupted, incredulous.

"Yes . . ."

"Well, that . . . that's just . . . that's crazy!" His nutcracker jaw worked convulsively for a moment; then he got it under control. "There was no sniper in the clearing," he said finally. "That was the story we told afterward."

No sniper. But that meant—

Jim was talking again, fast and earnest. "I know Frank was a friend of yours," he said, looking over her shoulder at Sam, "and maybe back here he was a reasonable guy. I don't know, I never knew him, but over there—" He paused for breath. "That . . . that situation turned reasonable guys into, um, exaggerations, what do you call it . . ."

"Caricatures?" suggested Claire, ever the editor.

"Yeah! Caricatures of themselves! Like, if a guy was kind of timid and a little unsure of himself back home, over there he might . . . freeze, under fire, and some people might think he was a coward. . . ." His eyes flickered to Claire and then he turned back to Sam. "And Frank Rodriguez. Back here on the Parkerville football field maybe he was . . . daring and high-spirited—but out there he was a sadistic monster! I mean it, Sam!" he said imploringly, straining to be understood.

There was a long silence. "Okay," Sam said finally. "I can see what you mean. Go on."

"O-ka-ay," LaSalle breathed, drawing the word out and relaxing as if Sam had bestowed absolution. Then he continued.

"Manny and I, we talked about it a lot. Killing the sar—Rodriguez, I mean. We each had our reasons. Only I figured it was just a way of blowing off steam; I never took it seriously."

Didn't you? thought Claire.

"But Manny's a very literal-minded fellow. I found that out that night on patrol, when the three of us were separated from the other guys in the unit. Rodriguez was standing near the edge of an open area where we thought we'd seen a VC, Manny had a clear shot, and . . . *blam!* Right through the throat!"

Sam grunted and Claire flinched. "He had took the hit right through the throat," Manny had said; she was replaying his story as she listened to LaSalle's. It was like a simultaneous translation, and reluctantly she was deciding that Jim's version was the more plausible—certainly in light of recent events, but even considering what she already knew about Jim. Could he really have exploited so coolly the possibilities of that night? Calmly shot that sniper, as Manny had claimed? Jim, who had to shore up his so-called manhood with shiny firearms and tough talk? Whose jaw clamped down on a perpetual scream of terror?

Uh-uh. Manny had lied to her and manipulated her, and she had gobbled it up.

"See, that was what got . . . exaggerated, in Manny," Jim was saying. "He liked to kill . . . things. He might never have found that out if he hadn't gone to Vietnam. Or he might have confined it to his job."

"His job?" Sam was puzzled.

"Yeah. At the packing plant. You know . . ." He drew his finger slowly across his throat.

"Oh," said Sam, and then after a moment. "Larry McKeever."

"Right, Larry McKeever," Jim repeated unhappily. "I swear to you, that was entirely Manny's idea. Wait, let me back up a minute—"

Now that he had found an attentive audience, Jim couldn't stop talking. When he got back to the States he avoided Manny Aragon, he said; in fact, they didn't meet for years. But he couldn't avoid Frank Rodriguez, as Frank's obscure family pressed their lawsuit against the Hanfords and achieved a kind of prominence, not to say notoriety, in the county. It was like a nightmare to Jim, a constant reminder of the person he most wanted to forget. And the possibility that the unpredictable Silvia and Carlos might decide to investigate their son's death hovered in his mind.

So he watched, fascinated, and then obsessed, as the Rodriguezes' fortunes waxed and waned. The orchard nearly failed, recovered, began to fail again—due, he decided, to those same deep flaws of character Silvia and Carlos had imparted to their bully of a son: sloppiness and ignorance overlaid by arrogance and bluff. And then he hit on his plan. Why not put them out of their misery? Maybe they would leave the county, and his troubled conscience, forever. Last year he began paying Larry McKeever to substitute lime for Benyl when he delivered the spraying supplies to Agua Dulce. It was an ingenious idea: nonviolent, effective, and even if the substitution were detected it would be attributed to someone's incompetence. But Tony Rodriguez saw the sacks Larry had prepared and stacked at Amargosa, and when he returned to investigate, Larry killed him, and called Jim in a panic.

"I never meant for anyone to get hurt," Jim said. "I didn't know what to do; all I knew was that Larry was out of control and I had to shut him up somehow. I'd run into Manny Aragon at the county fair, and I . . . I called him. He was just supposed to *scare* McKeever, that was all!"

Sam and Claire didn't comment. They all knew they were thinking the same thing: you don't call a killer just to scare someone.

"Well, you know what happened," he continued after a moment. "Manny called me, kind of pleased with the job he'd done, and I was terrif—well, I was upset. It was just like Vietnam; he'd done it, but I was responsible for it. And then *you*"—looking at Claire—"show up at this maniac's place, full of ideas, asking questions about Frank Rodriguez! Manny called me the next day and said you were a problem he was trying to solve. And I know how he solves—solved—problems."

He passed his hand over his face, and Claire felt a faint twinge of sympathy for him. "I couldn't shake him now," he said. "It was like being . . . haunted or possessed or like that story where the guy lets the imp out of the bottle and can't get him back in again. I told him I'd frighten you real good, so you'd stop asking questions. Guess he didn't trust me."

With an effort she said, "Thanks for trying." For a moment she searched for remaining questions.

"Did you break into my lab?"

"Yeah. It was a stupid thing to do, I realize. That's what put you on to me, right?"

She nodded. "You should have trashed the *Aspergillus* too; that was a giveaway."

"I know. I kept putting it off—and then I heard you in the hall, and hid in the closet. I barely got out that window. Just about left my behind behind, and my balls too! Pardon my French."

Out of habit she gave Jim her usual pained smile, and then remembered that her ineffectual, mildly unpleasant colleague had caused two—no, three—well, four, if you counted Manny—deaths. Murder was a lethal virus and Jim was a carrier.

There was a rumble and a squeak behind them, and Tom Martelli's black-and-white bounced to a halt.

He goggled for a moment at the tableau—the body lying in the dirt, Sam and Claire facing Jim LaSalle like a firing squad—regained his poise, and lifted an inquiring eyebrow at Sam.

"Well, folks," he drawled, "quite a—"

"You better get on the horn, Tom," Sam interrupted. "There's a black stretch limo on its way to LA with Buddy Hanford in it—"

"If he's not already lying in an onion field near Bakersfield," Claire cut in.

Tom didn't bat a blue eye. "Got a license number on the limo?" was all he asked as he headed for his car.

CHAPTER 23

Claire was struggling to prepare an elegant Back East Sunday breakfast in Sam's kitchen, without much success. The *Parkerville Sentinel* had to stand in for the Sunday *Times* and the cheese omelette kept sticking to the scratched aluminum bottom of what had once been a Teflon-coated saucepan. Cursing, she scraped up the eggs once again.

Sam, too dumb or too polite to notice the mess she was making, peered over her shoulder, said, "Looks good," and picked up the sports section. She grumbled, and thought longingly of her patented and extremely expensive French omelette pan, carefully packed away in Cambridge. Should she have her things sent out? Was she really going to stay here with a man who reminded her of her *mother?*

The smell of burning butter brought her back to the present. She prodded the yellow agglutinated mass, decided it was scrambled eggs, and turned it out onto plates.

"Eating and talking. No reading," she announced.

Sam wrenched himself away from the funnies. "I heard something about Agua Dulce yesterday."

"Oh?" Following the revelations about Jim LaSalle and Buddy Hanford and Venture West, Carlos and Silvia had received a great deal of sympathy. But sympathy didn't pay Kavoian's bills, and anyway their hearts weren't in Agua Dulce anymore. But they couldn't even sell—their buyer had, after all, withdrawn his offer, at least temporarily, and nobody else had made an offer.

"Good news or bad?"

"Good. Hey, did you put cheese in these eggs?"

"Yes," she said shortly.

"Oh. Well, it seems that one of the daughters has decided to move back to Agua Dulce and help out. And the money she made selling her house will just about cover their debts. I don't know how long it will last—"

"Rosario, right?"

"How'd you know?"

She had to have been right about something.

Actually, she had been right about something else—the time it was going to take to clear things up, to bring the outlaws to justice. But she hadn't anticipated just how unsatisfying this would be, especially when 1) the actual murderers were already dead, 2) the slimiest, most villainous player in the drama, namely Stephen Van Horn, was actually completely innocent of any wrongdoing, except for taking Buddy Hanford for a little ride, and anyway 3) Buddy himself was not a pretty sight, having committed arson and willful destruction of property. This left 4) Jim LaSalle, whom she didn't exactly like, but for whom she had a certain sympathy, and even gratitude. He had tried to save her from Manny Aragon.

But Jim had set up the dominoes and pushed over the first one, and in the eyes of the law this made him fully culpable. *Respondeat superior,* or something like that, the county prosecutor had said when she asked him what would happen to Jim.

"We're going after Murder One," he had added happily, "but . . . he'll bargain it down. They always do. And juries are funny."

Juries are funny, and the Law moves in mysterious and remarkably unscientific ways, Claire decided. You couldn't collect data over the years, submit it to analysis, conclude that there was a highly significant probability that Van Horn and Cardenas were slimeballs and deserved to be locked up, and pass the computer output around to the jurors; you had to negate such queasily ambiguous notions as "reasonable doubt."

It was the same with love. She had set up a proposition in her head: null hypothesis, if you weren't stuck in this wasteland you wouldn't think twice about Sam Cooper, and the sooner he and Kaweah County become colorful memories the better; alternate hypothesis, you love Sam, he's the best thing that ever happened to you, and if you really need a fix of haute culture you can drive to San Francisco once a month. Now just enter the data into the computer, "the data" being everything you've done, thought, and felt in the last six months— No, better be thorough, better go back to birth—run a few statistical analyses, and bingo! null hypothesis accepted, or, null hypothesis rejected.

Lacking this *Star Trek* technology, she just muddled along. She sort of moved in with Sam, but kept her house in town. She wrote up some preliminary results on the *Aspergillus* project and passed them to Jim, who was out on bail and so chastened as to be unrecognizable. She thought of an idea for her own IPM project—a method of biological control of a cute but pesky native plant called fiddleneck, *Amsinckia,* that infested alfalfa crops—and proposed it to Ray.

And in the afternoons after work she would frequently drive up into the Sierras, which even by August displayed a sort of travesty of autumn colors. The buckeye, so spectacular in spring, had already turned dull brown, and the tough resinous chaparral plants seemed to be grimly hanging on, waiting for the blessed winter rains. In this cockeyed place, winter was the season of renewal. So she hung on too.

At six on a Friday evening in late September Sam walked into the lab where Claire was bent over the microscope.

"Howdy," he said, kissing her on the nape of the neck. "Ready to go— What's wrong?"

The face she had lifted to him was somber.

"Mulcahey called me today," she said. "He wants me to deliver a paper at a symposium next month. In Cambridge."

"Great," he said, "your worth is finally being realized. So what's the problem?"

"He wants me to come back. I mean, he *really* wants me to come back; he was positively . . . genial!"

"Oh," said Sam. He walked to the window and looked out at the hills. "Guess the work here is getting kind of boring, huh?"

His stiff back was as eloquent as a caption. Claire walked up behind him and put her arms around him. Pressing her face against the stylish all-cotton sport shirt she had bought him, which he politely wore when everything else was dirty, she answered his real question.

"I'm completely crazy about you, Sam," she said, which, after all, was true. "As you very well know."

"But—?" he said, not moving.

"But this place!" she burst out, releasing him. "I'll never

belong here, I'll always feel like an exile, like I just landed on Mars! I miss my friends, I miss the seasons, I miss the . . . the whole way of life! I'm homesick," she concluded unhappily, sitting on the lab bench.

Presently she said in a weak voice, "You could come to Cambridge."

"Don't be ridiculous," he replied quietly, still looking out the window. It was ridiculous, of course. He would be as out of place in Cambridge as she was in Kaweah County, and with a degree in agronomy from a California state school no one in Boston had ever heard of, he wouldn't even be able to get a job. Besides—

Besides, she wasn't sure their relationship could stand transplanting. Here, he was perfect; there, he would seem gauche, awkward, inarticulate.

"I don't know what to do," she said miserably, holding her head in her hands.

After a moment, Sam walked to her and pulled her against him. "Look," he said, "when's this conference?"

"October twenty-third."

"Okay. You go to the conference, stay in Cambridge as long as you want. Stay for a month, or even more. It'll be all right with Ray; it's kind of slow around here this time of year. See how it feels, see how you feel about the station, about . . . me."

"And then?" said Claire, noting even in the midst of her distress that she had fallen apart at the first sign of emotional complication, while Sam had risen to the occasion. *You'll have to do the behaving for both of us,* she thought.

"And then decide," Sam said simply.

On November 20 Claire was stopped at a red light in Harvard Square, absently watching the hordes of fresh-faced college students swarm across the intersection. "That was my man, Charlie Parker," the ultrahip voice on her radio was saying. "And now, for all you cow-persons out there, here's the Bard of Bakersfield, Merle Haggard!" A few strummed chords, the railyard whine of a pedal-steel guitar, and then she heard a familiar rich voice. . . .

The light changed. The cars honked. Claire sat listening to the simple-minded, mawkish lyrics—"if you're tryin' to break my heart, you don't have very far to go"—while tears streamed down her face.

"Hey, you dumb bitch, get outta the fucking road!"

She roused herself. She made a precipitous U-turn in the middle of Mass. Ave., causing further vehicular consternation. She drove for several blocks, then pulled to a sudden stop in front of the Crimson Travel Agency, where she bought a one-way ticket to Fresno.